Vivid

By Jessica Wilde

Natalie,
To the trials we
face that make us
stronger. —
♡ Jessica
Wilde
xo

Other titles by Jessica Wilde

Every One of Me

Our Time

The Brannock Siblings Series

Leverage (The Brannock Siblings, #1)

Conned (The Brannock Siblings, #2)

Missing (The Brannock Siblings, #3)

Protector (The Brannock Siblings, #4)

Rise & Fall Series

Ricochet (Rise & Fall, #1)

Coming Soon

Reckless (Rise & Fall, #2)

Jessica
xx

By Jessica Wilde

Cover Design by: Jessica Wilde
Cover Images by: Shutterstock Images

ISBN-13: 978-1517372354

For all the men and women that make the sacrifice every single day,
even after they come home.

Vivid is a story that will always stay very close to my heart. I honestly wasn't sure if I would ever write it. PTSD and the struggles a wounded soldier goes through upon returning home are difficult to describe. It's impossible to come close to fully grasping the idea of it. This book in no way describes a general experience. Every person is different and each obstacle they face is unique. If you, your family, or someone close to you has experienced what it is like – whether by association or direct experience – my heart goes out to you. I truly wish that after reading about Merrick and Grace, or even *before*, hope comes within reach.

We are all broken, that's how the light gets in.
– Ernest Hemingway

There are song titles mentioned in this story. Each one is meant to capture an emotion that may add to the reader's experience. It is not necessary, but I highly recommend finding the time to seek out these artists and listen to these songs. The words are powerful and say so much about what Merrick and Grace are experiencing. A playlist is provided in the back matter of this book.

Vivid

Prologue

There are a lot of things a man can hear about himself that won't puncture his thick skin. A lot of things that won't make a difference in how he lives his life.

He's an asshole. I can say, with almost complete certainty, that every man hears those words at least once in his life. It comes with having a dick.

He's an idiot. That one sucks, but it can be overcome, and we all know why we are idiots. We think about sex every seven seconds. We think about a woman's underwear almost as often. Yes, we can be idiots, but only because our minds are preoccupied. We learn how to get around it, eventually.

He doesn't understand me. Well, of course we don't. If you don't tell us what the hell we are supposed to understand, we never will. It's not worth the drama, most of the time, but the times that you actually talk to us and tell us something that isn't spoken in code, we try to understand. We try to fix it.

He's awful in bed. Well, that one has an effect, but again, we just get better. Sleep with a few more women or learn a few more things, and voila! We are better in bed. That one is probably the worst to hear, but again, it doesn't change anything. We are still me. We will still *act* the same once we get it fixed.

It won't change us. We adapt and overcome. Then, we carry on.

But there comes a moment where something *does* change. We've done everything a man should do. We heard the shit said about us; we dealt with it and got over it. Then, we hear the one thing that penetrates after we've done the one thing that has already destroyed us.

"He's blind."

This isn't the metaphorical blind. This is the real deal.

For twelve years, we've had the discipline, the training, and the work. We've put on the gear and lived in a special type of hell, all for the purpose of protecting our country. Protecting our friends and family.

We've done it. We've sacrificed.

Now?

We were spared long enough to see a cloudy image of our friends being torn to pieces, shot at more times than one can count, and cornered, with the only thought being, *'How long will they torture us before God finally takes us?'*.

We see it all happen right in front of us, and we are helpless to stop it, no matter how hard we try. Then, suddenly ... everything goes black. The last image in our mind is our best friend bleeding all over us, crying to God to take him home to his wife and unborn child, and knowing without a doubt that it won't happen.

I should stop saying *'we'* because it doesn't happen to every man. Only a rare few.

But it happened to me.

And now, every hope of seeing light again is stripped away.

"He's blind."

Not only do I feel like I've been torn to shreds, burned to the bone, then slowly broken into a million pieces; I see nothing but blackness. Hear nothing but the sound of my mother crying softly in the corner of my hospital room. Feel nothing but the anger and disappointment in myself, knowing I could have done more. Knowing that because I was still alive, it was all my fault. I should have been the one to die. I should have been faster. Smarter. I *shouldn't* have been thinking about how fucking hot it was in that blistering sun or how long it would take me to get all the sand out of my clothes. I should have prevented it all from happening. It was *my* responsibility.

I lost two of my men, watched the others nearly die, and prayed, to the only God I knew, that it would end.

He ended it, but not the way I asked for.

He took away my sight. He took away my ability to see what was happening and my ability to fix it, to adapt and overcome ... to save my friends.

"Will he walk again?"

"With therapy and time, yes. His hand will be a difficult transition. We have another surgery scheduled for some hardware to be placed, but he will have the use of his hand, eventually. I imagine it won't be at one hundred percent, though."

"And his burns? How long?"

"We're treating him carefully. There will be scars. His burns are too severe for plastic surgery to help significantly. He will be in pain for a long time and will need to limit himself until he's completely healed, but he *will* heal, Mrs. Thatcher. He's alive."

I heard my mother sob; could almost hear the tears falling from her eyes. "And his eyes?"

A sigh, then the sound of clothing shifting. Doc was uncomfortable, that much I could read just by listening. "He'll need to see a specialist as soon as he's home. The shrapnel nearly destroyed his optic nerve, and I don't have any well educated guesses, but ..."

I didn't need to be able to see to know that the look on the doctor's face was resigned. He didn't think I would be able to see again. Ever.

I didn't need to hear otherwise.

My fate was sealed.

I was no longer the man I had been when I first joined the Army. No longer the man my unit saw when they followed me off base that day.

I was a result of war.

A consequence.

Lying here, in this uncomfortable bed, with my entire left leg immobile from snapping not only my tibia and fibula, but my femur as well; bandages covering the scorched skin on my left side; my arm feeling like it's been crushed; my face covered in bandages ... I know my life has changed. I know that the pain will last a long time. That the pain I feel now is nothing compared to what I will feel later.

The morphine may numb my body, but it sure as hell isn't numbing my mind.

I may be blind now, but I can still see my men falling. I can still see that desert sun shining down on us as we approached the bridge that would take us back to base. And I can still see the bright light shining on the dash of the MRAP. A reflection off the machete that signaled the bastard aiming that fucking EFP directly at us. Just one hundred yards away.

And I can still feel the panic. The knowledge that we had fucked up. No, the knowledge that someone we were supposed to be able to trust, had betrayed us. The helplessness to stop it. I should have seen the signs. I should have been more careful.

I can still see and feel and hear ... all of it.

And I still can't stop it.

Chapter One

Grace

Some may disagree, but there is nothing more humiliating to me than being twenty-nine years old and needing to move back home to your parent's house because you had been a fool. I wasn't embarrassed about the failed relationship or the failed attempt at becoming a mother. No, those things were devastating, not embarrassing. I'm embarrassed that the only choice I have is to move back to the room I spent most of my life in – where I spent most of my nights wishing for more – all because I couldn't hold it together.

I'm embarrassed that I need my mom and dad, now more than ever.

I know I shouldn't be. I know that shit happens, and I should be grateful my parents are the type of people to be there for me no matter what. I *am* grateful. Relieved, in fact. It's just that all my dreams came crashing down in a matter of seconds, then the rest of my world joined them.

It has been a year since I lost everything, since the man I thought loved me, walked out of my life forever because of something that was out of my control. A year since I lost my heart and soul in a delivery room, surrounded by strangers. Doctors and nurses that looked at me with pity in their eyes.

I couldn't even hold it together for a year. The depression had taken over, and if it wasn't for my mother, Alaina, I would probably be in a ditch somewhere without a pulse.

I didn't answer my phone for a week. The same week I lost my baby the year before. Mom came for me and didn't let go until I agreed to go with her.

"I know this is hard, Grace, but it's necessary. You stay with us until you find your feet again and if it takes longer than you hope, it doesn't matter. You work, you live your life, and you look forward to the future."

Mom was always positive and always throwing out a new motto to live by. She was loving and strong, but she didn't know what it was like to be me. I couldn't be mad at her for that, though, and I loved her too much to make it an issue. She was trying.

"I will, Mom. I'm okay, it's just been hard ... remembering."

"I know it is, sweetie. I know."

Alaina Samuelson, at fifty years old, didn't look a day over twenty-five. Her short, brown hair was colored religiously to hide her grays, and she was the only person – along with my father – who never gave up on me. She was a sweet, publicly-conservative librarian, and she loved her job. If she wasn't taking care of me or Dad in some way, she was reading a book.

My father, Jeff, was an ophthalmologist. It's kind of funny if you think about it. Mom loves to read, and Dad will always make sure she *can*. He adored my mother. She is smart, funny, and so beautiful. But standing at an inch taller than me and as curvy as I had always been, wasn't what made her so beautiful. She was always breath taking. Her face was consistently flawless, and her teeth were straight and perfect. All her life.

I had seen the pictures from her childhood. How pretty she was. That's why I always had such a hard time believing I was actually hers.

I couldn't count the number of times I asked if I was adopted. It got to the point where my mom threatened to kick me out if I asked again.

The only similarities between us were our noses and eye color. Small and hazel. My brown hair has never looked as vibrant as hers, and I looked like a teenager when it was cut short, so I always kept it past my shoulders. I had freckles, where Mom's face had a perfect complexion. My lips were fuller, but hers were the deepest shade of pink. I looked like her, obviously. She gave me these genes, after all. I just wasn't devastatingly pretty.

At least not naturally.

It took years of braces to fix my crooked teeth and the buck teeth I suffered with during my childhood, plus, an expensive salon to fix the bushes my eyebrows were and to teach me how to apply makeup. I still wasn't breath taking, but my face was improved by miles. My body was never skinny and shapely. The curves were always there, mocking me when my jeans shrunk a little in the dryer and shunning me when a dress didn't promise the hour glass figure all women want.

I guess I wasn't *overly* disappointed in my body, but it certainly didn't diminish any of my insecurities.

Jason thought I was pretty enough to be with, but not to marry. We dated for three years before I got pregnant. I knew, deep down, that was the only reason he was going to stay with me, and I didn't care. I would have a family of my own and I would be the best damn mother I could possibly be. Then, we lost the baby and Jason left immediately after. The hospital discharge papers weren't even written up before he walked away.

I was devastated but thankful that I wouldn't spend the rest of my life feeling inadequate, knowing the only reason he was with me was because of the kids.

As an only child, one would think I was spoiled rotten. That wasn't the case. My mother made sure I learned discipline and responsibility. I could be independent if I needed to. That was how I was raised.

Independence takes more than a wave goodbye and a nice apartment, though. And once there is loss, no one *wants* to be alone.

"I spoke with Emma Thatcher. She said there was an opening in homecare and therapy," Mom said, interrupting my despondent thoughts. "All you have to do is send in your application and she can almost guarantee you the job."

"Is she the one hiring?"

"No. She works in labor and delivery now," Mom answered, hesitantly.

I hid my reaction and forced the memories away. "Then how?"

"She's good friends with one of the administrators and with the homecare director. They need another nurse on staff, and fast. Plus, they trust her since she's been there so long."

I didn't have a problem with homecare and I enjoyed helping patients with their therapy, but I wanted to make sure I stayed busy. I needed the money so I could pick up the pieces of my life that were still scattered on the ground.

"Sounds like a good plan then," I replied, sighing as we pulled into the driveway of my parent's home.

Nothing had changed. Same colors, same windows, same curtains. It was like going back in time. My eyes moved to the neighbor's house, which looked only slightly different from my memory.

"Are the Thatchers still next door? I wouldn't mind talking to Emma about the job myself."

Mom shook her head and turned off the car. "They moved across town about two years ago, but they still own the house. Kept it for the kids if they ever needed it. Micah lived there for a while, but once he finished his residency, he bought a house in Ogden. Emma is staying there while Merrick recovers, though."

"Merrick? What happened?"

Hearing that name after so many years was like the strike of a match. Merrick Thatcher was the boy everyone gravitated to. The girls loved him, the boys wanted to be him, and I was always hopelessly in love with him. Major crush. One that almost made me fail several classes my junior year. It seemed so important at the time, but now I could see how immature I had actually been. Still didn't change the fact that the man was gorgeous.

I knew he joined the military right after graduation and became a kind of celebrity in our small town of Morgan, Utah. He served two tours in Iraq and was on his third the last time Mom showed up and attempted to bring me home. That was five months ago. I hadn't come back, obviously, but that didn't stop me from hearing about everything that was happening back home.

"I don't know the whole story, but he was hurt pretty badly," Mom said and turned her gaze to the old house I'd watched for so long when I was younger. "Came home about two months ago and has barely been outside since. The only time I see him is when I catch him moving past a window with Emma. She tries to open up the house, but he refuses to let people see him that way. The poor man is really struggling."

My chest ached, knowing that Merrick was so seriously injured. I was grateful he was alive and wished I had been a good enough friend so I could go over there and talk to him. Maybe even help him. But I wasn't a friend. In fact, I don't even think he knew I existed. He hadn't while we were growing up, why would he now?

Once, in all the years living next to the Thatchers, did Merrick ever acknowledge me.

It was the first day of my junior year and, with my ever wonderful luck, my car wouldn't start. Merrick had been climbing into his truck while I was in my driveway, furiously shouting every swear word I knew. Unfortunately, the commotion caught his attention; it wasn't my best moment. Then, he crossed our yards and asked if he could help.

That was the kind of guy he was. Popular, smart, kind when he needed to be, and a jerk when social rules required it. That day, he was the boy I couldn't get out of my mind. He fixed my car, said 'you're welcome', and drove away, already ten minutes late for his first class. By the time I'd caught my breath and remembered how to drive, I missed first period and had to have my mother call to explain for both of us.

Merrick hadn't cared about being late that day. He cared about fixing my car.

It was the start of girly fantasies that distracted me more than ever before.

We had three classes together that year, and not once did he speak a word to me. Of course, I was too shy to even look his way half the time. But all my focus was on the tall, muscular boy sitting in the back corner of the class, flirting with one of the popular girls.

It's my own fault. I never engaged him in conversation, and anytime he may have come close to even looking at me, I usually turned away.

"He's in a wheelchair right now. Fractured his femur and lower leg. Went through a lot of surgeries. He was burned pretty badly, too." Mom watched the house carefully, searching for movement. "You know how your dad is when *he's* sick, imagine a once perfectly able bodied man now *incapable* of getting around by himself."

I moved my gaze back to the Thatcher home and watched the front window. "I've seen plenty of injuries where the patient can still be independent, Mom."

"He's blind."

I certainly wasn't expecting that. "What?"

Mom turned and acknowledged my shocked stare with a nod. "I think it was shrapnel that hit his face. It took his sight. He can't do anything on his own right now."

"Oh my God. That's awful," I whispered.

She nodded again and opened her door, not saying anything else about it until we had dragged my two suitcases into the house. The rest of my stuff would arrive within the week since we left in such a hurry. It was all going to storage, but Dad had hired a moving company to do all the work for me. Just one more thing I still felt entirely too guilty to accept. Not that Dad even listened to my arguments.

"I can hear them every so often," Mom continued. "Emma tries to take care of him and help him adjust, but he keeps fighting her every step of the way. Refusing to take his pain medication, refusing to leave the house, except for the occasional doctor's appointment. And even those come with difficulty."

"He's angry, Mom. Like you said, it's hard for a man who can't get around by himself. Think of all he's lost."

She pulled a couple bottles of water out of the fridge and handed one to me. "You're right, Grace. I'm just upset for Emma."

Someone should be upset for Merrick, I thought to myself.

"Alright, you stay here and unpack. I'm going into town to get us a pizza from Deb's. Anything specific that you want?"

"No, whatever you get will be fine, Mom."

"Okay, dear. Be back soon."

I dragged my suitcases to my old bedroom located at the front corner of the house. This part of the house had definitely changed since I moved away. Mom and Dad turned it into a guestroom. It was boring with its white walls and neutral colors. The bed was new and bigger than the twin I'd slept in for years. The carpet was new as well.

I looked out the side window that was facing the Thatcher's home. Merrick had always been closer to me than he ever knew. That's if he even considered it in the first place. Our bedrooms were directly across from each other. In this neighborhood, the houses were built close together with the empty space between our rooms measuring only eight feet. It was easy to see his opened closet through the blinds.

I wondered if I would catch a glimpse of him one day. Maybe see the extent of his injuries while I silently hoped he would get better.

Hope is a funny thing. No one really pays attention to their ability to hope until it's all they have. And even then, it's not a guarantee for *anything*.

I dropped down on the bed and shut my eyes.

This last year had taken its toll on me, but I was determined to come out on top. Mom made a good point when she finally came to drag me back home.

"Your baby girl wouldn't want her mother to lose herself. She may not have seen you, Grace, but she heard you every day. Make sure you're still the woman you were when you carried her inside you."

I was going to become a better person for my daughter, and she was going to look down on me and see that I loved her more than anything on this earth. That the few minutes I held her still body in my arms, she was loved with every breath in me. She still is.

If she would have lived, would she have known unconditional love? From me, yes. From Jason? I have no idea. He didn't love *me* unconditionally, but a child is different. A child is a part of you. The fact that he left me just hours after I lost her, however, showed his true colors. A child shouldn't grow up in a family like that; with parents who didn't complete each other.

I would have done it on my own, but that wasn't in the cards for me either.

I was going to work hard, earn a living for myself, and move forward. I was going to make my baby girl proud of me from wherever she was watching.

I started to drift, thinking of all the things I would need to do before starting a new job. Homecare wouldn't be so bad. I was a good nurse, and caring for patients in their home made everything a little more personal. I was good with personal. I'd done it before and stayed busy. It's exactly what I needed. I didn't have to take the suffering home, but I could connect with someone and help them through it.

My thoughts strayed to Merrick Thatcher, and I wondered if anyone could make a connection with *him*. Mom said that Emma was certainly trying. I couldn't imagine what it would be like to see war and devastation. To watch your friends suffer along with you and have it all stripped away when you were injured so badly. Everything Merrick worked for, since he graduated from high school, was now over. He served his purpose, and my respect goes to any man who makes such sacrifices for his country. How many of them come back shells of their former self? How many of them have families waiting for them?

How many never make it home?

I drifted further, not realizing I had fallen asleep until I woke thirty minutes later. I didn't plan on napping and ,for a moment, was happy for whatever it was that woke me. Then, I heard the shouts.

"Son, you have got to stop this. I can't take care of you if you don't cooperate."

"I don't need you to take care of me. I'm fine. Just leave me alone."

Several thumps sounded before the voices came clearer and louder. I kept myself still, knowing that my window was wide open. If I moved, they would see me from his room. Well, Emma would.

"Merrick, you haven't been outside in weeks, you haven't showered in days, and I can't sit here and watch you waste away. You need to eat, you need to sleep, and you need to do your therapy."

Emma sounded desperate and on the verge of tears. I couldn't imagine how hard it was for a mother to watch her son return from war so broken.

"I don't need you wiping my ass all the time, Mom."

"Well when you can wipe your own ass, I'll stop doing it!"

"Jesus, just leave! Stop treating me like I'm some pathetic animal that needs healing."

"I don't. I am trying to do what I have to do so you can live your life."

"I don't *want* to live my life!"

I gasped and covered my mouth. Tears burned the back of my eyes, and it took everything I had not to sit up and look out that window. I heard the soft sound of Emma crying and another thump against a wall.

"Merrick," I heard her say softly, "let me help you."

"I can do it myself! If I run into something, who gives a fuck?"

They continued to shout at each other. Emma kept begging her son to let her help him, to listen to the doctors, and to stop pushing everyone away. Merrick kept telling her to leave.

I couldn't take it anymore. I didn't want to shut my window and make it obvious that I had been listening this whole time, so I did the next possible thing to try to drown them out.

I sang to myself and hoped they would carry on with no notice of me.

I don't know why I chose the song I did. I had always loved *Damien Rice*, but it was the first song, out of all the hundreds I had memorized, that felt appropriate for the moment. Maybe that was because it was how I saw myself from another's eyes. Or maybe it was because I knew it would be how a true friend would see Merrick. Wherever he was or however far away his troubled mind took him, there would always be someone that cared. There *was always* someone.

I took a deep breath and closed my eyes, stretching out on the bed and drowning out the anger just feet away from me with the song, *'I Don't Want to Change You'*.

Maybe my focus was somewhere else, but the sound of their fighting was gone. All I could hear was the music in my mind as I continued to sing. I wasn't singing for anyone else but me. There was no way they could hear me. It was just enough to drown out everything else.

I finally sat up and lifted my suitcase onto my bed. There was only silence coming from next door. I figured they had moved to another part of the house, or they were finally working things out a little less dramatically. I didn't dare look. I just started to unpack, singing through the rest of the song; about being there for someone in any way possible with no intention of changing them or the way they feel.

I stopped what I was doing as I sang the last line about a safe place where love has eyes. Where love isn't blind. I still don't know why I chose the song, and now it just seemed inappropriate. The slam of a window was the first clue of my mistake. They'd heard me loud and clear, and with my luck, that last line of the song was the very line they heard the clearest.

I turned and finally looked out of my window, only to see Merrick struggling to close the blinds with one hand while the other was in a cast and sling. I could only see one side of his face, a profile that looked even more handsome than it did all those years ago. His jaw looked strong, although unkempt, with a scraggly beard covering it. His hair was too long and hung in his eyes, and his shirt tightened around a muscular torso as he moved. He could barely reach the handle from his sitting position in what I assumed was a wheelchair.

I almost said something. What? I don't know. 'Hi', maybe. That just seemed superficial. I saw Emma standing in his open doorway, staring at me with wide, teary eyes. Looking like someone had just broken her heart.

I left my room quickly after that and stayed away from it for the rest of the night. It wasn't my place to interfere with Merrick. Not my place to do anything but lend a quiet support.

Mom returned with a pizza and other groceries, which I helped her put away. We sat in silence as we ate, and I refrained from asking any more questions about Merrick Thatcher or what happened to him. The man who used to be larger than life, was now withdrawn and cold.

If his own mother couldn't get through to him, who could?

Chapter Two

Merrick

"Merrick."

I hated the sound of my mother's tears. What I hated even more, was the fact that I caused them. I didn't realize she was still in my room, but Emma Thatcher was never one to back down from a fight. Especially if she hadn't won, yet.

I was in the middle of telling her to go to hell, like the bastard I was, when I heard it. I didn't realize I stopped screaming at her until halfway through the song. That voice. Bluesy with a feminine rasp. One that sent warm vibrations across my chest. For a moment, I thought I accidently turned on my stereo and was listening to the radio, but I quickly realized that the singing was coming from next door.

I knew my window was only feet away from the neighbor's. However, I didn't realize that someone other than Alaina and Jeff was living there. That voice certainly wasn't Alaina Samuelson. I had heard the woman sing before. She couldn't carry a tune to save her life; something pointed out on more than one occasion.

It couldn't be their daughter, could it? What was her name again? God, I could barely remember what I wore yesterday let alone high school.

I didn't know her name, but I knew the song. It infuriated me and calmed me at the same time. She was singing that specific song for a very specific reason, but whether it was for me or her, I had no clue.

While I sat in my chair, I listened to her sing and move around the room, trying to picture her face or anything that would prompt her name. I got nothing. Once she sang the last line, I didn't care anymore.

Slamming the window shut was painful. The burns were healed enough, but they still hurt when I moved too thoughtlessly, and my leg throbbed every time I breathed. I struggled with the blinds, appropriately named in this case. I was blind and couldn't find the damn handle to close them up tight. I must have looked like a fool, fumbling my way up the window. Mom would usually come to my rescue, but after the horrible things I said to her, I wouldn't have been surprised if she kicked me out of the house and left me on the street.

I didn't deserve to be taken care of. The pain reminded me of that every day.

So, I sat there, pointlessly staring at God knows what, while I listened to my mother's heavy breaths. She was hanging on by a thread because of me.

"Merrick..."

"Please, Mom. Just go before I say something stupid."

I heard the step she took into my room, and I tensed, every muscle in my body going stiff as a board. I didn't want her to touch me. I didn't want to feel her motherly tenderness. I just wanted to be angry and damage everything I could get my hands on.

My insides shook as the tight hold on my control started to weaken.

"Sweetheart, I know this is hard for you, but you can't shut down. You have so much to live for and that's all we want. For you to live."

I didn't respond. I just sat there like I always did, in my pathetic wheelchair, with my pathetic broken body that was unable to do anything on its own. For the love of God, I'm thirty years old and my mother has to wipe my ass for me.

I was done. If I couldn't take care of myself, what was the point?

"I'll be back tomorrow. Get some sleep and call if you need anything. You have your cell?"

I lifted the small black phone up for her to see, then tucked it back into my pocket. If I lost this, who knows what would happen? I had used it a couple of times already and hated myself for it. It was when I'd been trying to go to the bathroom and slipped out of the chair before I could position myself correctly. I ended up on the floor with pain shooting through every nerve in my body. The phone was in my pocket, and I had to call the only number that was programmed into it.

Mom.

She brought Dad along with her that night. I never felt more humiliated in my life. I couldn't see his face, but I could feel the pity and the sorrow. The last thing I wanted my dad to see was one of his sons getting hurt because he couldn't get himself on the toilet. I knew he loved me. I even knew he was proud of me, but in my mind, the pride melted away in that one moment of weakness.

I shook my head and forced the images out of my mind. They only made me emotional; that was unacceptable. Anger was the only thing I wanted to feel anymore. I could handle anger. I knew its weaknesses and its strengths. Plus, it welcomed me more than sadness ever did.

"I love you, Merrick."

Again, I stayed silent, and I wanted to strangle myself for it. Mom was only trying to help, but for the life of me, I just couldn't let her.

This was my penance. The consequence I had to suffer through to somehow make up for losing my friends. It would never make up for it completely, but it certainly was a start.

I listened to Mom making her way through the house, switching off lights that she turned on earlier in the night. It was a task I wasn't grateful to lose.

Who the hell misses turning lights on and off?

I do.

God, I missed it. I missed *light*. Seeing one flicker of light would bring me joy, but it would be short lived. Lights always turn off. The sun eventually hides away. So, why not embrace the darkness?

Because I have always hated the dark, that's why.

Who the fuck likes darkness? There couldn't possibly be a soul out there that would be happy with darkness every minute of every day. It was depressing and lonely and ... cold.

I listened to my mother shut and lock the door before hearing her car back out of the driveway. She wouldn't be coming back tonight; that's how our fight started in the first place. I was tired of needing a babysitter and I was fine at night. There was no need for her to wake up whenever I did, which was a lot these days.

I didn't move my chair. Hardly moved at all. I stayed right there, listening to the sounds of the house. The sound of my own breathing gave me a headache, but it was all I could do these days, and I heard *everything*. They didn't mention that my hearing would improve as well as my sense of touch. Of course, I'm sure they assumed I would already know that, but when you find out you're blind and there is nothing anyone can do, you don't think about the positives. You think about all the shit you went through before, and you think about all the things you'll never see again. And everything ... everything gets blurry until it is consumed and forgotten.

I knew it was late by the time I finally moved from my spot by the window. The new clock Mom picked up for me, announced the time every hour. All I had to do was push a button to hear the exact time. It was annoying as hell, but helpful. Funny thing is, I don't remember ever thanking her for it.

"That's because you're an asshole," I said to myself, grumbling every word.

I was exhausted and wanted to slip into the oblivion that was sleep. An oblivion that could somehow turn into a nightmare when my subconscious decided to hate me. Every sound woke me, no matter how small. The creak of the house sent a spike in my blood pressure, making me wonder if someone was breaking in. The screech of tires from a car made me sweat bullets. The slam of a car door. The clanging sound of a train passing through town.

All of it was a reminder. How does one accept so many reminders all at once?

They don't. They just have to suffer through them.

Before I left my room, I thought once more of that voice. Why would she sing that song? Why would she sing at all, knowing that I could hear her?

I rolled my chair right back to the window, thumping into the wall and bed a few times, before I reached out and groped for the handle on the blinds. The smooth plastic felt so fragile in my hand. How effortless would it be for me to rip the whole thing down? I wouldn't see it fall, but I would hear it and feel it. Funny how that just wasn't enough.

I twisted the handle and only opened the blinds a tiny bit, or at least I hoped I did. I lifted the window until only a small crack was opened, and I listened.

The heat of summer in Morgan, Utah, was nothing compared to the scorching heat of that desert overseas. No matter how much I wanted to shut out the rest of the world, I couldn't bring myself to keep this window shut. Not when the warm breeze blowing into my room felt so invigorating. Safe.

I didn't hear anything for a while. Just the sound of a car passing by and birds chirping in the trees. Were those trees taller than I remembered?

I'd never know.

When there was nothing else, I finally decided to use the bathroom and go to bed. It took a lot longer than it should have, and my anger boiled all over again. I knew I smelled like the dump truck that hauled away the garbage every Thursday. My breath was awful, too, and I had dropped my toothbrush – again – and couldn't bend down to find it with my leg stuck in a ridiculous immobilizer. If it wasn't for the pillow my mom strapped to my foot, I would be crying out in pain every time I bumped into a wall. The damn leg was up and straight, for now, since my knee repair had been recent. No way bending over to find my toothbrush would be worth the pain.

I rolled back into my room, ignoring the rancid taste in my mouth. In sleep, I wouldn't register the lingering spices from the steak Mom cooked for me. I could deal with waiting until morning no matter how much it irked me. I'd dealt with a lot worse just a few months ago. You get used to sleeping in a box and smelling your sweat and grime. You get used to not having much more than what you could carry.

And you learn to appreciate the fact that you are even alive.

I finally found the window again and sighed with relief. Almost two months of mapping out the house I grew up in and it still took me forever to find something. Mom tried to help me remember the layout. She even placed rough stickers on the walls throughout, signaling me when it was time to turn the chair. There were changes all over the place to help accommodate my situation. It was more than I could ask for, but it was still difficult to adapt to. Once my other arm was working, it would be easier.

Fuck that. It would never be easier because I still couldn't see!

"Stop whining, you asshole," I whispered harshly and took a few deep breaths to calm myself.

There is a reason for my survival. God does not give these trials to those that cannot endure them.

I repeated the words my post trauma therapist had given me, but didn't feel them no matter how hard I tried. Still, I kept at it because I wasn't a quitter.

I had been given a chance to pull myself together. The same people that paid for Mom and Dad to travel to Germany to see me were the ones that provided the counseling that would supposedly help me cope. I was grateful for the help, but doubtful of the success.

I sat by the window for a few minutes longer, listening for the sound of someone moving in that room. Had these two houses always been so close together? I couldn't remember the exact distance, and I could never remember hearing much of anything back in the day. Now, it was as if everything was happening in *my* room when I heard the rattle of a doorknob.

My muscles tightened, sending an immediate pain through my leg and arm. Was that her? What the hell was her name?

"Are you sure it's okay, Mom?"

"Grace, you need a car. I'll get a ride with Karla in the morning. It'll be fine."

Grace.

Grace Samuelson.

I remembered her, but only because we'd been neighbors since the third grade. I couldn't remember her face, though. Was she the blonde that always followed me around the cafeteria junior year? No, that was the chick who ended up dating my friend, Kyle Gale, later that year.

What about the red head who was in my chemistry class and whose shirts were always too tight? No, that was the chick who ended up pregnant for graduation.

I could only remember the name.

Grace.

I lived next to her for years and couldn't see her face in my mind.

I was an asshole of the highest order for treating my mom the way I did, but this one took the cake. What kind of dick did a guy have to be to not know what the neighbor girl looked like? Did I ever even talk to her?

I couldn't remember if I had.

Wait! I did remember helping to fix her car once. It had saved me from running into Shannon Connors that first day of senior year. Shannon always waited for me in the morning, and being late that day saved me a few more days of her *not* knowing where my locker was. The girl could be annoying as hell, but she had a body that most of the guys in school drooled over. Sleeping with her was still one of my biggest mistakes.

"Thanks, Mom. I'll see you in the morning then. Goodnight."

The sound of her door closing was the last thing I heard for what could have been more than five minutes. She was just standing there. I would hear if she moved, wouldn't I?

Grace sighed and that's when I heard her footsteps shuffle across the room, then the sound of a zipper. Was she undressing? No, the zipper sounded larger than one would on clothing. Was it a backpack or a suitcase?

A few more moments of silence. Then she spoke. "I'm sorry about the song. I won't sing it again."

She knew I was there, but I couldn't bring myself to move. She couldn't see me, could she? Hell, I could have opened the blinds too far and not realized it. Should I continue to stay still? Pretend I'm not there, just breathing and listening. What would I say anyway?

"I'm glad you're safe now, Merrick."

Those were the last words she spoke before I heard the sound of her window sliding shut.

"I'm not," I replied, quietly.

Because I wasn't. I wasn't glad that I was safe and my friends weren't. I wasn't glad that I made it home while one of my men was still deep in a coma at the hospital in Germany because every time they tried to move him, he crashed. I wasn't glad that my best friend almost didn't make it home to his wife and unborn child.

I was miserable here, and I would be miserable tomorrow.

I struggled to get into bed, quickly giving up on removing my shirt and pants. I would just have to sleep in them and deal with the fight in the morning when Mom came to help me change. I would have to shower, too. That just added a whole new set of humiliations. The last time my mom had to bathe me herself, I had no idea that war even existed. I was a child. Now, I had regressed back to that pitiful state, knowing more about war than I cared to admit.

Sleep never came easy. Tonight was no different. The nightmares plagued me off and on, and I woke too many times to count; the same image in my mind. My brothers, my friends, the men that risked their lives for me every day and whom I risked mine for ... they all surrounded me. But they weren't the smiling, laughing group I had come to know before that day. They were all dead, bloodied and broken. And I was left standing there, unable to close my eyes and block out the pain. I looked down at my body to see my flesh on fire, feel the blood running down my face. I saw my leg bent awkwardly in several places. Then I screamed, knowing I couldn't get to any of them. Knowing I couldn't help them.

That's when I woke up and forced myself to stay awake.

"I'm hiring a nurse."

I almost choked on the shitty oatmeal I had insisted on making for myself. Mom wasn't one to drop bombs before saying, 'Hello, sweetie. How are you feeling today?' No, she was officially done, and I only had myself to blame. It was two days since the blow up with my mother. She'd barely said two words to me in all the time she was here. She stopped staying the night, though, so I figured she was still upset that she actually lost that battle.

"You what?"

"I'm hiring a nurse to come help you. I've tried. You don't want me here, which hurts, but I can deal with it. I don't know what you're going through, and I can't pretend to know, but I can distance myself enough to let you deal. I'm hiring a professional to come and help you get cleaned up, take your meds, help with your therapy, and teach you how to adjust."

"I don't need a–"

"I don't care, Merrick. It's happening and I swear to God if you treat her badly, I will be back here wiping your ass and coddling you the very next day."

Well, she had me there.

"Her?"

"Yes, her. Homecare just took on a new nurse and I'm hiring her to come here."

"Who is it?"

"I haven't spoken with her, yet, but I have no doubt she will be able to handle you."

Handle me? Well, I guess she had me there, too.

"Micah is coming by in a few minutes to stay with you. I'm going to go interview the nurse and, if all goes well, she will be starting tomorrow."

I wanted to scream that Micah was the last person I wanted to see, but he was better than Mary and Mitch. My older sister and youngest brother could be annoying as hell, and they relished the idea of pissing me off. Especially since I'd done nothing but bitch and complain since I had gotten home. Their visits became less and less frequent, including Micah's. But he and I were always the closest, and I had a little hope that he would know to leave me the hell alone today.

"He was working the ER last night so go easy on him. Okay, Merrick?"

"Yeah," I grunted, digging back into my oatmeal. God, I sucked at cooking. If I couldn't make oatmeal taste like food, I was screwed.

I pushed the bowl of mush away from me and attempted to turn my chair toward the hallway. I missed it by inches and crashed into the wall. Mom didn't even hesitate. I felt her grab hold of the handles behind me and turn me before guiding my chair to my room. She wasn't going to let me go without a fight and, for the sake of my sanity the love she had for her second child, I would have to comply.

"You're getting in the shower."

"Mom, I don't want you to hurt yourself."

"You say that every time," she snapped and helped me take off my shirt. "I haven't hurt myself once. You may think you're a tough soldier, but you are still my boy. I don't care how heavy you are, I will always be able to lift my boy."

Mom was just tossing me left and right today. How many times would she put me in my place before Micah showed up?

A shower that should have taken five minutes, took thirty. I tried to dress myself, but it was no use. My hand ached, my leg throbbed, and my entire body felt like it was on fire.

"Did you take any medication this morning?" Mom asked.

I was suddenly grateful that looking her in the eye was *not* an option.

"I don't need it."

"You do."

It was the shake of a pill bottle that signaled my doom. Before I could argue, she had shoved them in my mouth and forced me to drink water. I hated the pills. I hated the heavy feeling, the numbness. And they made me groggy. It was uncomfortable to sleep in my chair, but when I took the pain meds, it's where I ended up. I wouldn't have the strength to get into bed.

"Right. I'm going to make you boys some sandwiches before I leave. I'm putting you by the window. It's opened."

The way she said it ... it was mischievous. Like she knew something I didn't, which grated on my nerves. Blindness was the worst thing that could possibly happen to me because I hated not knowing what something looked like or what was happening around me.

I'd always been that way, but after the things I saw during my tour, it became pure instinct. A need that I could no longer access.

I sat and brooded for a long time before I felt the pain meds kick in. They took longer and longer to work each time. It only made me hate them more.

My ears picked up the sound of movement on my right, the side the window was on. Mom had at least thought about that in her haste to leave me alone. My right side looked normal while the left side of my face looked ...

Fuck, I had no idea what it looked like or how many scars covered my cheek and jaw. All I knew was that my skin didn't feel like skin and my eyes didn't feel like they were even in my head anymore.

I heard it then. Her voice. It was sexy and smoky, and I could only imagine what kind of face came with a voice like that. She was only humming. The melody was familiar, but I couldn't place it. Not until she started singing and I realized how badly I needed to hear her after only one time.

'Say It Ain't So' by Weezer.

God damn. The first words of that song, in that voice.

How long had it been since I felt any movement down there? A long damn time. If only I could remember her face. I'm sure I saw her plenty over the years. Weezer was one of my favorite bands back in the day and for her to know that, well, I guess that just means she had seen *me* plenty, too. The fact that I even considered she was singing just for me showed how much of a dumbass I truly was.

I closed my eyes and just listened, not even thinking about seeing. The way she sang the song, one that normally sounded strange; she made it sound like a fucking prayer. She slowed the melody to a pace that could only be considered a love song. And the way her voice hit the notes, as if it had been written for her voice alone. Damn. It was phenomenal.

Peace.

I felt calm, sitting there listening to Grace Samuelson sing.

I felt like nothing else mattered, except listening to her voice caress each note, each word. It was serenity.

"Merrick! Can you hear me?"

I pointlessly turned my head, expecting to see my brother's face, but still only seeing blackness. Grace's singing abruptly stopped, and I knew I was caught. I didn't even know if the blinds were open as I shamelessly eavesdropped on her quiet moment.

I clenched my fists, embarrassed that Micah had basically ratted me out. "I can hear better than you think, Micah."

"I've been calling for you since I got here and when I walked in here, you looked like you were sleeping. You were so still. Had to make sure you were alive."

"Asshole."

Micah laughed, which made me want to laugh with him, but I didn't. I couldn't.

"Come on, man. Mom made some killer sandwiches."

I maneuvered my chair with one hand and my good leg, then rolled myself around my bed.

"Hey, isn't that Grace?"

I stopped and hoped he could see the glare I was supposedly sending his way.

"Hi, Grace. How you doin'?"

Closing my eyes didn't hide me, but I still hoped my brother was just playing with me.

"Micah Thatcher. I'm doing well. How are you?"

"Can't complain," my brother called a little loudly, making me flinch away. "I heard you were back in town."

"Yeah, for a while."

"We'll have to get together sometime and catch up."

"I'd like that, Micah."

I could hear the smile in her voice, and I instantly hated my brother. All she would have to do is look at me and her smile would be wiped away. The only chance I had with her was listening to her sing.

A chance with her? What the hell, Merrick?

"I'm hungry, Micah, so get out of my way."

I heard my brother sigh and felt his body move to the side of me. Without pausing, I rolled my way into the hallway, away from their voices. Micah was asking about something to do with the hospital and I shook my head. He needed to work on his flirting skills. He was at work all the time. Couldn't he just leave it there?

My bitterness only heightened by the time lunch was finished. Micah went on and on about Mary and Mitch, telling me what they were up to, that they said 'Hi', and they were worried about me. I stayed quiet and ignored the information, pretending not to hear his questions. Once I took my last bite of the delicious sandwich Mom made, I rolled away from the kitchen and placed myself at the window that looked out into the backyard.

At least, I hoped that was where I was.

There was no point in placing myself anywhere because the view was always the same, but Micah took the hint and left me alone the rest of the day. He only showed up in front of me to help with something I should have been able to do myself. I'm pretty sure he took a nice long nap, too.

No nightmares to wake him and no pain to make him suffer. But he left me alone and that's exactly what I wanted.

I was bored, groggy, and in pain. Wishing for sleep and dreading it all at once. By the time Micah left, Mom had returned and was helping me get ready for bed. She hummed to herself as she guided my injured arm out of the sleeve of my shirt. Hell, I could have been wearing pink all day and never known.

"The nurse is going to be here bright and early, Merrick. She's wonderful and I know you'll like her."

"What's her name?" I asked, suddenly curious about the woman my mother was going to trust her son not to kill. I completely ignored the voice in my head telling me why names were suddenly important now.

"Oh, I don't think you know her that well. I'll introduce you tomorrow and show her around. You better behave or I'll tell her where your guns are hidden."

I scoffed and rolled my eyes. The ache I felt each time I moved them was there, but it had dulled and the medication almost made it non-existent. Now, it just felt like holes in my head that throbbed on occasion.

"I spoke with Dr. Hopkins. He wants to see you next week and check your hardware. I scheduled it for the late morning."

"Sounds good, Mom."

I felt her flinch and knew she was shocked to hear me agree with her instead of argue. She didn't rub it in, and I was glad I couldn't see her face. She would have tears in her eyes, I just knew it.

Instead of acknowledging my acquiescence, she helped me into bed. I tried to relax as she fed me another dose of pain medication, but everything inside me wanted to slap them away.

"I'll see you in the morning. Cell phone is on the night stand and plugged in. There's a glass of water as well. I know you'll be fine, Merrick, but I'm your mother and I still worry, so please call me if you need anything."

"I will, Mom."

I was too exhausted to be angry, too drugged up to frown. All I could do was lie there and listen to my mother lock up before she climbed into her car and drove away.

I didn't sleep. In fact, with how tired I was, I was surprised I hadn't already fallen asleep and woken up to my nightmares. I tried to adjust my position and groaned when the throb in my leg morphed into a stabbing pain. I shifted again, sighing. Guess I would just be staring into nothing tonight like I did every night I laid awake.

I heard a rustle near the window and my body tensed. Was someone trying to break in? My pulse raced and my ears perked. Every muscle in my body stayed perfectly still, controlled, waiting for another sound. Waiting for an explosion or the raspy whistle of a mortar. The same sounds that haunted me in my dreams.

Then, as if a splash of cold water hit me in the face, I remembered. I was useless if there was a break in, so what the hell? Let them take everything and leave me in peace.

Another rustle and a feminine sigh.

Grace.

She started to hum, her husky voice reaching my ears as clearly as if she were right beside me. My imagination wandered. I could almost picture a beautiful woman lying next to me, playing with my hair or running her fingers over my chest. Blood slowly made its way down my body until I was at half mast. Grace continued to hum.

This is so wrong, Merrick.

It wasn't long before she stopped humming and took a deep breath. The silence almost made the pain worse, and the medication seemed to be fading faster than ever before. If I didn't fall asleep soon, I would be awake until the nurse showed up. Then, who knows what I would do?

"It feels like a Weezer kind of night, don't you think?"

She was talking to me, but I didn't reply. I would only say something stupid or rude when she was only trying to help me.

I knew that, deep down in my broken bones.

She sang about being terrified of everything, but seeing someone who was strong.

Her voice took the pain away. I wouldn't have believed it if I wasn't experiencing it for myself. Her voice took my mind away from my body until all I could do was listen. All I could feel was her voice. Not the aching in my limbs or the hollow in my head.

Just her.

'Hold Me.'

She sang it slowly, like a lullaby, and before I could stop myself, my useless eyes closed and my mind drifted away.

I slept.

And I dreamed of Grace.

Chapter Three

Grace

This was a mistake. I never should have agreed to this job, but I was *almost* desperate for work and *completely* desperate to keep busy. I figured the possibility of a non-stop argument with an abrasive and bitter man was better than waiting for a call to help an old woman or man who didn't want to talk.

A couple months.

I could do a couple months of that and come out of it alive.

When Emma had approached me the day before, all but begging me to help her out, I couldn't refuse. I hesitated, but I didn't say no. That should have told me something about myself.

Either I was a glutton for punishment, or I was just very, very stupid.

She looked worried when she left, and I could only imagine what she was predicting would happen. She knew her son better than I did. Right?

I didn't believe that Merrick was hostile enough to kill me. In fact, I think he kind of liked me. I sang whenever I knew he was in his room, and he stayed still and silent instead of grunting and groaning like I heard him do so many times over the last few days.

He treated his mother like shit, but she stayed with it. I admired her for that.

I hated to admit that I was purposely eavesdropping on their short conversation the night before. It had been as much of a surprise to me as it was to Emma that her son didn't put up a fight. Through the blinds covering my window, I'd watched as she helped him get ready for bed.

He slept in his underwear and that surely spiked my blood pressure to dangerous levels. Not just at the idea of him sleeping in so little, but at the sight of his still-amazing body. He was injured and, looking at him, those injuries stood out starkly. His scarring was still fresh and looked incredibly painful. The left side of his face that I could finally see, looked battered. There was no bruising like I expected, but I should have known better. It had been well over two months since his initial injuries, and although he wasn't healed, he was well on his way.

What fascinated me were the parts of his body that were *not* injured. He was still fit for being in a wheelchair and unable to do pretty much everything. His good arm flexed powerfully whenever he moved and his chest was a sight to behold.

Merrick Thatcher was one of the sexiest men I had ever laid eyes on. Dark brown hair that hung in his eyes only made him look more intense. His strength must have been massive before he was injured. He was still a soldier, hurt or not.

I couldn't get a glimpse of the boy he was before he went to war, before he went into the military. That care-free heart breaker was no longer in there. He changed and I'm not just talking about the change that war causes. He had become a man, and it was obvious he didn't think he was a *whole* man anymore.

Emma was just pulling into the driveway when I walked out of my house. At least I wouldn't need a car to get to my job, and Mom wouldn't have to worry about transportation.

"Hello, dear. Thank you so much again for doing this." Her dark, brown hair glistened in the morning sunlight while her smile lit up the rest of her face. Blue eyes beamed back at me and I wondered how she did it every day. Even under pressure, she glowed.

"It's no problem, Mrs. Thatcher. It's my job. I'm just happy to have one."

"Oh, Grace, you call me Emma and I know it's your job, but I have the feeling Merrick will make you work for it. That or he'll chase you away before lunch."

"I think I can handle him," I replied with a sweet smile.

She winked at me and led the way to the front door. I didn't think Merrick even remembered me, and if he knew my name at all, it was because Micah had greeted me in front of him.

"I haven't told him your name yet and I think it will be a shock to him, so just ignore any rude remarks he makes."

I giggled softly and shook my head. I should have known Emma would be sneaky about this. In fact, I was surprised she even told Merrick she hired a nurse in the first place. It was more strategic to just drop the bomb on him, wasn't it?

Before she could unlock the front door, I stopped her, placing my hand on her arm. "I do have one question before we go in."

"What is it?" Emma asked, looking worried.

"Why me?"

She sighed and nodded her head. "I understand that it might be awkward and that you and Merrick never really knew each other, but the other day, I saw something change in him. I think you might be the one to get through to him."

"But I haven't done anything. He doesn't even know me, why would he trust me?"

"Oh, but you *have* done something, Grace."

She didn't explain any further and opened the door. I was back to square one.

"Merrick, we're here."

Grumbling came in loud and clear, from the front corner of the house. I couldn't help but smile. He acted like a child most of the time. I could deal with a child. I was only nervous to deal with the man.

Emma quickly moved down the short hallway, leaving me awkwardly standing in the foyer.

"I need another toothbrush. Dropped it in the fucking toilet again. Maybe you should just stack them on my dresser so I can use a new one each day."

"Oh, calm down, Merrick. We'll figure something out. Maybe if you weren't banging everything around every morning you wouldn't lose your toothbrush so easily. And watch your mouth. The nurse is here and I doubt she wants to hear the filth you spew daily."

"Then she can fucking leave. I don't need her anyway."

I took a deep breath as they rounded the corner, Merrick in his wheelchair with Emma guiding it carefully.

"It's only for a couple months, tops. Maybe not even that long if you're compliant with your exercises and you stop trying to do everything on your own."

Merrick huffed and put his hand down to stop the wheelchair. Emma shook her head and came to stand next to me.

I kept my gaze on Merrick and felt like that mistake I was worried about before, was actually bigger than I originally thought. *He* was bigger than I thought. He dwarfed the poor chair, and his presence alone made me feel breathless. He was very intimidating, but it was when he finally raised his head that I saw a hint of vulnerability. His eyes moved to the side of us. The reminder of his blindness was painful.

Those eyes may not be able to see, but they were just as beautiful as I remembered. A light blue, clear and sharp. Although, looking at them closer, the color had almost dulled and the whites of his eyes were tinted red. I knew he didn't sleep much since I had to resort to shutting my window at night to keep out the sounds of his restlessness. The visual evidence of his exhaustion made me feel guilty for blocking it out.

The scarring on his face looked painful, like whatever happened was actually worse than one could imagine. His left temple and ear looked like it was burned, and the skin was red and raw. It was the jagged scar which started at the side of his neck, however, that reminded me how lucky he was to be alive. The puckered skin followed a direct path over his jaw, up his cheek, crossed over his left eye, and ended just above his brow. That's when I noticed his left eye looked slightly distorted. Whatever caused the injury, caused significant damage to whatever it touched. There was another small scar beneath his right eye, but for the most part, the right side of his face looked completely normal.

My gaze moved down to his good arm which flexed as he held his chair in place. I wondered why he hadn't gotten an electric one that would move around easier, but the scowl on his face answered that question for me. Either he pissed off the insurance company or he had flat-out refused an electric chair. Both were likely. Still, even with his injuries, he looked strong. Just tired. His shirt was twisted as if he was in a hurry to dress and couldn't quite get it right. And was it backwards?

Merrick's impatient sigh forced both me and Emma to snap to attention. Emma had been watching me carefully as I took in her son's appearance. I hoped I didn't disappoint her. His injuries were extreme, but it didn't draw away from his attractiveness. In no way were his scars repulsive to me, and my heart constricted at the thought of *anyone* feeling that way.

"This is my son, Merrick."

He waited for Emma to introduce me, but she looked at me expectantly. I only hesitated a moment before I introduced myself. "Hi, Merrick. I'm Grace."

His entire body stiffened like a board when I spoke, and his eyes widened in shock. I hadn't been expecting that kind of response, but then again, what *did* I expect? A warm smile and a handshake was less than likely.

Emma shifted next to me as we both waited for the explosion.

It didn't come.

I started talking again, Merrick's expression going from unbelieving, to complete and utter astonishment. As if reality had just hit him in the face. Hard.

"I'm going to help you as much as I can, as much as you'll let me, and I hope that it produces results."

"Grace," he whispered, so softly I almost didn't hear him.

"Yes, I'm Grace. I'm also your neighbor."

Merrick's lips pressed into a thin, tight line, and I was grateful he couldn't see me staring at them so intently. They were very nice lips, full and soft looking, even when they were strained in anger. He frantically turned his chair with one hand and one leg and rolled away as quickly as his body would let him, running into the wall several times before he finally stopped. Both Emma and I could hear his deep breaths coming from his room.

He was either furious or having some kind of episode, neither of which were acceptable in my book. I was itching to go to him and help him calm down.

Emma led the way to his room, and I watched as she picked up some clothes that had been lying on the floor. I stayed in the doorway, waiting.

Merrick seemed to gather his control when his mother said his name for the third time. "How could you do this, Mom? It's hard enough that a complete stranger will be seeing me like this, but the neighbor? Is she even qualified?"

"Shut your mouth, Merrick Isaiah Thatcher. Grace is very qualified and she is doing *this* instead of working something easier with much better pay. You show her some respect, and stop whining."

"Mom, I'm sure she can't lift me and what about the whole conflict of interest shit you're always telling me about? I don't think it's a good idea."

"I can assure you, Merrick, that I am very capable of doing this job," I said, firmly. He dropped his head. "And since you and I *are* practically strangers, I don't believe a conflict of interest is the case here."

"You aren't a stranger," he snapped.

"But I am."

"You—" he growled and raked his hand through his hair. His jaw ticked from grinding his teeth together. "Get out."

Emma didn't hesitate to move him further away from the doorway. Once he was out of the way, she exited the room and pulled me into the kitchen where she pointed out Merrick's chart. I had to admit, I was very curious about what had happened to him, but I was mostly curious about his injuries.

How many surgeries had he been through and what else was he going to be subjected to before he was out of that chair?

Emma sat on one of the stools tucked up against the island in their kitchen. "Give him a minute to warm up to the fact that an attractive nurse is going to see him naked."

I giggled and shook my head. "If he could see me, I think he would disagree with you."

Emma eyed me carefully before pulling a list out of her pocket. "Then I guess you're *both* blind."

The next hour was spent with Emma showing me around the house, making sure I understood my duties. It was the typical homecare nursing job, and she was obviously worried about leaving me alone with Merrick, who hadn't even come out of his room once.

"I think that's it," she chimed, sighing tiredly. "If you have any questions, please call me. I'm on shift tonight, but my husband, Nathan, will be available in the evening."

"That sounds good. I think we will be just fine."

"Good."

She spoke with Merrick for a few minutes while I went over his list of medications and required exercises. I left the chart for last.

He had been taking antibiotics early on for his burns and hadn't suffered with any kind of infection. It was actually pretty amazing he healed so efficiently. The kinds of burns he'd endured were usually very temperamental, but the skin grafts were remarkably successful, and the doctors had noted that they didn't expect any fallback.

The injuries to his left leg ... I hurt just reading about those. He had a comminuted fracture to his femoral shaft that was treated with surgery a couple of times. In the initial surgery, pins and plates were placed for a temporary fix until his other injuries could be treated. It wasn't long before they opened him up again to place a rod down his femur. His tibia and fibula had both been fractured near the ankle and the ligaments in his knee had been torn completely. No wonder he was still in a wheelchair three months after going into the hospital. The surgeries only just recently came to a close.

Merrick had been so busy dealing with his other injuries, there was probably no time to focus on his lack of sight.

Traumatic Optic Neuropathy. He was diagnosed shortly after returning to the states and by then, it was too late to do anything. According to his chart, the left eye was too damaged to even consider surgery. The questions about his right eye were still unanswered, but the words 'irreparable' and 'possible optic nerve damage' were enough of an answer to me.

The notes on his lack of compliance didn't surprise me either.

I'd only worked with one blind patient a couple years prior. It was in the ER and only for a few moments before the doctor took over. I had no experience with the blind, but from what Emma explained to me and showed me, it was pretty straight forward. I had an idea of what kinds of things could be made easier and decided to start there.

Emma knew my experience was limited and, for some reason, she still trusted me instead of an expert. I wasn't about to disappoint her.

I heard a few thumps down the hall, but didn't bother looking that way. Merrick was coming towards the kitchen. I was ready for the most part.

He rolled in and felt his way to the fridge before taking a moment to position his chair so he could open the door. He didn't grab anything out of it, in fact, I think he had forgotten that he couldn't see anything inside of it when he made the decision to look in the first place. It was a habit.

"I could make you something if you'd like."

"You're my nurse, not my maid," he grumbled.

I rolled my eyes and pushed away from the counter. "Nurses are capable of putting together a bite to eat."

He tried to slam the door shut, but his chair stopped it, making several items in the door rattle around. He breathed heavily, his face going red with anger. God, he was handsome and so intense when he was angry, but if he was this good looking when he was pissed, I don't think I would be able to handle a smile. Instead of making sure the fridge door was shut, he rolled his way back down the hall, thumping the wall a time or two before gliding into his room.

I watched him go and felt my nose start to sting. Seeing him struggle wasn't easy, and the compassionate girl in me wanted to cry for him, but she didn't.

He needed to move forward and learn to live again.

I shut the fridge door, but grabbed an apple and bottle of water first, then made my way down the short hallway to Merrick's room. I wasn't quiet about it, but he ignored me as if he didn't even acknowledge my presence. He sat next to his window, his eyes pointing down to his lap and his good hand bunched into a fist.

"This isn't going to work if you don't learn to trust me. I'm here to help and I know you don't need it, but the doctor has ordered it," I said, setting the apple and water bottle down on the desk next to him. "You of all people should know what it's like to follow rules and obey orders."

His head snapped up and he scowled at the space in front of him. "What the hell is that supposed to mean?"

I wasn't surprised by his anger, but his intensity scared me this time. "It means that you were in the military. You followed orders and you learned discipline. You should understand that what you learned there, can apply to your life here."

He sat forward in his chair, his expression rock solid. "What I learned there could never apply to my life here. What I learned there was that the man beside me could die at any moment and it was up to me to protect him. You have no clue what it's like to know that kind of failure."

His words were a slap in the face, a cold reminder that he was dealing with something much darker than pain. He was right. I didn't know war, but I knew loss. I knew failure. I knew what it felt like to have your heart and soul ripped away from your body, leaving you empty and alone.

"I know more than you think, Merrick Thatcher. Don't underestimate me, but most importantly, don't underestimate yourself." I took a step back and saw the stone cold expression on his face soften, only a little bit. "An apple and bottle of water are at two o'clock on the desk. Once you eat something, we'll get started on your exercises."

I turned and walked away before he could respond. I didn't care what he said at this point. He had no right to provoke me, and I wasn't going to make this easy for him. I needed this job and he needed *me*.

I let the anger fester for a short time before I made lunch. I ate alone since Merrick never came out of his room.

When I wandered into the bathroom across the hall from his closed door, I saw one of the problems that I could fix. The pedestal sink allowed space for a wheelchair, but it didn't allow for much of anything else. He had nowhere to set his toothbrush so it could be easily reachable. I would have to speak with Emma about that later. I inspected the shower and found everything I would need, readily available including a seat and handicap bar. I was also happy to see a tub mat already in place. Slipping would be horrendous with two hundred and thirty-plus pounds of naked man falling on top of me.

I switched off the light and made my way to the living room. The Thatcher's home was beautiful. Wood floors, expensive furniture, stainless steel appliances in the kitchen. According to Mom, they had renovated the house shortly after they moved across town, always planning to keep it for their children, should they need it.

I remember being in the house a couple times before, when Mom and Dad had been invited for dinner. Merrick was never there, but Micah always kept me company. He even spoke to me in school and whenever he saw me outside. The funny part was that he was the reserved one in the family. He was a shy kid for a long time, but never around me. Micah wasn't a charmer like his older brother, but he certainly had that look about him. He would be a successful doctor in the very near future, too. He was smart and compassionate and even being reserved, he was good with people.

I used to think that Merrick would become the one everyone in town gravitated towards. Maybe, for a while there, he actually was that man. He had a job, a life, and a purpose. He did his part and took responsibility. I could only imagine what coming home would be like, only to lose all of that.

I'd seen the people come and go over the last few days, hoping to visit with him and bring him food, only to be turned away.

Mom told me that when he first got home, there were lines of people across the front yard, all hoping to see him and thank him for his service. He refused to come out of his room and Emma handled the thank-you-come-back-when-he's-feeling-better speeches.

I didn't think anyone would come by again because I didn't think Merrick would *ever* feel better.

My mind wandered to the first conversation I had with him just hours earlier. He said I wasn't a stranger and I missed it at the time, determined to argue back just as hard. Now that I thought about it, I wondered what he meant. I *was* technically a stranger, but in ways, I guess I wasn't. We had been neighbors for most of our lives and even though he never acknowledged me or even saw me, he was aware of me in one way or another.

I mean, seriously. How can someone never know their neighbor? Especially one he was in school with.

I leaned back on the couch and, without realizing it, started to hum. I always loved to sing. It was a way to calm myself whenever I got too nervous before a test or whenever I was going to be in a big crowd. Singing was one of the things I looked forward to when I found out I was pregnant. I sang to my belly every night, and I wrote songs for my baby for the nights she would spend crying with a fever or just overtired to the point where she would scream. I had prepared for those moments and, in a way, looked forward to them.

But I would never have them.

I closed my eyes and hummed a random melody.

The thump on the wall in the hallway made me grin, but I pulled it back. I didn't stop humming, keeping my eyes closed. All the while, Merrick was trying to be stealthy and get closer without being seen. I glanced over and saw his leg poking around the corner. Amusement felt wrong, but everyone needed a little hilarity once in a while. He didn't know I could see him, and I didn't *let* him know. If this is what it came down to, so be it.

I started to hum a little louder and kept my eyes on the giant leg covered in a thick black immobilizer. Damn, that looked uncomfortable. I started planning out a therapy schedule in my mind to improve his movement and get him out of that thing as soon as possible. He didn't move from that spot as he listened to another random melody pour out of my mouth.

Maybe that was the key.

For a man who couldn't see, the sound of peace was the only comfort he would get.

Chapter Four

Merrick

Almost a week of this shit and I was no closer to chasing Grace away.

My plan to get rid of her, quickly and quietly, didn't work. In fact, a part of me didn't even want her to ever leave. She hummed with everything she did and when she wasn't humming, she was singing.

When she was singing, I wasn't hurting.

It took the anger away. The anger I needed, to get through each day without falling apart.

We didn't talk much, except for the occasional argument back and forth about being compliant and following orders. After she invaded my privacy by stealing my phone to add her number to the speed dial, I spent most of each day locked up in my room.

Avoiding her was easy, but holding my bladder together wasn't.

Grace didn't coddle me and she allowed me to make the first attempts by myself, but she was always close by. It was actually surprising how proficient I became at lifting myself out of the chair and onto the damn toilet, just to avoid needing her help. Once I was finished, she left me to myself until I needed her, which was more often than not. It was exhausting trying to dress myself, use the bathroom, or just move around the house. I didn't shower because I couldn't stand the thought of her seeing me that way. Seeing the scars that covered my body and feeling her pity. It just wasn't a step I wanted to take.

I was starting to ferment, though, and I couldn't even stand to smell myself anymore. That didn't stop my refusal. She didn't push too hard at first, either, which made me wary.

On the third day, she arrived to find me still lying in my bed. After arguing with me about getting up and starting the day, she finally left me to sleep for another hour before she threatened to call my mother. If I was any weaker, I wouldn't have been able to stop her from forcing the pain medication down my throat. She relented for as long as possible, but when I couldn't hide the pain any longer, she put up quite the fight.

For such a tiny woman, she sure did have a bite.

There were no more late night lullabies after that. I didn't need them anyway.

At least, that's what I kept telling myself.

I don't need them. I don't need them.

I used a washcloth, late one night, to clean the stink off of me, but it didn't do any good. I could still smell myself. It was Friday now, and I was almost desperate for a shower. It was obvious I looked like a moron, thinking I could win this battle.

I was still sleeping when she arrived, waking to the sound of her humming in the kitchen along with the rustle of papers.

It took more effort than normal, but I finally got out of bed and into the chair that controlled my life these days. I felt my way along the wall and, for the first time in a week, didn't bump into the door. It was getting easier to maneuver the bulky wheelchair, and a small weight lifted off of my shoulders when I made it to the kitchen *without* putting another dent in the wall.

"Good morning, Merrick. You reek."

My lips tugged into a grin when I heard her greeting. She was sarcastic and straight forward, but she always did it sweetly. I heard her gasp before I could pull the grin back.

"Your smile makes up for it, though. Don't worry, I won't tell. We wouldn't want to ruin your bad-ass reputation, would we?"

I wanted to laugh. This woman challenged me at every turn, and I had to admit, I really liked it. Instead of laughing, I turned my chair to the fridge, barely stopping myself before opening it. That was a hard habit to break.

"I've organized the fridge for you. Would you like me to show you where everything is now, or after you shower?"

I was still focused on the fact that she thought organizing the fridge would help me, so I almost didn't catch the animosity in her voice.

"I'll call my mother myself, but you aren't helping me shower."

"Then you aren't eating today," she said sweetly.

"Excuse me?"

"I think you heard me."

I wanted to be able to walk and see, just for a few moments, so badly. Just enough time for me to grab her and spank the living daylights out of her. She thought she could threaten me?

"Didn't anyone ever teach you not to make idle threats?" I warned.

"Oh, that threat is very much legit, Merrick. Everything in that fridge has been placed in a container that's easy to open and labeled in Braille. So, unless you've learned to read Braille in the last month, which I highly doubt based on your cheery disposition, you aren't going to know what you're getting into. Unless you want to sniff everything, but I doubt you'd be able to decipher what's what under that stench you're putting off."

I could do nothing but let my mouth fall open in shock. She was completely serious.

"I know you're probably asking yourself, 'how could she?', so let me explain."

I heard her slip off of her stool and walk toward me. God, she smelled good. I could smell her sweet scent over my own stink and no matter how hard I tried, since that first day, I couldn't get it out of my mind. Was it vanilla or honey?

"You're going to let me help you shower today or you aren't going to eat at all. Now I know you need your food, but with your mother's approval, I'm laying down the law."

"What law?"

"The shower law."

"I'm a grown man."

"I'm a grown woman."

"This is childish," I bit out.

"*You're* childish."

"Seriously?"

"Stop pushing me away, Merrick," she said firmly, but I could hear the emotion she was trying to hide. My chest started to ache. I was stubborn, but up until now, it only hurt *me*. Mom didn't even let it get to her, most of the time.

Now, that stubbornness had penetrated Grace's soft skin and, instead of chasing her away, I was only making her life harder. *I'm officially at Top-Asshole status.*

"Stop trying to erase everyone from your life and stop trying to slowly kill yourself. You want to honor your fellow soldiers? Live for them. Get better *for them*."

If I could just see her face ... that would be the end of it. I'd never been one to go for a stubborn woman, but Grace just had something about her that challenged me. The way she put me in my place was refreshing. It was effortless to like her and too easy to fall for her. Even when I tried so hard to push her away.

Why the hell hadn't I noticed her before?

"Now, are you going to let me help you or are you going to ferment a little more?" she asked.

I shifted my eyes up, hoping to catch a glimpse of whatever expression she was throwing my way. All I could see was ... nothing. I didn't even know if my eyes were pointed at *her*. I swallowed down the lump in my throat and forced myself to get it together. It was pointless to hope for something that I knew would never happen.

Something that *couldn't* happen.

Grace sighed. I felt her hand on my good arm a moment later, and her voice came from below me when she spoke. She was crouched down in front of me.

"I'm a professional first, Merrick. I know it's awkward to let someone help you with the basics, but right now, it's necessary. Soon, you'll be healed up and won't need anyone's help and I'll be out of your life forever. Until then, I'm running the show, okay? And I promise to be respectful."

Out of my life? I didn't want that. Not at all. But I was too much of a chump to admit it out loud. She was right. It was time to start cooperating. "Respectful?"

"Yes," she replied. "I'm not going to grope you, I promise. I'm more desperate to stop smelling you."

"I stink that bad?" I asked, feeling a twitch in my lips as I fought the grin.

She chuckled softly and stood, keeping her hand on my arm. "Yes. You smell like a garbage truck."

I dropped my head to hide the smile forcing its way through. "Then I guess I better get cleaned up."

"Good idea."

She was walking away when I spoke. "Then maybe you can grope me after."

Her steps silenced. A few tense seconds passed before her laughter reached my ears. A sound she could easily sell to the darkest souls out there.

"He jokes! I'm in shock over here, Merrick," she said through her laughter. Then her steps moved farther away.

She thought I was joking.

Let her, Merrick.

That's when it hit me. She won. I didn't even see it coming. Just a few words out of her mouth and I was basically her bitch now.

Is it bad that I didn't really care?

I turned my chair to follow Grace, but I was in too much of a hurry this time. Before I could reach out to the wall, the chair smacked into it. I grumbled a curse and tried to shift, but the damn thing wouldn't budge.

"The pillow dropped, Merrick. It's stopping the wheel. Here let me get it first."

Her scent surrounded me once more, and she brushed up against my good leg as she pulled the pillow out from under the wheel. My earlier joke was now at the forefront of my mind and slowly trickling downward. *Not now. Not when I'm about to be naked.*

That had been my biggest worry since she showed up. An erection popping up while she was helping me shower, was *not* going to be my finest hour. Not that I had many of those anyway.

Would she run screaming if she knew I was attracted to her? And how the hell could I be attracted to her if I couldn't even see her?

Because you know, Merrick. You know she's beautiful. You can feel it in your bones.

"All set. I'm heading to the bathroom. I'll meet you in there."

She didn't offer to push me down the hall, and she didn't doubt that I would follow her in the first place. I'd bet my savings account that she had a sway to her hips when she walked. I would probably crash into the wall with that kind of distraction anyway.

Damn, I missed seeing a beautiful woman. Seeing the teasing curves of a *real* woman and being on the other end of a sensual smile. That's the kind of thing that should be keeping me up at night.

As I turned the corner, my ears picked up the sound of Grace moving things around in the shower. I rolled into the bathroom and waited. My good hand was balled into a fist and the need to fidget was stronger than ever. Do I just start trying to undress or do I wait for her help? Was she going to watch me? Did I *want* her to watch me?

I was in uncharted territory now. The decision to cooperate was much harder than the arguing, but she was right. I had been childish. For some reason, this woman made me want to change that.

"Alright, Merrick. I don't know how your mom did this, but my way is going to be pretty easy. Let's take your shirt off first," she said, her tone professional. Her hands landed on my shoulders, letting me know she was there. When they quickly dropped down to my chest, I felt like the wind was knocked clean out of me.

"You okay?" she asked, her hands faltering.

I'd never been a heavy breather, but fuck if I could control it in that moment.

"What are you doing?" I asked, shakily. My voice sounded like sandpaper since my mouth had gone dry just seconds ago.

"I'm helping you remove your shirt. I just want you to know where my hands are so I don't startle you."

Oh. Well, that makes sense.

"Okay."

"Okay," she said, then took a deep breath.

"Proceed," I said as casually as I could. Her soft laugh didn't help the situation at all.

Those gentle hands moved to the hem of my shirt, and lifted. Cool air hit my stomach and I felt goose bumps trail across my skin. She adjusted my shirt until I could pull my good arm through it, then she lifted it over my head. I felt a few tugs on the sling protecting my other arm. Once it was free, she gently maneuvered my arm so she could remove the shirt completely.

My good hand absently scratched through the scruff on my face. I needed to shave soon or it would take me even longer than it already did. I could feel the patches that were more scraggly than others. There was no way to make it even and I'd forced Mom to stop doing it for me. Getting used to the feel of it without seeing it would take a while.

Why do you even care?

I closed my eyes, feeling extremely exposed without my shirt. I couldn't see her, but I didn't want her to see *me*. Not when my emotions were hanging by a thread. Was she looking at my scars? At the mangled skin of my upper arm and my left side? Was she frowning or grossed out?

I shouldn't care. She was my nurse and I shouldn't care. I should have been a man about it and faced it head on. I. Shouldn't. Care.

But I did.

"Now, let's remove your shorts."

I couldn't stop the words from leaving my mouth, and no matter how childish it sounded, I needed to know. "How disgusted *are* you? On a scale of one to ten."

She sighed and moved my arm aside so she could reach the waist of my shorts. "That's not a very good joke, Merrick."

"I'm not joking, Grace."

She stopped moving, but stayed close to me. I could feel her quick breaths on the skin of my chest. It was doing things to me that I hadn't felt in a long time.

I must be coming down with something. A fever maybe?

"There is no need for a scale because I'm not disgusted. You're scarred, Merrick, not ruined."

"They're the same thing."

"They aren't," she snapped.

I dropped my head, hoping my eyes were close to meeting hers or at least her face. "Then why does it feel like they are?"

Her small hand touched my cheek, the warmth from her fingers making me ache for more. She cupped my scarred jaw before running her fingers back, behind the damaged skin of my ear. I couldn't breathe. I didn't want to. Not if it meant the moment would be over. Her gentle fingers followed the scarring up to my eye and over my brow. Her touch felt intimate, but more compassionate than anything else.

She hummed softly as her fingertips drifted back down to the scruff on my jaw. "It feels like they're the same because you haven't healed yet. Feels like your life is over because you've lost so much, and it hurts to even breathe." Her hand cupped my cheek again, and I wondered if this was her idea of being professional, because I'd double the pay if it was.

"Grace..." I breathed.

"Being scarred by something so horrible isn't the same as being ruined. You can only ruin yourself, Merrick, and that kind of destruction doesn't leave any visible scars."

I wanted to say something, anything that would make her see me as something other than a damaged man, but I couldn't think of anything. Maybe it was because she didn't really see me that way at all.

"Shorts," she said and helped me lift off the chair so she could remove them. My boxer briefs were left alone, and I felt her move my chair forward until I'm sure I was only a small distance from the shower door.

"I'm going to cover your lap with a towel and remove your underwear, then I'm going to cover your cast and leg."

I nodded, flinching when the towel landed over the semi erection I still had going on. *Think of something gross, Merrick.*

I pictured everything I could that would possibly gross me out, but Grace would have to leave the house for that to work effectively. She still smelled good and her hands were still on me. I swear I'd been partially aroused for the last week, and it was starting to get to me. Her tiny hands yanked on my underwear as I attempted to help by lifting myself off the chair a little. The soft towel kept me covered, but I couldn't stop my hand from checking to make sure I wasn't pitching a tent.

Grace busied herself with wrapping my arm and leg. Before long, she was lifting me out of the chair. I tried to balance on my good leg and put as much of my weight on it as possible, but I was too busy trying to hold the towel up.

"Help me out, Merrick. Don't worry about the towel, I've got it," she said, her voice strained with the effort of holding me up.

A few grunts and painful groans later, I was finally on the seat inside the shower with nothing but the towel over my lap. We were both out of breath, but I was shocked she could even get me out of the chair let alone through a shower door. "It will get easier once we get the hang of things," she mumbled.

My leg was lifted and propped up on something inside the shower that was never there before. "What's my leg on?"

Grace adjusted me a little more and checked the covers on my limbs before answering. "I snagged another seat from the hospital to make it easier for you. This way you're a little more stable so you can shower by yourself if you want to."

My muscles ached and the throbbing in my arm and leg was almost unbearable, but I couldn't concentrate on the pain. Grace was making it possible for me to take care of myself. I couldn't thank her enough for that.

"Thanks?" I said, shaking my head when it came out as a question.

"You sure about that?" she teased, handing over the removable shower head. Dad had it installed the day after they brought me home, in the hope that I would use it one day. Up until now, I'd barely touched it. Once my fingers securely wrapped around it, Grace let go.

"I am. I appreciate it," I declared, emphasizing the sincerity in my voice.

"You're welcome. I'm only here to help make it easier for you to transition and to make sure you don't do too much damage to yourself in the process."

"You mean the damage I could cause in that stupid chair?"

"Exactly," she said, her voice giving away a smile. "You've been doing better driving the last couple days, though." She turned on the water and adjusted the temperature, then lifted my arm and guided the shower head to its hook on the adjustable slide bar, being sure not to let the water spray us. "We'll start with basics for now. Here is the hook. If you hold the shower head down by the hose part, you can feel it slide into the hook and make sure it's secure."

She made me practice a few times before she was satisfied. It was difficult with the water on, but she assured me that practicing that way would be better since I was going to be showering by myself, for the most part. It was a strange thing to re-learn something I never even thought was necessary before losing my sight.

Once the shower head was secure on its hook once more, she shut off the water and lifted my arm to a shelf next to the slide bar, guiding my fingers to a couple bottles. "The shampoo is in the square bottle," she informed me and waited for me to feel its shape enough to memorize it. She moved my hand to the other bottle, "This one is the body wash. It's round." Again, she waited patiently while I memorized its shape. "And here is a wash cloth. I'll stop at the store tonight and get you a bath sponge. It will lather better, plus, it's easier to hold onto."

She slowly moved my hand back and forth so I could feel where everything was, then she let go and waited for me to do it on my own. The loss of her touch made my brain misfire and my first attempt knocked over both bottles, sending them clattering to the floor. She replaced them and told me to try again. I moved slower this time and was able to find them on my own without sending them crashing again.

"There. You just need to be patient with yourself and the things around you."

I nodded and pressed my lips together. I could do this part, I just needed to practice. Once my left arm was useful, it would be a cinch.

I reached for the bottles once more and one of them fell to my lap.

"I'll let you get that," she stuttered.

Control yourself, Merrick.

Didn't help that I was almost completely naked in front of this woman. It also didn't help that her voice made it harder and harder to suppress my erection. No pun intended.

"Would you mind if I stayed in the bathroom while you showered? I want to be close by in case you need me this time," she declared, casually. Her tone was very clinical and I wondered how many people she had done this for already.

I nodded my permission and she turned the water back on. It was when I felt her step around me that I realized I was actually scared to do this alone. I wanted her close by, but no way I was going to admit that and scare her away. I settled for teasing instead. "You just want to make sure I get clean enough, don't you?"

She chuckled and her hand landed on my bare shoulder. "You caught me. I don't trust you enough to get rid of that awful stench without some kind of supervision."

I dropped my head and felt a full on smile stretch across my lips. My first full smile since that awful day. My cheeks ached. Seriously? Had it been that long since those muscles were used? Since I smiled enough to stretch them?

"That right there," Grace whispered. "That's the Merrick I like to see. He's very handsome."

Heat spread up my neck to my face, but I was still smiling. Strange since I knew she was lying out her ass.

"And he blushes, too? Careful, Merrick. You might make people fall for you."

With that, she exited the shower and shut the door tightly. The squeak of her shoes on the bathroom floor was the last thing I heard before I bathed myself for the first time in months.

Chapter Five

Grace

Why did I say that?

Why in the world did I even think that was *appropriate* to say?

"You might make people fall for you."

It was unprofessional, and it was foolish ... and it embarrassed Merrick. I was sure of it. He was in no position to be on the other end of my flirting, but it came so naturally. Flirting was never my strong point, but being with Merrick, it was more natural than it ever was with Jason, and I wasn't sleeping with Merrick. In fact, I was barely his friend. We argued more than anything and the times we weren't arguing, we *weren't* speaking.

Why, then, did I feel closer to him than I ever had to anyone else?

That first week was difficult with his constant grumbling and arguments. He refused to try anything new and refused to practice any sort of patience with me *or* himself. After a few days, it reached the point where quitting would have been a definite possibility and completely justified. I hadn't been able to get through to him and he didn't care if anyone did.

It was clear as day. Merrick didn't want to be fixed because in his mind, it just wasn't possible.

Then he opened up. What started as a minor argument – almost an insult to me – became something else entirely, whether it was intentional or not. We'd both experienced a horrible loss. It was a connection he didn't know we had and it changed everything.

I didn't pretend to understand the horrors he'd seen or the shit he'd been through, but I could connect to the feelings of loss that he dwelled on every day.

It had taken me months to finally be myself again. Even then, it wasn't real. Not until Mom said what she did and showed me that I was only hurting myself.

I didn't act as if I was all better, because I wasn't. I still hurt every day, but it was getting easier to handle. Easier to accept. Locking myself up with dark memories was not going to help me get what I wanted out of life.

The differences were vast when it came to Merrick and what had changed his life forever. I wasn't the one who saw my brothers fall all around me, and I hadn't experienced the kind of pain that leaves those deep scars, both physical and emotional.

I had never seen war so close, and I probably never would. Not like Merrick had.

Spending each day with him helped me understand him a little more. His frustrations were warranted, but the feeling that he wanted to give up so easily, put me on edge. Getting through to him had looked less and less likely, until that day in the bathroom.

Once he started to trust me, being with him each day was like walking out into the sun. It was warm and bright, and I looked forward to the hours I spent watching him adapt to his limitations. I looked forward to watching him conquer his demons.

And the days I wasn't with him, like today, I spent my time doing laundry, reading a new book, and wishing I *was* with him.

No. At work. Wishing I was *at work* ... with him ... God, I couldn't even fake it with myself.

I shook my head and slammed the dryer door shut.

"Hey, now. Be nice to my appliances," Mom called from the kitchen. "They need to last or I won't be able to talk your father into getting me new ones later on."

"Sorry, Mom." I tossed the laundry basket into my bedroom and found her sitting in the kitchen drinking her afternoon cup of coffee. "Shouldn't you be at the library?"

She shook her head mid sip and raised her eyebrows. "I came home for lunch. Wanted to make sure you weren't too bored."

I grinned, weakly. Staying busy was easy with Merrick, but she was right. I was bored out of my mind and that wasn't good for anyone.

"I'm fine, Mom." I opened the fridge and stood in front of it, just staring at the contents. This definitely *was* a hard habit to break. I wasn't even hungry.

"It's Saturday, Grace. Shouldn't you be out of the house? I know that Keara is waiting for you to call her. She misses you."

I sighed and leaned against the counter, looking down at my feet. I wished I hadn't been such a horrible friend over the last year. Once I lost the baby, my desire to talk to *anyone* just disappeared. I couldn't handle the condolences being sent my way and I didn't want to drag my friends down with me.

That was no excuse to cut off my friendship with Keara. We had been like sisters since junior high when she was the only girl in my biology class that spoke to me. She was also the only other girl in there that actually knew what was going on. We were both good students and neither one of us cared about being popular. Plus, Keara was the only girl I knew that kept her crush on Merrick a secret, same as me.

We used to spend a lot of nights 'studying' in my room when we were really just waiting for Merrick to get home from a party or from a practice. The poor guy had no idea there were a couple of peeping toms next door.

"How would I even talk to her, Mom? It's been almost a year and I ignored her so many times," I stated, regretfully. I was disappointed in the way I handled things and I lost a best friend because of it. I knew she only wanted to be there for me, but I just couldn't ...

It was too much.

"You just do it, Grace," Mom answered, gently. "You go see her and you tell her how sorry you are for not being around and how hard it was for you to deal with what happened. You tell her that you love her. Keara will forgive you, sweetie. She's just waiting for you to make the first move."

Mom was right. I needed to suck it up and take responsibility.

"She works at your father's office. Just started there a few months ago. She couldn't stand working at the hospital anymore and she's good with the administrative stuff so your father hired her on immediately."

"Thanks, Mom."

Mom leaned forward and cupped my cheek. "You've been through a lot, sweetie, but that doesn't mean your life is over."

I nodded and smiled down at her. "That's the same thing I said to Merrick yesterday."

"Well," she smiled proudly, "it's very good advice." She took another sip of her coffee and blinked a few times, indicating that she was about to ask a question I may not like. "Are you okay over there? Is he being nice?"

I rolled my eyes and laughed. "Yes, he has a bark, but no bite. He's just upset and no one could even begin to understand what he's going through. Not even me."

"It's okay for him to be angry," she said.

"It is and he probably will be for a long time. Once he adjusts, it will get better."

"You're good for him."

"What?"

"As his nurse, you're good for him, but he needs a friend, too. Just ... be careful," she said, her brow furrowing in concern. "I don't want you to get hurt."

"Mom, he's my patient. And believe me, I don't think he would want anything to do with me in any other way."

She grumbled something under her breath about looking in the mirror, then stood as she picked up her purse. "That boy may be blind, but that doesn't mean he can't see you."

"That makes no sense."

She rolled her eyes and rinsed her empty coffee cup in the sink. "I thought your father was blind as a bat when I first met him. Well, technically he *was*," she said with a chuckle. "Had those thick Coke bottle glasses. I knew, in my mind, he was seeing what he wanted through those things. But that man didn't take his eyes off me whenever I was in the room." She sighed and got a faraway look in her eyes, like she was replaying the very first moment she fell in love with my dad. "He couldn't see a damn thing without those horrible glasses. That's how he knew I was the one."

I frowned. "I don't understand."

She smiled and wrapped her hands around my shoulders. "He said to me, 'Alaina, I know you're the one because when I can't see you, I still feel you. I still love you more than I did yesterday and not nearly as much as tomorrow'. And you know what, Grace?"

"What?" I whispered.

"I finally believed him."

She stared into my eyes as if she was waiting for something. Anything that would make me understand.

"He fell in love with the pieces that weren't visible. I had to learn to accept that, sometimes, it's not about beauty. It's about the heart of someone. You have the biggest heart I've ever seen, Grace. That boy over there feels it."

"How do you know?" I asked, skeptically.

"Because he wouldn't be waiting by his window every night for you to sing."

My mouth hung open in surprise. "That's ... how ..."

"Mom's know everything," she said, shrugging as if I should already know that by now. Her arms wrapped around me and squeezed tightly. "I love you, Grace. You're beautiful, inside and out. Just be smart. That boy may look strong, but he's extremely fragile."

I sighed. "It sounds like you're more worried about *me* hurting *him*."

She shrugged again. "Go see Keara. Dad left the Honda for you to use today. I'll bring home some sushi tonight."

"YES!" I shouted with a fist pump.

Mom laughed her way out the door while I was left in the kitchen debating on whether to go see Keara now or invite her over for sushi later. If I went now, I wouldn't dwell on my mother's words and the thought of Merrick ever feeling anything for me that wasn't in the realm of a patient-nurse relationship.

But then, sushi always fixed everything.

My phone rang before I could decide, Emma's name flashing across the screen.

"Hello?"

"Grace, hello dear, how are you doing today?"

"I'm good, Emma. How are you?"

"Oh, I'm good. Just trying to decide if I should strangle Merrick now or let you do it on Monday."

I chuckled into the phone and walked to my room to finish folding laundry. "Is he having a bad day?"

"God, yes. If bad is even the right word for it. He's locked himself in his room and told me to go away. I was only trying to help him with Braille and he got frustrated."

I loved Emma Thatcher, but I understood Merrick's frustration. She could be a little overbearing with her children and that's exactly what made her so wonderful. No matter what they did, she was first in line to love them. My mother had always been the same way.

She continued talking as I glanced over at the window, seeing Merrick's blinds shut tightly.

"I was wondering if your mother had anything at the library that may be able to help. I know sometimes there are resources that make it a little easier."

"I'm sure we can find something and if not, she can get it ordered in no time. I'm actually going to head into town in a few minutes, so I can stop by and look."

"Oh that would be wonderful. Thank you so much. Nathan and I have a dinner with some friends that we've put off too many times and I just want to get it over with, you know?"

"I understand, Emma. I'll let you know what I find and if I get a chance, I can take it over to him tonight."

She sighed and I could hear the relief in her voice. "Thank you so much. You are a life saver."

"It's no problem."

"I think he would actually like to see you for a minute tonight. You seem to have the magic touch. He never cooperated with me like he does with you."

"Well the threat of starvation will do that," I said, jokingly.

She laughed and confirmed how right I was before saying goodbye.

I glanced over at Merrick's window again and noticed it was cracked open now. Had it been that way a moment ago? I was sure he was sitting there listening. I didn't want to admit it, but it made my stomach flutter knowing he was curious enough to eavesdrop on my phone conversation.

"You should be nicer to your mom."

There was a long moment of silence before he sighed. "She doesn't understand," he said so quietly I almost didn't hear him.

"She wants to."

"That's the problem."

I sat on my bed and stared at the wall in front of me. He was right. Sometimes people try too hard to understand us when, in reality, we just don't want them to. The pain is too immense and we have no choice but to carry it. We don't want someone else to be weighed down, especially the people we love most. We just need their silent company.

"Do you regret pushing her away?" I asked.

"Every minute of the day," he admitted.

I wanted to hug him, to see his face and tell him it would be okay. I wanted him to see that there were people who cared about him and wanted him to get better. People that were proud of him.

But he *couldn't* see.

"Sometimes the regret is what keeps us angry, Merrick."

He didn't speak or move, but he was still there. Processing.

I pulled on my shoes and grabbed my purse.

"Will you sing to me tonight?" he asked.

Warmth spread through my chest and butterflies swarmed my belly, making me smile. "If you stop being a jerk to Emma, I'll sing to you whenever you want."

He didn't reply, but he didn't really have to.

"Talk to you later, Merrick."

I shut the window and walked out of my room, forcing myself not to look back. I had to go find Keara and follow my own advice.

My father's office was always immaculate. He was a stickler for cleanliness, especially when it came to his patients. He cared about every single one of them. It's not easy for any doctor to remember personal details about their patients right off the bat, but Dad was different. Simple notes about the patient would spark his memory, recalling details like names of children or what vacation a patient had been planning to go on after their last appointment.

Jeff Samuelson had a knack for being social, which is strange since, according to him *and* Mom, he was one of the biggest nerds around.

He was good at his job. Loved it *and* the people. He even stayed open one Saturday every month. Sometimes two.

"Grace, I didn't know you were stopping by today," Dad said brightly when he saw me at the front door.

"I hadn't been planning on it," I replied.

He nodded and glanced over his shoulder before leaning forward to speak quietly. "Keara is in the back right now. I'll have Mandy run the desk for a while."

"Thanks, Dad."

He winked at me and smiled.

My dad may have been a nerd, but he was certainly handsome. Being his daughter made me a little biased, but I saw the eyes that followed him whenever we were out in public together. He was tall and strong without being overly bulky. His eyes were like mine, not one color, but interesting enough to be special. His face was always clean shaven, and even with the thinning hair on top of his head, he looked younger than his age. He had started to shave his dark brown hair recently, so it was just fuzz. Mom said it made him look like a sexier Bruce Willis and women in town seemed to agree.

Mom never let it get to her that women admired my father from a distance. I figured she was damn proud to have a man like that standing beside her, and she never doubted their love. Neither did anyone else in this town. They may look, but they knew her husband was off limits.

The fact that he never noticed anyone but Mom certainly helped.

I wandered past the desk and down the hall to the back offices. Patient charts lined the walls of one room while extra medical supplies and instruments covered the shelves in another. Keara was standing in the middle of the room with all the charts, looking like she was about to climb Mount Everest.

"Need any help?" I asked, shakily. Why the hell was I so nervous to see my best friend?

Keara let out a tiny squeak of surprise before jumping to the side in a spin move I had only seen in the movies. Her hand went to her chest and the folders in her arms went tumbling to the floor. "Sweet mercy, Grace! You almost gave me a heart attack."

I smiled and tried not to burst out laughing at the look on her face. "You must have really been concentrating, huh?"

"Well, there are about a billion Smiths that come to see your dad and like ten of them are named Sandra. I'm trying to find the right one."

"I can help with that."

Keara finally smiled at me, her eyes filling with moisture. "Thanks."

Neither one of us moved as we stared at each other with goofy grins on our faces. I decided it was my responsibility to make the first move.

"I'm sorry, Keara."

She didn't even hesitate. She stepped all over the papers lying on the floor in order to get to me, and I barely caught her without tipping over. Her honey blonde hair covered my face as she tackle-hugged me. It was the greatest tackle-hug I had ever experienced.

"I missed you, Gracie."

"I missed you, too." I hugged her back and felt a sting in my nose. All the memories of our friendship came rushing back. I wanted to bawl for coming so close to losing it all completely.

Keara pulled back and lightly smacked me on the shoulder. "Don't you dare do that to me again. I've been worried sick. A girl needs a phone call now and then."

"I'm sorry, Keara."

"A year!" she shouted, ignoring my words. "A year of not hearing one word from my best friend. Do you have any idea how embarrassing it is to be asked how you're best friend is doing by random people and not have a clue?"

"I'm sorry."

"And then I had to listen to Laura talk about how Jason just left you and how you deserved it for what you put him through. Do you know how long I had to wear the stupid cast after I broke my hand from punching her? A long time. It looked horrible and it would get all gross. And it itched like a bitch. I almost went psycho and cut it off myself, but it reminded me that I had finally gotten in a good one. Finally!"

"Wait! You punched Jason's sister? When was this?" I asked, trying to get her to hear me over her ranting.

"It was like a month after ... you know ... and he came back here all smug and shit, before he moved to God only knows where. I hope he's in Hell." She took a deep breath and met my shocked stare. "Laura was telling everyone that you faked the pregnancy to keep him and that he felt bad leaving so he stuck with you. Then, suddenly you were really pregnant. Said you cheated on him."

"WHAT?"

"I know! I knocked out one of her teeth, then ripped out a chunk of that nasty hair. If Josh hadn't pulled me off of her, she would've been eating it out of my hand."

I was still reeling from the fact that Laura had spread those lies about me. I thought we had been friends. She was a snooty bitch, but when Jason and I started dating, she was always so nice to me. We spent a lot of girl's nights talking about more than our fair share of secrets. Her betrayal stung. Badly.

"No one believed her, Grace. Especially when you spent most of your life being so sweet to everyone in this stupid town. No one believed you were capable of something like that. Not even Laura, but she was trying to cover up the shit her brother had done."

Keara calmed down and was hugging me again before I could get a word in. "Don't worry, my hand is all better and the doctor was a stud. Josh ended up coming with me to the last appointment to make sure he didn't make a move on me."

I laughed, my shoulders shaking both of us as we hugged. Then Keara started laughing and suddenly, neither one of us could stop.

"I would have paid good money to see you punch her," I gasped between fits of laughter.

She covered her face with her hands, but she couldn't hide the blush that spread over her cheeks. "Josh thought it was the hottest thing he'd ever seen."

"Of course he did," I stated. "How is he, by the way?"

"Wonderful. Amazing. Sexy. Mine." She bit her bottom lip, her grey eyes twinkling. "I think he's going to ask me to marry him."

"Seriously?" I all but shouted.

She nodded and I gave her another hug.

"Oh God, Keara. I'm so sorry about everything. I abandoned everyone, thinking it would be easier. I just couldn't handle it."

She pulled back and cupped my face in her hands. "That's because you didn't have me. You can handle anything with me, I'll make sure of it."

We were both crying. Tears of happiness, tears of regret. It didn't matter because I had my friend back.

A few minutes passed before we finally got a hold of ourselves.

"Now, help me clean this up before your dad fires my ass for messing up his charts. I don't know why he doesn't just go electronic like everyone else."

I chuckled and helped her gather the papers still sprawled on the floor. "He doesn't want anything to be missed. He has notes in these charts that he wrote down years ago and thinks it will all be distorted once it's scanned in."

"True. Your dad is amazing. Did you know he just did surgery on an eight year old that probably saved the kid's sight? It was a last minute thing. He was here seeing patients and all of a sudden he burst out of his office and raced to the hospital while he called the kid's parents. Told them he knew exactly what was wrong."

I smiled, proudly. "That's my dad."

"That's your dad," she agreed.

Once we had all the charts squared away, I helped her find the one she was looking for while we chatted about anything and everything. She asked about the last year and I told her the truth. Not much had happened. I worked, I barely ate, and I barely slept. She scowled at me while pursing her lips and giving me the evil eye. The one look that always told me she was about to beat my ass.

"I'm done with that now, Keara. Mom came and knocked some sense into me. I'm not better, but I'm happier. I know what I did was a way of grieving. Pushing everyone away and not taking care of myself. I know I took it too far. It won't be happening again."

"Good," she said with her arms crossed over her chest. I followed as she led the way back to the front desk.

Mandy greeted me with a smile and a hug before she went back to her post. The employees my dad had working for him were always genuine and kind. Not once did any of them say anything negative about their job or the people they worked with. I think that was one of the reasons why my father was so successful. His employees were happy there.

"So, tell me what's going on with you and Josh."

Keara looked like her face was about to crack with the massive smile that covered it. "We moved in together about three months ago."

"Really? That's awesome. And how is that going?"

She blushed and turned to her computer. "It's fantastic!"

"Come on, Keara. Give me details."

She looked around us to make sure no patients were within ear shot before she leaned in and whispered, "The sex is even better, now that we don't have to wait to see each other every night. I wake up in the morning because of the orgasm he gives me and I fall asleep at night because he's worn me out."

I giggled right along with her as she gave me the details of how they ended up moving in together. It was like no time passed while we were apart. Exactly how it had always been between us.

Josh Colson and Keara Brighton had been dating since right after high school. They ended up at the same university together and hit it off immediately. They'd been inseparable ever since and if it wasn't for the busy schedule they both followed through school and work, they would be married already. Josh ended up getting a full ride football scholarship to Washington State in the middle of their sophomore year at the university. They lived apart for a couple years, managing a long distance relationship full of questionable Skype sessions and freaky weekends indoors. When Josh tore his ACL, his football career was officially over, but he didn't really mind all that much. They wanted to be together and he always wanted to become a paramedic. Both of them got their dreams and they were slowly working toward their next one.

"Does Josh know that you want a destination wedding?" I asked.

"Yes, he loves the idea. I mean, we haven't talked about it much, but when I mentioned it last year he thought it was a great idea. He said once we were both done with school, there was nothing to stop us. I think Daddy really scared Josh when he said he would hang him if I didn't finish school. Josh apparently wasn't taking any chances, but that's okay. We are both really happy," she said brightly.

"I'm happy for you, Keara. You both deserve a good life."

"So do you, Grace."

I grinned and nodded. "I'll get one. It will just take some time."

We spent the next hour goofing off in between patients until Dad finally came to the front and made us both go home.

"If I have to hear another giggle session while I'm shining a light in someone's eye, I might go crazy," he said, trying to be serious. The grin on his face gave him away.

"Sorry, Dr. S. Your daughter is the culprit," Keara said, throwing me under the bus.

Dad seemed happy about it. "Well, in that case, go get your mom and have a girl's night or something. You all need it, apparently."

Keara and I both started giggling before we could leave. Dad just shook his head, waving goodbye. We stopped at Keara's car and decided to leave mine for my dad to take home. I texted Mom, who was leaving the library in ten minutes, and told her to bring enough sushi for the three of us. Keara drove us to my parent's house, and we settled in with a couple glasses of wine before Mom showed up with her arms full of bags of sushi.

"I'm starving," she said when we started tearing open the boxes. "I got so busy with story time this afternoon that I forgot to have a snack after lunch."

"Oh shit!" I shouted. "I was supposed to go to the library and see if I could find anything to help Merrick with Braille. Do you guys have anything like that?"

Mom tapped her chin with a slender finger, tipped with a bright red nail. She was always so put together. "I'm sure we do. And your dad might know some people who can help, too."

"Merrick?" Keara asked.

"Merrick Thatcher. Next door."

"Aahh, that's right. I knew he was injured, but I only briefly remember someone telling me he had lost his sight. Why are *you* helping him?"

"I'm his homecare nurse," I shrugged.

Keara's mouth hung open and the piece of sushi that had been dangling from her chopsticks, fell to her plate. "Seriously?"

"Yeah. He's in a wheelchair until his leg is healed, and his left arm and hand were in a cast until this last week, but he still needs a little help until he adjusts."

Keara and Mom exchanged a look and ... was that a smile? "What?"

Keara took a sip of wine before gently placing her glass on the table and leaning forward. Her eyes locked with mine, her brow furrowed in concentration. My fingers started to fidget with my chopsticks the longer she stared at me.

"You're Merrick Thatcher's homecare nurse. You get to touch that fine specimen of a man almost every day, hell, you've probably seen him naked, and you didn't think this was important to tell me before now?" Keara's voice got louder and louder with each word and I couldn't stop the laugh that burst out of me.

"She thinks this is funny, Alaina. Is this funny?"

My mom started to laugh right along with me. "Oh goodness, I forgot that you two had massive crushes on him back in the day."

Keara grumbled something about her having a bigger crush than I did, before she shook her head and got back to the point. "This should have been the first thing you said to me right after 'I'm sorry'," she demanded.

"Really? I was supposed to walk in and say, 'I'm sorry for being a horrible friend, Keara, but I get to see Merrick Thatcher naked and I think we should be friends again.'"

"Yes!" she yelled. "In fact, you probably wouldn't have needed to say you were sorry. It wouldn't have mattered after hearing the words 'Merrick Thatcher' and 'naked' in the same sentence."

She crossed her arms and looked away from me as if she was angry and didn't want to even look at me.

"Keara, I don't even see him completely naked. I help him get into the shower, but I never see anything."

"Why not?" she demanded.

"Because I cover him with a towel. He doesn't need me looking at his ... you know, when I need to be helping him as a nurse."

She looked disappointed, but quickly decided I was right. "Are you going to tell me what he's like then? I mean, all those years and he never really spoke to us. I always wondered if he was a complete asshole or if he was really the funny and sweet guy everyone said he was."

I thought about my answer for a moment and decided to give her the truth. "He's angry right now. He went through a lot and he's in pain all the time. That will make *anyone* angry. There are moments, though, where I see the old Merrick. The one everyone adored. He can be really funny, but most of the time he's just intense. He's a good man, though. He sacrificed for his country, for *us*. That alone makes him amazing."

My cheeks flushed and my stomach fluttered as I talked about Merrick. I busied myself with stuffing more sushi in my mouth so I wouldn't have to see Keara and Mom's reaction.

"What are his injuries?" Keara asked a moment later.

I sighed and took another sip of wine, glancing at my mom who looked just as curious as Keara. I hadn't really spoken with her about his injuries since it wasn't really my place to share that information because I was his nurse.

"He was burned. Broke his leg in a few places. His left hand was pretty messed up, I'm guessing since he had several surgeries on it. Without telling too much, I think the left side of his body was closest to whatever explosion went off that day."

Keara seemed to sense that I couldn't say much more about Merrick without violating his privacy. What I had said were things the whole town already heard about him. Without seeing him, one wouldn't really know about the rest.

"Can they fix his eyes?"

I shook my head. "Not that I know of, but he isn't very compliant right now as far as doctor visits go. I think the only reason he went to his last appointment so easily was because he wanted that cast off."

"I can imagine," Keara said around a sip of wine. "Those things are the worst."

"Your father said that he was looking into his condition," Mom chimed in, surprising me once more. "He talked to Merrick shortly after he returned home, and although Merrick didn't think it would go anywhere, your dad is still making as many phone calls as he can."

"I had no idea," I breathed.

Mom nodded, "Our families were neighbors for years, Grace. Emma and I became good friends. Jeff and Nathan did as well. Merrick was always a nice boy and had so much going for him. Still does. His time in the military only added to it."

I ruminated on that information for the rest of dinner while we chatted back and forth about weddings and engagement rings and the story about how Dad asked Mom to marry him. I hadn't laughed so much in my life and it felt good to finally feel like I could look up. I had a piece of my old life back, but it was better than the old. It was now and it was needed.

I only hoped that Merrick could one day find that kind of peace. Even if it meant starting a whole new life.

"So, what are you doing for the Fourth of July?" Keara asked as I walked her out to her car a couple hours later.

"I'm not sure. It's this coming Friday, right?"

"Uh huh. Josh is on call, so we can't really plan much, but we were thinking about going to the high school to watch the fireworks. I know you and your parents usually watch them from here, since you're so close, but if you want to come with us ..."

"Maybe," I said with a shrug. "I don't know if I'm quite ready to mingle with so many people. Too many questions."

"I get it. I do. But don't lock yourself up too tightly. It only makes things worse."

I nodded, knowing she was right. It was just easier said than done.

After a brief hug, Keara climbed into her car and poked her head out the window, sending a playful smile my way. "Or maybe you'll be too busy with Merrick."

I rolled my eyes and waved goodbye as she pulled out of the driveway. When I turned to walk back to the front porch, my eyes wandered over to the house next door.

The Fourth of July hadn't even crossed my mind in the past couple weeks since I'd been working with Merrick. I couldn't imagine he would be up for the celebration since he barely left the house. It was another item to add to my list of things to ask Emma.

He may not want to celebrate, but I would make sure he wasn't alone.

Chapter Six

Merrick

I used to love Independence Day.

The parades, the food, the softball games. Even the people.

It was a celebration for the sole purpose of just being free. An honoring of the sacrifices made for that freedom.

Now, it just felt like another day in Hell.

Just the thought of being around so many people made my skin crawl. The smells, the sounds ... it was all too much for me. I could feel everything through my bedroom window. The taste and smell of smoke rising from grills in every backyard, laughter and delight in every voice. It was sensory overload for a man that couldn't see what was happening.

Mom spent the entire week begging me to at least consider joining them at the fairgrounds once the parade was over. I begged her to just leave me alone. Spent the whole week trying to prove that I was just fine. That nothing was wrong.

"Just this year, Mom. Just give me this year. I can't do it yet."

She was reluctant, but who was going to deny a blind man this one request. "Okay, son. We'll be around for the fireworks."

"Don't bother. I'll be fine. You can check on me throughout the day, but all I'm going to do is get some rest."

This, of course, led to several questions about why I wasn't sleeping and why I was so stubborn. Mitch and Micah didn't let it go until Dad finally put his foot down and told everyone to stop treating me like a child.

I wanted to hug him and fall at his feet for the gesture. I just wanted to sleep through all of it.

Grace tended to agree with my mother that I shouldn't be alone on such an important holiday. She didn't give me crap for it, though, and she had all week to do it. I think she understood, in some ways.

The day passed without incident. Mom checked on me every hour by phone and stopped by the house every *other* hour to make sure I was still alive and kicking.

I kept telling her not to worry. I'd be fine.

That's before I remembered that in Morgan, the fireworks could be heard everywhere.

I'm not talking about the small ones everyone and their mother lights on the streets. Those made my muscles tense, but I could handle them. I'm talking about the ones that make those puny ones look like glitter bombs.

I was sitting by my bedroom window, like I always did, waiting for sleep to take me since Mom had shoved a couple pills down my throat again. It was the very first loud *boom* that made everything inside of me try to claw its way out.

I wasn't okay.

BOOM! POP! BOOM BOOM! POP!

It all happened so fast. Instinct kicked in, along with a massive dose of adrenaline. I was on the ground before the next one went off. The pain in my leg and hand was intense, but nothing compared to the pain of what I knew was coming.

Voices and shouts mixed in with the explosions. Shouts I couldn't understand. And suddenly, I was back on that fucking truck, hoping to God that tonight wasn't the night we all gruesomely died.

The crackle of flames and the whiz of bullets, filled my ears. I covered my head, riding out three more *booms* before my body went on autopilot.

Cover. Find cover.

I didn't know where to go, where I even was. I just needed to find cover.

I pulled myself along the wall, crawling over my fallen wheelchair, searching for anything to give me safety to ride it out. Instead of the cold metal of the chair, I felt the sand between my fingers. Instead of the warm breeze of a summer night, I felt the blood running down into my eyes.

I couldn't see anything in front of me as I reached over for a gun that wasn't there.

Images flashed in my mind, and every *boom* sent my heart racing. I squeezed my eyes shut, waiting for the impact.

It was coming. It always came.

A muffled voice reached my ears. Then I was surrounded by something warm and soft. Something that didn't smell like the sand and blood I knew, without a doubt, was covering my skin. It held me tight. Covering my head and protecting my body from the imminent impact of whatever was being fired at us.

A humming sound filled the silence between each *boom* and *pop*. They kept going, but the melody slowly began drowning out the crackling in my ears. I opened my eyes, but saw nothing.

I was either dying or dreaming. Either way, I was no longer in reality.

"You're here, Merrick. With me. Nowhere else but here. It's the fireworks. Nothing else," the voice said, trembling like my body trembled. "You're here and you're safe. I'll keep you safe."

An angel then. It had to be.

I wrapped my arms around her, sensing the need to protect her from whatever was coming, but I was too far gone. I couldn't protect anyone if I couldn't see. I dropped my head to her chest and squeezed my eyes shut again, riding it out in a cold sweat. All the while, she hung onto me, humming her song through every explosion.

When it was finally silent, all my working senses seemed to give up on the memories. I couldn't smell any fire or burning flesh, just a sweet, familiar scent. I couldn't feel the sand and blood, just a softness against my cheek. I couldn't hear anything but that sweet voice I knew, only too well.

Grace.

Breathing came easier, but the aches in my body only intensified with each inhale.

"You back?" Grace whispered.

For the first time in a long time, I actually wanted to be. I wanted to be home instead of paying my penance out there. I wanted it to be over instead of re-living every moment.

"I'm back," I rasped.

But for how long?

Three weeks later and I still hadn't thanked Grace for what she did that night.

How does one thank a person for metaphorically saving one's life? They can't.

Well, *I* can't.

We tiptoed around each other those next few weeks. Conversation was stilted, but there. Nothing personal or enlightening. Grace never said a word about what happened and I couldn't bring it up without feeling weak. On the outside, as far as we were both concerned, it never happened.

She didn't tell Mom. I was sure about *that* at least. Otherwise, my mother would have been a blubbering mess of guilt for not being there for me herself. Another thing I needed to thank Grace for.

It was when I opened my mouth for the hundredth time, trying to say something – *anything* – that she finally took pity on me.

"Let it go, Merrick," she'd stated.

The memory of her arms around me, keeping me safe when she didn't need to, made me ask, "Why?"

She never answered, but then, she didn't really need to.

I was saved by Grace once more.

It was getting more and more difficult to keep my mind off of her. She was so soft and warm and smelled so fucking good. I wanted to reach out and touch her when I knew she was close by, but I never did. Her clinical touch would have to be enough, for now.

I was getting better with transitioning in and out of my chair. Grace helped me find a more comfortable way that put less stress on my legs and used more of my upper body strength. With my left hand free of a cast, it still wasn't easy, but it was a little more convenient to have another limb, even if it was still weak. The removable arm brace that Dr. Hopkins ordered me to wear was a pain in the ass, but at least I could take it off and scratch the tender skin underneath.

Feeling the scars crawling over the skin of my arm and hand was a constant reminder of the pain I had endured while dragging Ryan away from that burning truck. I'd felt the pain, but it didn't matter at the time. All that mattered was getting my friend away from danger.

Ryan was alive and holding his baby girl now because of this hand. I was proud of myself, but it still hurt. I lost too many that day, and even though Ryan was important to me, the rest of them had families and children, too.

Just another painful reminder that I should have been taken that day. Not them.

Don't underestimate yourself.

Grace's words, undeniably, had an effect on me. Everyone told me to stop *hating* myself. The thing was, hating myself came too effortlessly. It was simpler to believe I was inadequate, but she was right. I was underestimating myself from the very beginning, and although I still wanted the easy way, I was starting to think that hating myself *was* the weakest part of me. Not my damaged body.

Grace constantly spoke about her friend, Keara, and the soon-to-be fiancé, Josh Colson. I knew Josh back in the day, but we were never friends. I couldn't really remember Keara that well.

This was no surprise to Grace. "We both kept our heads down and neither one of us ever got invited to the crazy parties you went to."

"Seriously?"

"Seriously. We never fit in with those kids, so we stuck together. I don't feel like we really missed out, though."

"You didn't," I informed her. "Those parties were nothing but kids trying to find a way to get drunk. That gets old after a while."

"Then why did you go to them?"

"Because my friends went. Because I was expected to go. They were fun most of the time, but not worth the hassle afterwards."

She stayed silent for a moment before she asked, "Did you know you were going to join the military all along?"

I wasn't prepared for that question, and I was even less prepared for the answer. My decision to join wasn't really a mystery to me. From the very beginning, I knew I didn't need the money for school and I'd never been interested in the extreme training we all went through. It was just something inside of me that needed to be a part of something important. A part of something incredible. A part of me also wanted the discipline and the responsibility. Life was always so easy for a kid with a straight path carved out in front of him. Friends and girls that wanted him. I wanted something unpredictable, something difficult.

I was always proud to serve my country. The first day I arrived at basic was like coming home. I belonged there and knew I could make a difference.

Those reasons changed quickly. It was no longer about the challenge or the purpose, it was about the man next to me and the one next to him. It was about my brothers in arms. It was about protecting them and fighting for them, because they were fighting for *me*.

Grace didn't hear any of those reasons, because I didn't tell her. I couldn't find the words to explain it to her, and even if I did, she wouldn't understand. So, like the inconsiderate jerk everyone thought I was, I just shrugged and rolled back to my room. The sanctuary that was no longer a sanctuary.

She didn't ask again and ended up staying away from the topic altogether.

I wasn't ashamed or scared to talk about it. It's just hard to describe something like that. It's hard to explain to someone that, out there, you've already accepted your death. That it's not about *you* anymore.

Maybe one day I would tell her. Maybe one day she would just know, because she knew *me*. Or maybe one day, the reasons would change and I wouldn't feel so much regret.

The days passed in a blur. Pretty soon, July was gone and the heat of August kept me inside. Not that I wanted to be out there anyway. There were days that Grace sat on the back porch, 'soaking in the sunlight'.

"You'd feel better if you felt some sun on your face. It's refreshing," she said.

I was tempted, but knowing I would still be in the dark while my face felt the warmth of the sun ... it was like falling into a nightmare all over again. I couldn't risk it. Not if I wanted everyone to leave me alone.

Grace kept the windows opened and I didn't argue. She wanted light, she'd have it. Enough for the both of us.

I started a more intense level of therapy for my hand. It was as much of a pain in the ass as I expected. The stiffness in my fingers didn't let me do *anything* without pain, and every time I tried to grip something, it was like starting from scratch. I could barely lift a fork to my mouth without trembling.

I was sick of the limitations I still had and I hated not being able to use my body. After all the work I had done to take care of it, to hone it into a weapon to be used at will, it was hard for me to accept that it would never be the same.

Still, I kept trying. I'd already established that I was an asshole so why not add stubborn to the mix?

Grace helped with the therapy and with basic things that were still too difficult to try without hurting myself. She also kept trying to feed me the pain medication that no longer numbed the pain. I fought her every step of the way and she dealt with my continued stubbornness, but she did it sweetly. Anyone else would have smacked me in the face by now, but not Grace. Her patience was almost Godly.

The hardest part was adjusting to the blindness. Grace had done my mother's bidding and found me a better way to learn Braille. It was difficult and frustrating. My thick fingers made it hard to focus on one line at a time, but I was making progress even if it was only a tiny bit. I had Grace to thank for that, but she insisted I thank my mother.

Which I did.

I didn't earn any son-of-the-year awards lately, and Mom didn't deserve the treatment she had gotten from me over the last few months. Dad ripped me a new one more times than I could count, but Mom always stayed calm.

I didn't deserve her.

I told her this, which resulted in her ripping me a new one on her own. Guess she gets pretty pissed when her kids don't understand how much she loves them.

Grace also organized my closet. Thick plastic hangers for sweaters and jackets, smaller hangers for T-shirts. She used the same techniques she had used in the shower, patiently guiding me through the process of finding my own clothing.

"Touch is your friend, Merrick," she said while she clutched my immense hand in her tiny one. Her skin was so soft, I could scarcely restrain myself from running my thumb over the back of her hand just to feel more.

Touch *was* my friend, but touching Grace would be the death of me. I barely processed what she was telling me in my attempt to shut down any sexual thoughts about her. I wouldn't say they came out of nowhere, but they were certainly unexpected.

"Let your fingers find the details that tell you the information you need to know. The feel of the hanger, the feel of the shirt. Memorize them."

She spent the next hour going through each of my shirts and telling me what they looked like as I ran my hands over the material. By the time we were done, I could identify two of my favorite shirts without her help, and I could tell the difference between a few of my sweaters.

Don't get me wrong. There were still times I felt like *nothing* would help me, but Grace always proved me wrong. She was good at finding new ways to get through to me, and I was getting better at cutting back on the swearing and frustrated exclamations.

I even stopped grumbling when Mom started to coddle me, reminding myself that pushing Mom away would only push Grace away. That and she was my mom and deserved my respect and love.

But I couldn't lose Grace. Not now. Not when her voice was the only thing that helped me fall asleep at night.

I don't know if Grace sang just for me or if it was something she *always* did. I certainly don't remember hearing her when we were younger, but there were a lot of things I overlooked back then. Regardless, it was the peace I felt when she sang – or even spoke – that made me desperate for more of her.

We were having dinner together on a Friday night. I was listening to Grace talk about my appointment the next day and what to expect from the new hand therapist I was being sent to. I didn't want to have an endless schedule of doctor appointments, but Grace told me to stop being a baby and deal with it. The promise of finally being able to grip something in my left hand, without feeling like a sapling, kept me from arguing any further.

I had been overdoing it on the exercises this last week and could barely move my hand when I woke up each morning. Grace started to hide the therapy ball I was given to strengthen my grip. The little spitfire only brought it out when it was time for my therapy. Tonight, she made an exception.

Grace had started cooking more often and Mom was grateful for her help. She was a good cook and she let me help every so often to make me feel like I was contributing to my own care. Sometimes I felt like a child all over again. I would never be able to cook well by myself, but that wasn't the problem. Not anymore. The problem was that I didn't *want* to be alone anymore.

Mom apparently saw this and started talking about Grace every chance she got. When Micah stopped by earlier in the week and asked about her, I knew without a doubt Mom was meddling. My family wanted me to be happy, but they just didn't understand that someone like me could never be with someone like Grace. Not anymore.

She deserved someone better. Someone whole.

Didn't help that she was being paid to spend time with me in the first place.

"How do you like the spaghetti?" Grace asked, interrupting my negative thoughts.

"It's delicious," I replied, lifting the fork with my good hand and taking another bite. Her shoulder brushed against mine and I lost my grip on the ball. It fell to my plate with a *splat* and I felt spaghetti sauce splatter onto my shirt.

"Ah, fuck!" I grumbled and dropped my fork, sending it clattering to the floor without thinking. I shook my head and tried to push away from the table, but Grace's hand on my shoulder stopped me.

"No harm done, Merrick. Just a little less sauce on your pasta is all," she said cheerfully, removing the ball from my plate. I heard her move around the kitchen and open a drawer before she put another fork in my hand.

Running water and the sound of her humming made my ears perk. I assumed she was cleaning the ball, but I didn't ask and I didn't move. When she sat back down beside me and handed it over, the anger I felt a moment ago faded into nothing.

Accidents happen to the best of us and even though they would happen to me more often than not, Grace proved that it wasn't a big deal. It could be cleaned up, swept away, and forgotten in a matter of moments.

Yes, the anger was gone, but the despair was still ever present. I wanted to watch her smile at me and tell me it was okay. I wanted to see the patience in her eyes for myself.

But I couldn't.

I didn't even know what she looked like and it finally hit me that I hadn't ever asked.

"Grace?"

"Yeah?"

I cleared my throat and slowly took a sip of water before carefully turning toward her. "What color is your hair?"

She obviously wasn't expecting this question. Her shocked silence was proof of that.

"Grace?"

"Oh wow, I never even thought to tell you what I looked like," she said, a smile in her voice.

"I've never asked," I pointed out.

She shifted in her chair and slid her plate away, the sound making me more anxious. Then, I felt her touch the front of my shirt, wiping some of the sauce away.

God, if she only knew what that did to me.

"Umm, it's brown."

"What kind of brown?"

"The only kind of brown there is?"

I shook my head and rolled my eyes. "There are lots of browns. Light brown, dark brown, reddish, golden."

"Dark brown. Darker than yours," she said quickly.

"How long?"

"Just past my shoulder blades."

I nodded and lifted my hand to point at my own eyes. "And what color are your eyes?"

She took a deep breath and let it out slowly. "They aren't really one color. Hazel, I guess."

I needed more than that. I needed to see her in my mind, to capture some memory of what she looked like. I knew I'd seen her all those years ago. I *had* to have seen her.

"Describe them for me."

She chuckled dryly. "What? How?"

I kept my eyes pointed forward and shrugged. "Go look in the mirror if you have to, but I need you to describe them for me."

"Why?"

"Please."

I don't know why I couldn't just accept her simple answer. I could picture a pair of hazel eyes lined with long, black eyelashes. I could see them in my mind so clearly that it could have been her eyes I was actually imagining. But I needed to be sure. I needed to picture them exactly how they were. Nothing else would satisfy me in that moment.

Grace rose from her chair and her footsteps moved down the hallway. I took another bite of spaghetti while I waited and tried to calm my nerves. I shouldn't be asking what my nurse looks like because it was only going to exacerbate my situation. I already had feelings for Grace that I couldn't quite understand. Feelings that I didn't have any business feeling for her. We were neighbors most of our lives and not once did I truly see her. I'd been an inconsiderate bastard.

Now?

Things were different.

Grace returned a moment later, sitting in her chair and brushing up against my arm again. I felt my grip on the exercise ball go a little slack once more, overwhelmed with the feel of her so close to me. This time, I kept my cool.

"They're a golden brown close to the pupil, then they change to a grayish-blue. The outside edge is more of a greenish-blue. And there are little specks of brown throughout."

In other words, they were eyes I could fall into, if I could fucking *see* them.

"How tall are you?" I asked, feeling her image form in my mind. "Normally I would be able to tell, but the chair ..."

"I'm about five feet three inches. Not very tall at all."

Tall enough to fit perfectly against my chest with the top of her head probably just reaching my chin when I could stand.

"And your nose?"

She laughed softly. I could imagine she was shaking her head, but there was no other way to find out what she looked like. Instead of arguing about it, she seemed resigned to answer all of my strange questions. "I don't even know how to describe it. How do you describe a nose?"

I shrugged. "Is it small and narrow? Straight? Crooked?"

"It's straight. Kind of small I guess. I always felt like it points up a little bit. It's covered in freckles."

My lips tugged into a grin. Those are the details I needed to hear. "Your ears?"

I heard her shift in her chair and assumed she was touching her ears. I balled my hands into fists to resist the urge to touch them for myself.

"They're just ears. Not too big, not too small. I like to wear dangly earrings. The lobes are normal size?" She said it as if it were a question and I felt her arm brush mine again when she shrugged.

"Are you sure about that?"

She sighed before saying, "Yeah, I'm sure."

There weren't any other questions I could ask without sounding like a creeper. How full are your lips? Do you have dimples when you smile? Is your neck slender and soft? And don't even get me started on the questions I wanted to know about the rest of her body.

"Anything else, Merrick?"

I cleared my throat and pushed away from the table. There was only one other way for me to *see* her, but I didn't want to make her uncomfortable. "Umm, no. Nothing that will ..."

I felt her hand rest on my arm, stopping me from rolling away and getting the hell away from her before I said something stupid.

"I know you don't remember me from before, but I ..." Her words trailed off, her fingers constricting against my skin.

God, if I could just touch her, I wouldn't need to ask questions. I would be able to feel every soft curve and edge, and I wouldn't need anything more than that. If I could just *touch* her.

"I was never one of those girls that you found yourself with all too often."

I frowned and leaned forward, waiting for an explanation. I had no idea what she was talking about. Of course she wasn't one of those girls. She was real and sweet, compassionate and smart. Those other girls were just fake. The pretty was only on the outside.

"I was never really pretty. At least not the pretty that everyone would have *seen*. I was kind of awkward and nerdy, but rounder in areas where other girls were flat. Still am. Does that make sense?"

I hesitated before nodding my understanding, grinning when I envisioned her. "So you're telling me that you look like a real woman and not a stick?"

She gasped and pulled her hand away from my arm. "I didn't say that."

I waited for her to continue. Anything that would give me a better picture of her. She stayed silent. I was starting to feel like the air around me was too thick to breathe.

Grace cleared her throat and shifted in her chair. I wanted to know what she was doing with her hands. Was she wringing them together? Were they in her lap? In her hair? Was she looking at me or trying to avoid that?

"I'm just me," she said, quietly.

"You're beautiful." The words left my mouth without my prompting, but there was nothing inside of me that wanted to take them back.

She released a self-deprecating laugh and, again, I wondered what she was doing with her hands.

"I may be blind, Grace. But I can still see *some* things."

Silence.

I had no idea what I was doing, but fuck if I could stop it. The last few weeks had been pure torture. A stunning agony that I wanted to end and last forever. It was a peace in some ways. Being with her forced everything else out. I didn't want to give that up.

But in her words, *I'm just me.*

"I'm tired. I think I'm going to go to bed," I mumbled. My left hand ached as I clung to the cold metal of the wheel. I turned the chair away and felt my way around the table. The sound of Grace's movements reached my ears as she started picking up the plates still on the table. I shook my head and cursed under my breath. I didn't want her to clean up my messes, but I would be no help anyway.

"I'll be here Monday, Merrick. Have a good night."

A good night?

A good night would be spending the rest of it talking to her and listening to her talk about her friend and her parents. Listening to her talk about her love of music and telling her about the things I loved ... the things I *used to* love.

It wasn't late at all. In fact, I was sure it wasn't even six o'clock by the time I heard Grace finish in the kitchen. The ringing of her phone perked my ears, the muffled sound of her voice almost as soothing as hearing her sing.

I sat in darkness and listened for a moment, but my senses heightened when I heard the panic in her voice. Footsteps moved quickly as she made her way to my room and I turned my chair when I heard her reach my door.

"What's wrong?"

She took a deep breath and her footsteps moved closer. Her small hand grasped mine and she placed the cell phone against my palm, curling my fingers around it.

"It's your father. He needs to talk to you."

I lifted the phone to my ear and before I even said a word I could hear the commotion in the background.

"Dad?"

"Merrick, it's your brother. Mitch was in an accident and he's on his way to the hospital right now."

Mitch?

My little brother was in an accident.

What kind of accident?

How injured was he?

Was someone else with him?

Endless questions swarmed my mind, but there was one that stood out among the others. An image flashed before my useless eyes, and I saw them again. My friends, the fire.

I could hear my mother crying and my father trying to calm her. I closed my eyes and pretended that was the reason I was able to push the image away. That it would stop me from seeing *everything*. My insides churned, my grip on the phone tightened. The sound of the plastic creaking under the pressure was the only thing that kept me grounded. "Is he ..."

"He's alive and Micah seems to think he will be fine, but he has some pretty serious injuries."

"Is everyone else okay?"

"Yeah, they are. He was alone and the other driver is alive, but that's only because he's about five times over the legal limit. It's not even six and the guy was already drunk."

This piece of information made me angry. I could handle anger. I could focus on anger. "Where are you at? Can you come and get me?"

"We are on our way now. Be there in two minutes."

I let my hand fall away with the small phone still in it, but the clatter I heard indicated my grip had failed. I don't remember how, but suddenly I was standing and reaching out for a wall that I could swear was next to me. My breaths were choppy and the ache in my leg started to feel like a ten ton boulder was sitting on it.

I didn't care. I needed to get to my brother.

I needed to get to the son of a bitch that hit his car, and I needed to make him pay for his attempt at trying to take something else away from me, away from my family.

"Merrick?"

Grace's voice cut through the roaring in my ears. Her arms surrounded my waist, pulling my mind back into my body.

"Merrick, what are you doing? Sit back down."

"I have to go." I steadied myself on my good leg and she supported me with a shoulder tucked against my side.

"I know and we'll get you to your brother, but hurting yourself won't get you there any faster. Come on, let's put you back in the chair and I'll help you to the car, okay?"

One of her hands moved to my stomach while her other arm stayed wrapped around my back. She turned me and my will finally gave out. The dizziness killed my balance and we both came down hard, me in my wheelchair and Grace nearly in my lap. On automatic, my hands reached for her and kept her from falling to the floor completely. She cursed and steadied herself before fixing my injured leg and making sure the immobilizer hadn't been moved too much. The pain was intense, but almost an afterthought, and I couldn't get control of my breathing. My face started to feel like it was covered in cobwebs while my neck could barely keep my head up.

"Breathe, Merrick. I need you to try to calm yourself so you can get a good breath in."

Rubbing my shoulders, she stayed in front of me, her body brushing against my knee. I wanted to pull her into my arms and cling to her. I had no idea why I was reacting this way. Shaking off the panic seemed impossible. Shutting my eyes ... it was no use. The images came back anyway. My brother injured and unconscious, covered in blood, and smashed inside of his mangled car. The car suddenly changed to a Humvee, then an MRAP, and his body slowly disappeared from my view as the fire consumed everything. The white-hot, melting metal curling in on itself. I could feel the burning in my flesh and I could smell the blood, the smoke, the gunpowder.

"Merrick!"

There was a tapping on the side of my face, then a pair of cold hands gripping my head. The cobwebs started to fade, the burning in my arm and at my side stopped, but I was trembling. A familiar, cold sweat had broken out over my entire body. The ache in my leg was still there, but all my mind could focus on was the feel of Grace's breath on my face as she spoke to me.

"I'm right here, Merrick, and you're right here with me. Nowhere else but here. Come back to me," she demanded, only her voice didn't sound like the Grace that threatened to starve me if I didn't shower. She sounded scared. "Come back, Merrick. You're here with me. Nowhere else but here."

She repeated the mantra over and over until my body stopped shaking and my breaths finally slowed down. Her fingers shook as she gripped my face and moved my hair away from my eyes. I was scaring her.

The reminder of what she did for me just a few weeks before, the reminder that I still had issues ... it made me want to demand that she leave before I did something that would hurt us both.

But in my gut, I knew that I would never hurt her.

"Grace, it's okay. You don't have to be scared."

She sighed with relief while her hands tilted my head slightly. Enough that I knew I would have been staring right into those unique hazel eyes she described to me. I would see the specks of brown she mentioned and would give anything to be able to count them.

"I'm not scared anymore now that you're with me," she stated. "Come on, big guy. Let's get you to the car. Your little brother needs you right now."

Grace Samuelson didn't know it, hell, *I* didn't even know it at the time, but that was the exact moment my heart irrevocably devoted itself to her.

Chapter Seven

Grace

I slept awful the next couple nights.

I spent hours worrying about Merrick and the reaction he had to Mitch's accident. It was almost as if the shock turned into living it. I was terrified I wouldn't be able to pull him out of it like I did the night of the fireworks.

Mitch was badly hurt and stayed unconscious for a while, but the doctors felt confident that he would be okay. Thank God. I couldn't imagine what would happen if the situation had been any worse.

Mitch had been on his way to pick up his date for the night when a drunk driver T-boned his car at an intersection. The impact sent him spinning until his car smashed into a cement irrigation diversion dam or whatever the hell they were called. Either way, the car didn't stand a chance against it. The other driver was in a diesel truck and Mitch was in his tiny Corolla.

Emma called me Saturday afternoon and told me the details of what had happened. I asked her if she needed my help in any way.

"I don't think so, dear," she said, tearfully. "Merrick is staying at the hospital and refuses to leave until Mitch wakes up. It's his head that's causing the most worry. I'll keep you updated."

Emma was upset and exhausted, and I wished there was some way I could take a piece of her burdens. She constantly worried about Merrick and now with Mitch in the hospital ... well, I could imagine her nerves were completely shot.

It took everything in me to not call her every hour to check on them. On Merrick especially.

When I took him out of the house to meet his parents in the driveway, it was officially the first time I had pushed him in the wheelchair myself. I don't even think he remembered the short trip outside. His mind was somewhere else, and once he was in the car with his chair stowed away in the trunk, he looked like he was carrying a thousand pounds on those shoulders.

By Sunday morning, I was more worried about Merrick than ever. His brother was okay, but he wasn't, according to Emma.

Keara and Josh talked me into attending a barbeque at their house to get my mind off of it. It didn't really help since the urge to look at my phone was stronger than ever.

"So, did you hear from Emma again today?" Keara asked, draining a giant pot of boiled potatoes.

"I did. Mitch woke up, but he'll have to stay in the hospital for a few days longer," I replied and continued cutting strawberries.

"It still pisses me off that some douche bag was already tanked at six o'clock. Josh said Mitch's car was just so mangled, he didn't even know how they got the poor guy out as easily as they did."

Josh hadn't been on that call, but the other paramedics described the scene to him in detail. Apparently, it was pretty bad.

"What about Merrick? How is he handling things?" Keara asked.

"He's still there at the hospital. Emma said she convinced him to go with his dad to their house and get some rest and a shower last night. She also said that he put up quite the fight and she almost called me."

Keara turned away from the potatoes and raised an eyebrow. "And that would have helped?"

I shook my head and shrugged. "I doubt it, but she seems to believe Merrick feels better when I'm around. She said she's seen a difference. I think he's just getting more adjusted and it's a little easier for him to deal with his situation."

Keara stared at me with her arms crossed over her chest. I kept cutting strawberries until there were no more to cut, but I didn't meet her eyes. After a long moment, she sighed and turned back to the potatoes. "You going to his house tomorrow?"

"As far as I know."

She nodded and kept her back to me.

My shoulders slumped as I sighed, knowing she was waiting for me to ask. "What is it, Keara?"

She finished up the potatoes and placed them on the table next to all the fruit and sides she'd been making all morning. When she sat down across from me, I knew she was going to start saying things I might not want to hear, but this was Keara. She was always honest and very rarely held anything back when it came to important things.

"What did Jason do to you, Grace?"

My chest constricted and a lump started to form in my throat. "What do you mean?"

"I mean, what the hell did he do to my best friend? You used to be more confident about yourself, although you've never once thought you were beautiful – which you *are*, by the way. You're gorgeous, Grace. You have hair I would kill for and curves everyone else would kill for. You're smart and giving and you are the nicest freaking person I have ever known. When you started dating Jason, I thought maybe you'd realize all of this, but you never did. And now? It's like that girl is gone completely."

I looked down at the bowl of strawberries and tried not to react to her words. She was right. She was *always* right.

"I just want to know what he did to make you feel like you're insignificant, because I would give anything to convince you otherwise," she added.

I curled my lips between my teeth and breathed through the anguish that wanted to climb out of me. Jason had taken away any kind of confidence I may have had. It became a way of life to always try to be better than I was. It was when I got pregnant that the woman I could have been went out of my reach. I knew the only reason Jason ever even came to see me was because of the baby, but I also knew I wasn't the only woman he went to see.

I hadn't been enough. The baby hadn't been enough. That's what ripped my heart to shreds.

"I just need some time, Keara," I stated quietly, my voice quivering on the word, *time*. Time hadn't been enough either.

Not yet.

"Okay, Grace. Just know that I'm here for you. I'm here to listen if you ever want to talk about it, but I won't push you. Even if I want to, I won't."

"Thank you."

She stood and made her way around the table, then wrapped me in her arms. "I love you, Grace. You're amazing and I hope one day you see that for yourself because everyone else does. Even the man who *can't* see."

Josh stepped into the kitchen and paused a moment before walking towards us, wrapping us both in a hug.

"I didn't know it was group hug time. You should have hollered for me. I'm good at this," he said playfully.

Keara and I both started giggling while Josh held us together, both literally and figuratively. When we finally separated, my smile was making my face ache.

"Thanks, Josh. Keara is very lucky to have you, you know that?"

He shook his head and wrapped an arm around Keara's waist before tugging her against his side. After placing a wet kiss on her cheek, he said, "Nah. I'm the lucky one. She has to put up with my grumpy ass all the time and she does it with a smile."

"You aren't grumpy," Keara protested.

He smiled wickedly. "Not when *you're* done with me."

Keara's cheeks reddened and her eyes got a faraway look. I couldn't help but giggle with glee for my best friend. She was happy and deserved every moment of untainted joy she could possibly wring out of life. Josh was a good man and would give her the world. I just hoped he asked her to marry him soon or I was going to have to step in.

Keara loved him and would wait patiently, but anyone could see that she was anxious for their life together to officially start.

"Where's Gary and Michael?" Keara asked as she slapped Josh's hand away from the steaming bowl of mashed potatoes.

"Setting up some chairs out back," Josh replied and kissed her cheek once more before smacking her butt.

Keara had practically begged me to come and hang out while Josh's family was there and not because she needed my support. A party without the Colson's was no party at all. Fortunately, Josh's brothers were all very cute. Unfortunately, they were all very married.

It wasn't long before the men filed into the kitchen through the back door, the smell of cooked meat engulfing my senses.

Funny how the first thought I had was if Merrick liked barbeques.

Gary, Michael, and Josh looked like they could be triplets. They all had the same short cut of dark blonde hair, and each of them owned a pair of piercing blue eyes. They were all pretty tall, but I was sure that, compared to Merrick, none of them would reach his height. Regardless, Gary, Michael, and Josh Colson were the heartbreakers in town and were all completely taken.

The brothers were close while growing up. Closer than your average siblings, and it showed in everything they did. They gave each other a hard time any chance they got, but they would take a bullet for each other, too. The kitchen seemed so much smaller with the three men dominating the space. It wasn't long before Keara had to shove them outside before they knocked something over. All I could do was laugh.

I helped Keara haul out the rest of the food and the barbeque was well on its way.

We spent the afternoon chatting and laughing with Keara's *future* sisters in law. That is, if Josh would hurry it along with that proposal.

Christie was Gary's wife and pregnant with their first child. She was what you would call a blonde bombshell. Pregnancy did nothing to change it. Her green eyes sparkled whenever Gary looked her way, and her excitement about the baby was contagious. She let me rest my hand over her swollen belly until I could feel the baby kicking. It was difficult to keep my emotions at bay, but the joy wafting off of Christie didn't allow for sadness.

They all knew my situation, but none of them pressured me to speak about it. Instead, Christie smiled brightly and asked about my parents, whom I was more than happy to talk about.

Jen was Michael's wife. She stood out with her nearly black hair and dark brown eyes. She towered over the rest of us at five feet and seven inches, and if I didn't know any better, I could swear she came off the pages of a Victoria's Secret catalogue. The couple had just married a few months before. They were still in the newlywed stage and couldn't keep their hands off of each other anytime they were within touching distance. More than once, I caught Michael with his hand on his wife's butt while he whispered something in her ear that made her flush and look a little lightheaded.

I should have felt like the odd one out, but I didn't. The Colson's were well known in this town and growing up with them made it easier to include myself with them. We talked about the stupid things we all did when we were kids. They shared stories about Josh and his football career. Josh didn't seem disappointed that his career was cut short and anytime Keara came up in the stories, he gave her a look that made her blush all over again.

Once everyone ate, the men volunteered to clean up while the four of us women sat back in our chairs and admired the view. It wasn't long before we ended up arguing about which of the Colson brothers was hottest. Keara stuck with Josh, but the other women couldn't quite decide, which had us laughing all over again.

"We need to do this more often," Christie said with a sigh as she watched her husband clear the table of food covered dishes.

"I agree," Jen chimed in. "Why don't we make it official. The last Sunday of every month, let's have a barbeque. We can rotate houses."

"That's a great idea," Keara exclaimed.

"What do you think, Grace?" Christie asked.

I smiled as I watched her rub her belly. "I would love that. As long as you guys are okay with me tagging along."

Keara clapped and grabbed my hand. "Of course! I wouldn't have it any other way."

We all agreed to get together the last Sunday of every month and the only way out of it was if we were on our death beds. Josh joined our group a minute later and agreed it would be a good time. Christie and Jen gave me their numbers and we promised to have a girl's night soon.

It was nice to have something to look forward to. How long had it been since I'd just relaxed and let myself have a good time?

The air started to cool as evening approached and we each went our separate ways. Josh walked me out to my car since I was the last to leave and Keara was jumping in the shower. She had been cooking all day and couldn't stand the smell of food saturating her hair.

"Thanks for coming, Grace. I know Keara missed you a lot and I'm glad you two worked things out."

"Me too," I replied with a smile and opened my door.

"Can I ask you a favor?"

I looked up at him, noticing that for the first time in his life, Josh Colson looked nervous. He shoved his hands in his pockets and glanced back at the house before looking at me with a pleading expression.

"Of course. What's up?"

He cleared his throat and quickly glanced at the house again. "I'm going to pick out a ring and I need some help. You know Keara best. I want to surprise her so I really don't want to ask her what she wants. I have an idea, but I don't want to get it wrong."

He was speaking so fast that I almost missed what he said.

I put my hand on his shoulder. "Breathe, Josh. I have no doubt that you would pick the perfect ring for her, but I'll be there to help you. Just call me and let me know when. I work long hours during the week, but I can get away here and there if you need me."

He nodded with a beaming smile and pulled me into a friendly hug. "Thanks, Grace. You're an amazing woman, you know that?"

I chuckled and stepped out of the hug. "I've been told that a time or two."

"It's true. Merrick's a lucky man."

My eyes widened with shock, "Oh, we aren't together, I'm just–"

"I know, but it doesn't mean something won't happen. I see Emma all the time at the hospital. She told me that Merrick has improved tremendously since you've been there. I saw how he was when he first got back. I've got to say, I didn't think *anyone* would get through to him."

"I haven't gotten through to him either, Josh."

"But you have. You may not know it, but everyone else does."

I stood there in stunned silence before he said goodbye and walked back to the house. By the time I pulled out of the driveway, I was almost hyperventilating. I had to see Merrick the next day and I already felt the pull of attraction between us, even though I knew the majority of it was one-sided. Knowing now what everyone else saw, though, my nerves tightened.

I didn't sleep well that night either. Knowing that Merrick was no longer several feet away from me, made my mind wander more often than it ever had before. I wondered if he thought of me the same way I thought of him.

After our conversation on Friday, I knew our friendship was starting to become a little ... more. In fact, I had the feeling that being his nurse was no longer the only motivation for my being there.

His questions about what I looked like caught me off guard, and it was slightly embarrassing that I couldn't describe myself in detail for him. He got frustrated when I gave my answers, needing more detail. His balled fists had made me wonder if he was thinking the same thing I was; if he could touch me, he would be able to see me in his own way.

The thought made my stomach flutter. Merrick was a strong man. His body was toned and fit even if he couldn't get around very well. He kept up on exercises that had nothing to do with his therapy, and I could guarantee that the minute he was healed, he would be training extensively to get back to where he was before he was injured. His fingers could crush my arm if he wanted to, but they could be so incredibly gentle. Watching those fingers learn the feel of objects around him always made me lightheaded. If those fingers ever learned the feel of *me* ...

I threw the blankets off my body and fanned my heated skin in the darkness. My attraction to Merrick Thatcher had only gotten worse. I thanked God he couldn't see the affect he had on me each day.

It wasn't just that Merrick was an attractive man. It was the way he apologized when he knew he screwed up. The way he thought about what he wanted to say when he explained something or answered a question. It was the way I clung to every word that came out of his mouth.

I felt like I could be myself around Merrick and he wouldn't judge me. Of course he was abrasive when he got frustrated and sometimes he could be a little frightening with his intensity, but he never insulted me for just being me.

His scars looked painful, but they didn't take away from his attractiveness. They added to it. As silly as that sounds, I couldn't see Merrick without them. They told a story about his life and what he went through, and even if I wished I could take those painful experiences away, they made him the man he is today.

A man that was more whole now than he had been all those years ago.

Monday came and went. Merrick didn't speak much, and knowing he was worried for his brother kept me from pushing him. After going through his exercises, I left him to himself for periods of time here and there while I just tried to stay busy.

We ate lunch together in silence, and he excused himself to his room to practice his Braille. The program my mother had ordered for him was amazing, allowing him to spend time on his own, learning. I could hear the silly voice translating what he was reading and wondered if he thought it was as annoying as I did.

I smiled to myself and continued to leave him be. My worries about Josh's previous comments faded away. Dwelling on what he said wouldn't help anyone, so I made a promise to myself. I just wouldn't think about it.

Merrick continued his silence throughout the day. Emma was stopping by earlier than normal, so I left his house around five after an awkward goodbye.

I was worried about him, but there was nothing I could say or do. It was just something he needed to work through on his own. Talking would probably speed it along, but Merrick wasn't much of a talker.

Mom was just pulling into the driveway when I opened the front door to my house.

"You want to go to a movie, Grace?" she asked the second she climbed out of the car.

"Sure. What movie?"

She shrugged and said, "Something romantic. I feel like a cheesy romance and since your dad has an emergency surgery, he won't be home for a few hours."

We changed into more comfortable clothes and Mom drove us into town. We spent the next couple of hours munching on popcorn, crying when the characters in the movie finally discovered they had been in love all along.

We stopped for some ice cream and picked up some food for Dad who called and informed us he would be home soon. It was nice to have some time with my mom. No questions or concerns.

By the time we made it home, I was ready to go to bed and Mom looked like she was ready to go out and party.

"You feeling alright, Grace?"

I put Dad's food in the fridge and turned back to her, seeing the curious expression on her face. "I'm fine. Just tired. Didn't sleep much over the weekend."

"How is Mitch doing?"

"He's recovering. I think they're discharging him in the next couple of days. I offered to help with his homecare, but since he lives with Emma and Nathan, she said they could handle it."

"Poor Emma. Having two sons so hurt is too much. I couldn't imagine you being injured like that. I don't know that I would stay sane knowing my baby had been hurt so badly."

I watched her frown and shake her head. She rounded the center island and pulled me into her arms.

"You go to bed. I'll wait up for your dad. I love you, Grace."

"I love you, too, Mom."

When she finally let me go, I didn't quite feel any better. My worry for Merrick was ever present, but it was the worry for his mind that kept me up at night. He still suffered with the trauma of what happened in Iraq and probably always would. He may have a strong body, but his mind was still very fragile.

The amount of nights he woke up screaming seemed to be happening less and less, and I just hoped that Mitch's accident didn't cause a setback. Merrick loved his family. His little brother had looked up to him his whole life.

Not having siblings myself, I couldn't imagine what it would be like to lose one or *almost* lose one. But Keara was like a sister to me, and imagining losing her made me completely lose my breath.

I washed my face and brushed my teeth, then sat on my bed and found myself staring out the window of my bedroom. It was strange knowing he was there but no lights were on. I started to hum as I undressed and found a tank and sleep shorts to wear. I jumped when I heard the blinds pull up at Merrick's window, covering my naked breasts out of instinct while I let out a squeak.

"Sorry, did I scare you?" he asked.

"Yes, I was dressing and–" I immediately stopped talking and closed my eyes. My blinds were mostly shut, but even if they were pulled up completely, Merrick wouldn't see me dressing.

"Damn!" he said, amusement in his tone. I pulled on the tank and shorts and moved toward the window, raising the blinds and leaning against the window sill. I strained my eyes to see in the darkness of his room and could barely make out the outline of his figure.

"Damn what?" I asked.

"I would have liked to see that," he replied, sighing dramatically.

I swallowed, the action harder than it should be, and opened my mouth to ask why. He didn't give me the chance.

"How was the barbeque yesterday? I'm sorry I didn't ask earlier."

I shrugged off the shock and decided to box his comment up so I could address it later while lying in my bed thinking of him anyway. "You have a lot going on, Merrick. I didn't even realize you knew I went."

"Mom told me."

I grinned. "Well, I didn't even know *she* knew I went."

Merrick chuckled softly, and I wished I could see the rare smile that would have been on his face at that exact moment. I dashed over to the switch and flipped off my light before resuming my position by the window. It only took several seconds for my eyes to adjust to the darkness, but I started to see him more clearly.

A sliver of moonlight was shining on his handsome face and instead of sitting with only his right side facing me like he always did, he was turned towards me. I could barely make out his features, but it was enough.

The smile was still there.

"So?" he asked.

"It was a lot of fun. The Colson boys know how to entertain and Keara is always fun to spend time with."

"Aren't both of Josh's brothers married?"

"Yes, and their wives are hilarious," I said, a beaming smile stretching across my face just thinking about them.

He grinned again before suddenly furrowing his brow, frowning. "So, were you there alone?"

"Are you asking me if I brought someone?"

"Yes," he answered without hesitation.

Curious.

"I didn't take anyone with me. I don't really have anyone to take." *Oh shit, did that sound pathetic? Why did I say that?*

Merrick's features were becoming more visible as the moonlight continued to light up his face. He looked unsure about my answer. "How is that possible?" he finally asked.

"How is *what* possible?"

"Not having anyone to take with you."

"Pfft, it's easy," I said dismissively. "I stay too busy to really meet anyone."

He nodded his agreement and I could have sworn I saw a grin on his face. He knew exactly what – or whom – I stayed busy with. "Have you ever been serious with someone?"

I had no idea where this was coming from, and I really wasn't prepared for these kinds of questions. Discussing my love life with Merrick seemed out of the realm of possibility, but he was sitting several feet away from me, *asking* me to discuss it.

My discomfort must have been shamefully obvious because Merrick shook his head and raked a hand through his hair, grumbling, "Never mind."

I thought about all the things Merrick had endured over the last few weeks with me. He wasn't really a talker, so the sharing of secrets wasn't the issue, but he trusted me with things that a man usually never has to trust *anyone* with. I had seen him vulnerable, which clearly wasn't easy for a man like Merrick Thatcher.

I could give him this. He trusted me, so I could trust him with this.

"I've been serious with someone before. Just one man," I rasped. "I've been too busy lately to really put much thought into anyone else and Jason wasn't really the kind of man that ... well, he made me doubt relationships altogether."

Merrick nodded, confusion clouding his expression. He patiently waited, giving me the chance to say more if I wanted to.

I took a deep breath, quickly filing through what was appropriate to tell him. "It wasn't a very good situation. He stopped loving me, and keeping him happy wasn't worth the heartache it caused," I informed him, hoping that the hurt I felt over a year ago wouldn't come back with a force that could knock me over. Not now.

Merrick was quiet for a long time, obviously ruminating on what I just told him. He was fighting something, but I couldn't figure out what. I wanted him to say something, *anything* that would make me feel less exposed to him.

"What if it was?" he finally asked.

"I'm sorry?"

"What if it *was* worth it? What if it was still a lot of work, but he *made* it worth it?"

I pictured Jason and everything I went through to try to make him happy. I believed that a relationship takes sacrifice from both sides, but I was the only one sacrificing while he lived the life he wanted. If he had been any different, made me feel like I was special to him or like I was important to him, would I still be with him?

No. I wouldn't be. What we had wasn't love, it was obligation. It wasn't real. Not for one minute.

"The answer is in the question, don't you think?" I said, shrugging. "Love ... *real* love ... is worth anything."

This time, it was me who waited. Merrick seemed to think my answer was strange if the look on his face said anything at all.

"Do you, umm ..." He cleared his throat and scratched his cheek. The scruff he had a hard time taming was sexy on him, but I could tell he wanted to shave, badly. He just didn't think he could. "Do you think, maybe, you could do me a favor?"

I smirked because Merrick Thatcher didn't ask for help, but I wasn't about to complain. He had changed the subject, after all. "Sure."

He scratched his cheek again, dropping his head forward so I couldn't see his face anymore. "My parents are coming over for dinner tomorrow night and their bringing someone kind of important. I, uh, I want to make sure I'm presentable. I guess."

"Okay?"

He sighed and shook his head as if he was chastising himself for being nervous. "I don't think I can shave on my own without cutting myself or missing something. Do you think you could ... I don't know, maybe ..."

I smiled because, again, Merrick wasn't a talker, but tonight he was rambling. Never in my life had I seen something so adorable, and I would bet my meager savings account that his cheeks were pink.

I was tempted to put him out of his misery and say, *'Yes, of course I'll help you shave'*, but this was much more enjoyable.

"Fuck, I'm so bad at this," he murmured.

I had to slap a hand over my mouth to keep from laughing out loud. The harshness of his words were in complete contrast to the utter vulnerability that was radiating off of him. My laugh slipped past my fingers and I could no longer contain it.

"Oh Merrick, you're adorable, you know that?"

He lifted his head, sending a dramatic scowl my way. It only made me laugh harder.

"Adorable? I'm *not* adorable."

"You are, though."

"I am not," he argued.

I shook my head and let the laughter die out. The poor guy had no idea how appealing he actually was. His typical grumpiness did nothing to hide it.

"I'll help you shave, Merrick. I would love to help you. Even though I know you could do it by yourself."

He sighed, those broad shoulders slumping with relief. "Thank you, Grace. This is important to me."

"I can tell."

We both sat in silence for a few minutes. The moon still shined on his face and I continued to lean against the window sill, getting my fill of him. The cool breeze outside swept my hair back and made me smile.

Peace.

I hoped Merrick was feeling the same way.

It was several minutes before he finally spoke again. "What other songs do you know?" he asked softly.

His deep voice sent a pleasant shiver up my spine, making my stomach swarm with those raging butterflies. "Lots."

"Will you sing for me tonight? Please?"

It was in that moment I realized I would do *anything* for him if he asked me like that.

"Yeah, Merrick. I'll sing for you." The lump in my throat felt impossible to swallow, but I pushed past it as I laid on my bed.

The man underneath all that tough skin – scarred skin – was still just a human being. He wanted peace just like the rest of us. It was just a little harder to come by these days.

I sang until I couldn't keep my eyes open any longer. Merrick listened.

Chapter Eight

Merrick

I believe there are only a few things in this life that should make a man truly nervous. This doesn't include actual fear, like the fear of losing a loved one or the fear of being shot at. Those are completely different.

I'm talking about that very distinct anxiety one has to make sure everything goes well. That deep concern that causes a quivering ball to sit heavily in his stomach.

First, is the apprehension a man feels when he makes the decision to serve his country, in any capacity. There should be pride and determination, but the underlying apprehension of getting seriously injured in the process is always there. This will not usually deter him, but it's there, and it's usually replaced with the adrenaline rush of purpose.

Second, is the unease a man goes through when he truly wants a woman. That *special* woman that makes him forget his name. He wants to ask her out, kiss her, or ask her to marry him, but he hesitates. It's the possibility of rejection that lies at the forefront of his mind. A guy might *say* that he isn't nervous, he might even *look* like he isn't nervous, but he most definitely *is*. The dread of rejection can make a man seriously reconsider his decisions.

The third thing applies to all men, too. It just comes in many different forms.

Facing the man that knew all of his weaknesses.

I've never been more nervous about my appearance and attitude than when I knew my CO was going to be around.

Captain Lee Bowman contacted my parents recently and wanted to check in on me. They invited him for dinner at the house. With the lack of sleep the night before and the added stress of Mitch being in the hospital, I didn't think I would make it. The captain had given his condolences for my little brother and said he would have rescheduled for another time, but he was leaving the country in a week and wanted to see me before then.

Lee Bowman was thoroughly involved in my training and that of my unit. He was a respected officer with a reputation for being subtly deadly. He was blunt when he needed to be, but the man was powerful with the simple act of silence. He planted seeds in the mind instead of throwing grenades of orders. He taught with lessons and punishment, but not one man who was under his command held any hostility towards him, no matter what he made them do.

He was a hero and a role model for every kid that ever entered the military and was given the incredible opportunity to meet him. The man who, for a solid week, forced me to carry around a fifty-pound rock named Respect.

I had Respect with me when I slept, when I ate, and when I trained. If anyone asked why I carried it around, I was to answer with, "To replace the respect I lack."

To someone on the outside, it didn't seem like a punishment, but every man there knew exactly how humiliating it was, and they made sure to ask about Respect every chance they got.

Needless to say, I learned an important lesson. One I must have forgotten in the last several months since the attack.

Captain Bowman was going to be disappointed when he realized the kid he'd taken under his wing was now lost. I was terrified I would lose his respect by lacking mine.

"You look like you're going to throw up."

Grace's voice was no help for my nerves. She was a prime example of that second anxiety and it was starting to give me ulcers. You'd think a man who had been in the line of fire, saw most of his friends killed, and was nearly burned to a crisp, wouldn't fear very much. But she terrified me. The way I felt when she was close had become a drug. One I couldn't imagine giving up.

"Nah, I'm fine," I said, clearing my throat after my voice cracked. If it wasn't already obvious to her how nervous I was, it was now.

We spent all morning getting the house ready for the captain's visit. Well, *she* did most of the work, and I tried to help where I could. Mom told her not to worry about it, but Grace insisted and told my mom to stay at the hospital with Mitch a little longer while we took care of things. I don't think Emma Thatcher could love Grace anymore than she already did.

The thought of my little brother lying in that hospital bed sent a shiver through my limbs. I don't remember how I got to the hospital that night. In fact, I don't really remember much after I spoke with my father on the phone. The only thing I know for sure is that Grace was there and she had reached into my chest and kept guard of my heart. A heart that I felt breaking more and more every day.

It isn't easy to shake off dread, but Grace swept it off my shoulders like she was dusting off a shelf. Once we took that first step – or roll – out of the house, it had been up to me to keep it off. I went through hell those couple nights in the hospital, unable to see if my little brother was truly going to be okay. I didn't sleep, I barely ate, and every sound in that cold hospital room took me back to the first day I woke up in Germany. I felt the pain, the grogginess from the useless narcotics, the panic of whether or not I was the only one to survive.

I heard the family members of other patients walk by Mitch's room with smiles in their voices. Laughter. Relief that their brother, sister, son, or daughter was going to be okay.

And the worst part? I was angry about it. They had no idea how many were lost. They had no idea the list of names that had already given their lives for *them*.

I couldn't stand to hear the happiness of others when so many of my brothers would never smile again.

It was the thought of Grace that kept me from shouting at them. It was the thought of Grace that kept me from completely losing it. She was a light in the only dark I could see.

Now we were both in the bathroom, me with no shirt and a face covered with shaving cream, and Grace standing over me, waiting for me to steady my breathing. She saw my struggle and had the most incredible amount of patience. She never pushed, just let me work through the pain.

"Merrick?"

"I'm fine," I breathed.

"Whatever you say. I promise I won't cut you with the razor," she teased with a smile in her voice.

"That's not the problem."

"Oh good. Because I've done this before."

Instant jealousy tightened my chest when I thought of her touching another man. I wanted to find the guy and pound his face to a pulp. "Who?" I snapped, tightly clenching my fists to control myself.

"When I did a rotation in geriatrics, the few patients I took care of were men. They wanted to look nice for some of the older nurses that worked there," she said with a chuckle. "I'd go in early and help them shave because they had a hard time keeping their hands steady."

I wasn't sure whether to be relieved or in complete awe of her. It made me realize that Grace was not just a good nurse, she was more compassionate than I originally thought.

She lifted my chin with her gentle fingers and said, "You ready?"

The feel of her warm breath on my face made me wonder if she would care about getting shaving cream all over her when I finally kissed the daylights out of those lips. I was sure they would taste like sugar and I would give anything to get just one look at them.

I nodded my head, under no condition to speak, and I felt her lean in close. I imagined the space between her eyebrows would be wrinkled with concentration and her bottom lip would be trapped under her teeth. The first swipe of the razor was slow and steady, and my fingers started to tremble in my lap.

My CO coming over for dinner was no longer the issue. The semi-erection I wouldn't be able to hide right now, was.

Grace moved closer, shifting her body so she could reach my face more easily. She ended up practically standing between my legs, brushing up against my injured one whenever she rinsed off the razor.

"Take a breath, Merrick. I haven't cut you. Not yet," she chuckled.

I breathed in her sweet scent, my head swimming with arousal. She had no idea what she was doing to me. All those months shaving with a tiny mirror stuck to the wall in my CHU had been frustrating as hell. I couldn't see shit in that thing. Now I very literally couldn't see shit and she was in front of me smelling like she did, being as gentle as she was, and all those memories didn't seem like such a horrible thing.

Because now I was experiencing something even more torturous.

She positioned the razor under my nose and expertly removed the coarse hair above my lip. What would she do if I just leaned in and devoured her mouth? Would I miss her lips completely or would she meet me halfway?

She gently turned my face and started on the other side. I didn't think having her shave my face would be this intimate. In fact, I was planning on it being annoying as hell since I thought she wouldn't really know what she was doing. Asking my mother had been an option, but I didn't want her leaving Mitch either.

"Almost there. You need a haircut, too." Her voice was rough and sexy, and I had to hold back a groan when it sent blood rushing straight to my groin. "I can style it for you so it stays out of your face, but I'm no good with cutting hair."

"That sounds good," I replied. God, if she didn't finish soon, I was going to do something stupid.

She raised my chin and carefully shaved my neck. When her fingers stroked my skin to check for any areas she missed, I swallowed thickly and lost the battle completely.

My injured and stiff hand found her wrist, slowly pulling the razor away from my skin. Her gasp sent my semi-erection shooting straight up to painfully hard. The skin of her wrist was like silk under my fingers, the tiny bones so fragile. I worried that if I was too insistent, I would hurt her with just a touch.

"Merrick?" she breathed, her sweet breath caressing my chin.

"Grace ..."

I felt her racing pulse under my fingers and pulled her forward until I could feel the heat of her face so close to mine. I raised my other hand to her waist and made a cautious path up, until I gripped the back of her neck. She didn't struggle or protest, and I hoped her accelerated breaths were telling me that she was feeling the same intense pull I was.

My dry throat finally found the strength to speak, even if it was just a whisper. "I would give anything to be able to see you right now." I pulled her face closer, until the tip of her nose touched mine. The sound of the razor falling to the floor, briefly registered in my mind. "I want to—"

"Merrick? We're here, son."

Grace startled at the sound of my mother's voice, quickly pulling back and forcing my hold on her neck to slip away. The sudden awareness of what I had almost done was like a punch to the gut. I wanted her more than I wanted my next breath, but what did *she* want?

Grace was still standing in front of me, but neither of us spoke.

"Merrick? Grace? Where are you?"

The tension in that bathroom was stifling. I haven't felt my heart thump like that since the first day of basic. It was making me dizzy. If I could just reach out and find her, touch her, I might be able to explain myself. If I could explain myself ... then what?

Grace took a deep breath and stepped around me, picking up the razor and placing it on the sink. "I'll let your mom finish up," she stammered.

I nodded, refusing to turn toward her voice. It was a memorable moment for me; the first that I was actually grateful for my blindness. I didn't want to see the rejection on her face.

"Good luck tonight," she whispered. Then her footsteps faded away and I wanted to punch something.

I heard her and my mother speak to each other before the sound of the front door opening and closing. Moments later, Mom walked in and my heart still clamored wildly. Had I completely destroyed everything? Would Grace come back or had I run her off like I tried to that first day?

"What did you do?" Mom asked, her voice filled with unease. Was her concern for me or for Grace?

I closed my eyes and shook my head. "Nothing. Why?"

"Grace looked like she was about to burst into tears. Did you say something to her? I thought you liked her?"

I turned my chair toward the shower, away from the feel of my mother's prying eyes. "I do. That's the problem."

She must have understood because she didn't push for more. I opened the shower door and pulled myself out of the wheelchair. It bumped against the tiled ledge of the shower and started to roll backward. I would be happy to get rid of the damn thing soon. But then it would be crutches, which were almost just as bad.

"Do you need my help?"

"No, Mom. I got it," I answered a little too harshly. I cringed and encouraged myself to stop being such an asshole. "Thank you for offering."

I sat myself on the shower chair, pulling the door closed. I started to tug my pants off, grunting when my leg smarted. Mom was still in the bathroom and it must have been pure torture to watch me struggle. Once my leg was propped on the other chair, I took a deep breath and tried not to think of Grace.

"You look nice with a clean shaven face, Merrick. Grace did a wonderful job."

I dropped my head and sighed, because it was pointless. I ran my hand over my face, feeling the smooth skin under my fingers. "Yeah, she did."

The sound of the bathroom door shutting was the only sign I had that Mom left the room. I tossed my pants out of the shower and closed the door again.

Captain Bowman was going to arrive soon. I needed to pull myself together.

I had hoped Grace would be around, but it seemed unlikely now. She helped me over all the previous hurdles, but maybe I had to do this on my own. Regardless of whether or not I was ready.

The sound of Captain Bowman's loud voice sent a rush of dizziness to my head. The deep breaths I'd been taking since his car pulled into the driveway weren't helping at all. I was hoping to be able to take a moment to compose myself once I was ready, but even with another hand and much less pain, it took me forever to accomplish the act of getting dressed.

Didn't help that I stopped to listen for Grace every few seconds.

I dropped my head into my hands, raking my fingers through my hair for the hundredth time. I never noticed how soft hair could feel, never even thought of it until I couldn't see it. Even my aching hand could feel the texture and length of it.

Grace was right, I needed to cut it soon.

My ears perked when I heard footsteps to my right, the side where Grace's room was. Suddenly, the dizziness disappeared and all that blood in my head went straight down. I could still feel her breath on my lips and knew if I could go back to that moment in the bathroom, I would do the same thing all over again. Only, I wouldn't hesitate.

"You look very handsome, Merrick."

The air in my lungs rushed out with relief and my eyes closed. At least she was still speaking to me. At least she was still keeping her window open. I didn't know what I would have done if it was winter instead of summer.

"Thank you, Grace."

"You aren't going to throw up are you? Because I don't think that would impress your CO very much."

I chuckled and tugged at my hair again. When I opened my eyes, the laugh died. After all this time, I still expected to see *something* when I opened them. The disappointment was always so powerful.

"Will you come over?" I asked, licking my dry lips and praying to God she said yes.

"For dinner? With the guy who just the thought of is making you look like you could run on a broken leg? Umm, let me think about that."

I heard the smile in her voice and it felt good to be teased about it. Grace was an expert in sarcasm, but she was never impolite.

"He doesn't bite, I promise."

Her laugh sent a shiver down my spine. "I'm sure he doesn't, but I still don't understand why you want me there. You're a tough guy. You got this, Merrick."

If she only knew. I wasn't tough anymore. In fact, I felt like a helpless child most of the time. I felt fear every morning I woke and fear every night I fell asleep. But with her, I felt like myself. Like I could move on with my life and look forward to the future. Then she went home each night and the reminder that she probably wouldn't be in that future, haunted me.

"Regardless, I have plans tonight," she added, making my stomach drop.

"Oh, what plans?" I shook my head. I shouldn't have asked but couldn't help myself. If she had a date, it was none of my business.

None. Of. My. Business.

"I'm not supposed to tell anyone, but if you can keep a secret ..."

"Who am I going to tell?"

She didn't laugh, even though I meant it as a joke.

Footsteps sounded in the hallway and I knew it was time to see Bowman. I wouldn't make it through the night if I was picturing Grace on a date with some asshole that didn't deserve her. "Now or never, Grace," I stated, thickly.

"Josh is asking Keara to marry him. I'm helping him look for a ring tonight."

The relief was immense.

It was like that first step on American soil after months in the dust and rubble. Taking that first step off the plane at Dallas Fort Worth for my visit home. Feeling that small sense of peace, knowing I wasn't in danger. That my friends were safe as well. The worry was always there, but there's just something about knowing, feeling the stillness in the air even with a crowd surrounding me. That crowd welcomed soldiers home all the time with a reception as far as the eye could see. Almost like a parade, lined up with smiling faces.

I'll never forget that feeling. That serenity.

"Good."

It was all I could say. Grace stayed silent and the sound of my door opening, cut through the room.

"Captain Bowman is here, son." Dad sounded nervous enough for the both of us. He heard the stories, and if Bowman still looked anything like he did before, I could pretty much guarantee Dad was intimidated.

"Good luck, Merrick," Grace said, quietly.

I wanted her with me, to somehow ground me and remind me to be polite, but she wasn't going to be able to hold my hand through this.

"Is that you, Grace?" Dad said, stepping in front of me.

"Hi, Mr. Thatcher."

"Well, look at you. I haven't seen you since you've been home, but Emma told me you were all grown up. Little Grace Samuelson, you're a beautiful woman, my dear."

"Thank you, Mr. Thatcher."

"You call me Nathan. Thank you for helping my boy out, he seems a whole hell of a lot happier since you started bossing him around."

"I'm glad to hear it," Grace replied with a chuckle. Her shyness spoke volumes even though I couldn't see her.

I smiled, picturing Grace's blush. Would it travel down her neck and arms? Would I be able to feel the heat of it if she was standing next to me?

"We'll see you soon, Grace," Dad called.

"Have a good night. And Merrick?"

"Yeah?"

"You got this."

I sighed. Would the hope of seeing her face, ever go away? I could feel the comfort in her words, but seeing it would be a completely different thing.

I rolled my chair out of the room with Dad following behind me. The captain's booming voice was coming from the kitchen. I guided myself with a hand on the wall and my good foot on the ground. It was getting easier and easier to keep the chair steady. Crutches would come as soon as I finally perfected this shit, I just knew it.

"Dad, will you please hold onto the chair when we get to the kitchen?" I asked, knowing he was itching to help me out somehow.

"Sure, son. But why?"

I didn't respond because I didn't want him to try to talk me out of it.

"There he is," Mom said.

"Merrick, you look good, boy. If I didn't know any better, I'd say you were faking all those injuries of yours," Bowman said.

I grinned because I didn't expect anything else from the man. Most guys didn't have the kind of relationship with their CO that allowed them to poke fun at each other. Most of the time, the only thing you talked about was orders and respect.

"Sir, not faking, just milking it out a bit."

His booming laugh made the wheelchair rattle. "Sounds about right. It's good to see you, Thatcher."

I braced both my hands on the arms of the chair and used my good leg to raise myself up and out of it. Dad was there, holding the chair steady so it wouldn't roll away from me. Once I was standing, my left leg stiff and pulsing when my foot touched the ground, I saluted my captain. I wouldn't see his return, but I knew he would give it.

Respect.

If I had lost everything else, at least I tried to come back with a little bit of that.

"Merrick." My mother's gasp was quickly silenced and I felt my father's movement from behind. He must have given her the not-now gesture. I would have to thank him for that later.

"I would love to shake your hand, son," Bowman said from right in front of me and I raised my right hand to offer it to him. The feel of his warm hand in mine was a surprise and a shock. How long had it been since I'd shook a man's hand? Since *I'd* touched anyone?

"You'll get through this better than any other man possibly could, Thatcher. I know it. I feel it. I see it in you and so do you. Don't give up on that."

The captain's firm words hit me deep. I did know it. I just needed a reminder here and there.

"Let's eat, shall we?" Dad said, his voice thicker than normal. God, I hoped he wasn't getting emotional. That would ruin all my preparation for the night.

I found my way back into my chair and felt my father's hand on my shoulder, squeezing tightly with support.

I may not be able to see it, but I could feel it.

Hope.

I had hope.

And damn if the only thing I could think about was that I wished Grace would have been there to feel it right along with me.

Chapter Nine

Grace

Merrick seemed different after that dinner with his superior. I hoped it would stick and so far it had. Two weeks went by and his progress was insanely fast. The strength he still had in his muscles helped to counteract the weakness in others. His therapy was smooth, and half the time I didn't even really need to be there.

His hand was doing remarkably well. Once he finally got enough strength back in his grip, he was switched to crutches with mild weight bearing. Some of the grumpiness returned for a day or two, but he still seemed lighter than he'd been in the beginning.

"Fuck!"

Well, most of the time.

"How the hell am I supposed to use these if they keep rubbing my armpits raw?"

I held back the chuckle because I had already discussed this issue with him. He swore he could use them without a 'stupid kitchen towel' wrapped around the top of them. He was beginning to realize that he was wrong. Especially since he would need them for a while.

"Do you need any help?" I called from the kitchen.

He showered and dressed by himself like he'd been doing for weeks already. Every time he finished, I could hear the deep sigh of relief coming from his bedroom. It took a long time, but he could do it. That sigh hadn't come today. Not yet.

"No, I'm good. I just ... ah, shit!"

The sound of his painful hiss made my feet move. I scurried into his bedroom only to find that he hadn't dressed himself, except for his boxer briefs, and he was standing in front of his bed with one crutch, looking like a God. I'd pretty much seen him naked a few times in the beginning, but it was all so clinical that I never truly noticed how ripped the man actually was.

Those abs could seriously cut some glass and his chest was chiseled and hard. Glorious. The scars did absolutely nothing to distract from his beauty. They were there, visible and many, but *'there'* is all they ever really were.

"Are you still here?" he asked, his eyes pointed straight ahead at the wall beside me.

I cleared my throat and shifted on my feet. How long was I staring? "Yeah, are you okay?"

His lips tugged into a grin, "Why were you so quiet? I wasn't sure if you left when you saw me naked."

"You aren't n-naked."

"I'm not?"

"No?" Why did it have to come out as a question?

"Are you sure?" he smiled. Those teeth were so straight and added so much to the already panty-dropping smile he was shooting my way.

I took another look, slowly grazing my eyes down his body. Just to be sure.

"Yes."

"So, why were you staring at me? I know it isn't because of the scars. You've told me they don't bother you. Were you lying?" He seemed amused, but the question was certainly serious.

"No, I wasn't lying. They don't bother me."

"So?"

"So, what?"

He sighed and shook his head. "Why were you staring at me?"

"I wasn't."

He laughed.

The man actually laughed. And not the chuckle that he graced all of us with now and then. No, this was a full on slap-your-knee-stomach-clenching laugh. The sound of it speared straight into my chest, swirled around a few times then changed its course downward.

God, it was a sexy laugh. Deep and rough. Sultry enough to send vibrations down into my feet.

He needed to laugh more. For the lives of all available women in the world, he needed to laugh just to keep their hearts thumping.

"Grace. Were you checking me out?"

I blinked several times before I processed what he just asked me. "What? No! I mean, yes. I mean ... damn it, Merrick!"

He kept laughing. I just stood there taking in that incredible sight with my arms folded across my chest. He may not be able to see the annoyance in my stance, but I needed to show it somehow.

And it *was* annoyance. Not arousal.

Not. Arousal.

"Are you done yet?" I snapped.

He shrugged those massive shoulders and let the laugh die out, that smile still on his handsome, still clean shaven face. A face he had attempted to shave on his own a few times until he was forced to ask for my help again. I knew he thought about that almost kiss two weeks before. I hadn't ever *stopped* thinking about it.

Would he try it again?

God, I hoped he did. If Emma hadn't walked in when she did, I would have been all over the man. Just like now. If something didn't interrupt us soon, I was going to climb him like a tree. His rare silliness only added to my uncontainable attraction to him.

"Now, tell me what the hell happened that made it sound like you hurt yourself. You look perfectly fine to me."

Oh, shit. That smile only got bigger.

"I do?"

I stomped my foot, trying not to smile. "Merrick!"

"Okay, okay. Sorry, it's just nice to know that you find me attractive."

He was baiting me. I knew it, but I couldn't stop myself from latching on. "Of course I do. I've always found you attractive."

This time that smile was accompanied by the deepest – and manliest – shade of pink in his cheeks. God, the man was beautiful. The scar slashing through the left side of his face did nothing but make it harder for me to look away. I swear I could stare at him all day and never get tired of it.

"These damn crutches are painful." Merrick lifted an arm as he spoke.

My eyes widened at the sight of raw, red skin under his arms. "Oh my God, Merrick, why didn't you tell me?"

He shook his head and rolled his eyes. Of course he wouldn't tell me. He was the master at keeping things inside.

I moved closer to get a better look. The irritated skin looked painful, reddening some of the scars from his previous burns in the same area. I could only imagine how much they actually hurt.

"It wouldn't be so bad if I could move from the shower to the room without the damn things. Am I walking on them wrong?"

I shook my head and lifted his arm, trying in vain to ignore those thick muscles of his under my fingers. "You're doing just fine on them. This happens more often than you think, but normal people tell someone *before* it gets this bad."

"Yeah, well you know better than anyone that I'm not normal," he said, his tone soft.

I looked up into his face, seeing that his eyes were aimed down at me, as if he was actually looking at me. The distant and empty look in them made me want to growl in frustration. It was the first time I wished with every fiber of my being that he could see. The first time I wished the past hadn't happened for someone else.

I felt his breath fan my face, not realizing how close I was to him until that moment. It would only take a slight movement to press my lips to his. If he knew how sexy he actually was, I don't think he would care *what* I thought of him. But the look on his face told me that he *did* care, and he was worried.

"You're better than normal, Merrick."

Neither one of us breathed, the air around us sizzling with electricity. I could almost hear the crackle, and I sure as hell could feel it.

Letting his arm drop, I stepped away from him before I lost my mind. The smell of his body wash did crazy things to my stomach, not to mention the things that happened a little further down.

"I'm going to get some ointment. You should probably stay off the crutches for a little while so you don't make it worse."

He nodded and felt around for his bed before slowly sitting down and tossing the crutch aside. "Would you mind finding me some clothes then?"

I swallowed, barely getting past the lump in my throat. "Sure."

A few minutes later, Merrick was dressed and I was sweating bullets. Touching him was getting more and more difficult to do without feeling like I was going to burst into flames. I needed to talk about something to take my mind off of his body.

"So, Josh is asking Keara tonight," I blurted out as he adjusted the brace on his leg.

"Really? That's great."

"Yeah, he's taking her to Salt Lake. Fancy dinner and a show."

Merrick grinned. "He isn't going to hide the ring in her food is he?"

"Oh, God. Probably," I laughed. "He was nervous as hell and had no idea when he would do it. He said he'd just wing it."

"Uh oh. Do you think that's wise?"

I shrugged. "At this point, I don't think Keara cares *how* he does it."

Merrick chuckled, a wide smile stretching through those lips as he adjusted the final strap on his brace. "Good for them. You didn't spill the beans, did you?"

I scoffed, completely offended by that question. "Excuse me?"

"I'm just asking," he said quickly, holding his hands up in front of me to hold off my attack. "You seem excited about it and I know how you women like to talk."

"Yeah, but I can keep a secret if I need to."

He shrugged, looking every bit the nonchalant he was going for, and shifted on the bed until he could reach the wall.

"Why did you just shrug?"

"What?"

I crossed my arms over my chest and popped my hip out. This kind of thing worked with my father all the time and Mom was a pro at the hip pop. Merrick couldn't see it, though. Didn't stop me from doing it because, damn, it felt good.

"You shrugged," I pointed out sharply. "Like you didn't believe me."

"I believe you," he argued with a smile.

Teasing me seemed like the only thing he actually enjoyed these days, but instead of annoying me, it was only making me like him more. This was the Merrick I used to stare at in class. The Merrick everyone gravitated to. The Merrick I drew a heart around in almost every year book I owned.

"I don't believe you," I said with an almighty glare that would have had other men shaking in their boots.

This caused another laugh that took my breath away. "Oh, Grace. You're adorable, you know that?"

His use of the same word I used to describe him was intentional, but instead of arguing about it, I smiled and kept my voice matter-of-fact. "I know."

He stepped forward with a hand on the wall, smirking playfully. Then he put more pressure on his leg than he should. The painful grimace on his face made me roll my eyes.

"Okay, tough guy. You aren't going anywhere right now so sit back down. We'll do your exercises in here."

He did as he was told, that same mischievous grin appearing on his face. "I can think of plenty of fun exercises to do on my bed, but I'm assuming you aren't into that."

I felt my face flame, because I was *very much* into that, but he didn't need to know that. "What a charmer."

I walked out of the room, leaving him chuckling on his bed, hoping I had enough self-control to touch him without actually *touching* him.

"This is going to be a long day."

"You'll be happy to hear that I have plans this evening."

My head snapped up so quickly, I was sure I strained several muscles in my neck. Merrick was standing unsteadily in the doorway of the kitchen a few days after the nonsexual-exercises-on-the-bed episode. I still couldn't get the image of him standing in the middle of his room, in nothing but his boxer briefs, out of my head. So, suffice it to say, the first thing I saw when I looked at him was that he was definitely wearing clothes.

I didn't even try to stop the frown.

Did he just say he had plans?

"I'm sorry?"

Merrick smiled and slowly made his way through the kitchen, counting his steps along the way until he reached out and grasped the edge of the counter where I was sitting. He was doing as much as he could only using one of the crutches and before long, he would no longer need them.

"I have plans tonight."

"You do?" I asked with a small squeak.

"I do. With my sister."

God, I really wish I could have held back the deep sigh of relief, but it came out so fast. There was no covering it up or taking it back.

With Keara and Josh finally getting engaged, for some reason I just felt like everyone was settling down and I was still in limbo. What would happen if Merrick found someone?

"What kinds of plans did you think I'd have?"

I shrugged and turned back to the book I'd started reading the night before. It was no surprise that with everything on my mind, I still hadn't finished the first chapter.

"Grace?"

I hesitated a moment, then looked back at him. His eyes were pointed down at the counter top and his hand was close to mine. I wanted to slide mine right over his and feel the strength in that hand.

"I don't know. I thought maybe you'd be going out with friends."

He laughed dryly. "What friends?"

"You have friends here, Merrick. Lots of them."

"And not one of them wants to deal with a blind man."

"Merrick ..."

He slid his hand away and pulled it through his hair, his lips pressed together in frustration. "I'm sorry, Grace. I know you're trying to help, but I don't think you realize that all the friends I used to have are no longer a part of my life."

"What about the friends you made in the military? Do any of them live close by?"

Merrick's expression suddenly dropped altogether. No anger or surprise or even thoughtfulness. Just empty. His face was pale and his good leg started to shake. I grabbed his arm and forced him to sit, hoping against hope that I didn't just open a can of worms for him.

It was a long time before he took a deep breath and told me something I wasn't expecting at all.

"There's one friend that lives in Mona. A few hours from here. Ryan Warner."

"Were you close with him?"

Merrick nodded his head and clenched his fists. "He was my best friend. We did everything together."

I knew then that this wasn't just a friend he made and hung out with when there was down time. This Ryan was *there*. He was there when everything went to shit.

I decided to take advantage of his sudden willingness to talk. "Have you talked to him since you've been back?"

He slowly shook his head and closed his eyes.

"You haven't called him? He hasn't called you?"

The regret on Merrick's face said enough, but he told me anyway. "He called the first week I was back. And a few times after."

"And?"

"And what? I haven't talked to him."

"I don't understand," I said, feeling like I was completely missing the point.

"We'd spoken once or twice in the hospital in Germany, but neither one of us were in any condition to be chummy," he said bitterly. "I didn't take his call and I haven't called him back."

"Why not?"

He shook his head and tried to push away from the counter, but I stopped him with a hand on his arm. "Why not, Merrick?"

The cords of muscle in his arm went hard, trembling under my fingers. "Because I don't deserve his friendship. It's *my* fault we ran into the shit storm that killed the majority of my men. *My* fault he almost didn't make it back to his family."

"But he *did* make it back. I can't imagine he would blame you for any of it."

"He doesn't have to," Merrick snapped, the scowl on his face reminding me of the first day as his nurse.

I stayed quiet. I didn't want to provoke his anger, but I didn't want to tell him it would all be alright. It wouldn't be alright because he still blamed himself for so much, and he still struggled with moving on.

How long would it last? How many reminders would he get before he finally started to work through the painful memories?

Every screech of tires, every slam of a cupboard, even the loud whir of a lawn mower made him tense. It all made him remember.

Merrick's face was aimed in my direction, but his eyes were looking at ... nothing. Nothing at all. It caused a massive lump to form in my throat, thinking of what he must be going through, what he must be seeing in his mind at that very moment. He wouldn't feel comfort just by seeing the sincerity in my expression, and no matter what I said, it wouldn't change anything.

"I'm sorry, Merrick. I won't ask any more questions."

The anger on his face softened with regret, and he shut his eyes, cursing under his breath. "No. I'm sorry, Grace. I shouldn't have snapped at you like that."

"It's okay. I shouldn't have pushed."

"No. Don't say it's okay. It's not." He sighed, slumping his shoulders. "I know you want to help and I know I'm being irrational. It's just too hard to think otherwise."

I reached for his hand and squeezed his fingers. They were cold and trembling, and it made the tightness in my chest twist and turn. "You don't have to think otherwise, Merrick. Not yet, at least. No one should tell you how to feel because no one could possibly understand what you've been through. We just want you back. Your parents want you back, and I ..."

His head slowly raised, those captivating blue eyes staring straight ahead. It was obvious he still expected to see something whenever he opened them.

"You what?" he asked, his voice just above a whisper.

I drew in a deep breath and tried to keep my voice steady. I had no idea what I wanted to say, but I knew what he needed to hear. Exhaling slowly, I carefully chose the right words. "I want you back, too. I saw the old Merrick and I know he's still in there. We don't expect you to be the same as you were before, but we want you to *be* here. To be with us any way you can. To know that we're here right beside you."

Merrick's fingers constricted around mine and his thumb circled around the back of my hand. My mouth went dry, my stomach fluttered. Did he already know?

"I just think you need to take your own time," I added a little breathlessly. "Just remember you aren't alone, no matter how long it takes."

"How do you even know what the old me is like?"

"Because I saw you all the time. Saw you with your friends and family."

"But we never talked, never spent any time together. Hell, I couldn't even remember your name. I know that makes me an asshole, but that just makes me wonder all the more."

"You didn't need to know who I was. Doesn't change the fact that I still saw you."

His right eye darkened, the dilation of his pupil making the blue all but disappear. At the time, I didn't think about what it meant for his eye to react to anything at all. All I could think about was the way his hand kept hold of mine, and how much I wanted to move into his strong arms, and stay there forever.

"I see you now, Grace," he said, moving closer until our chests were just inches apart. "I–"

"Yo! I'm here, Merrick."

We both startled at the voice coming from the front door. Mary, Merrick's older sister, had arrived to pick him up. The timing couldn't have been more awful. Or should I say better?

Merrick slowly released my hand. I stepped away from him, trying to catch my breath. Mary walked into the kitchen and abruptly stopped when she saw us standing next to each other. I don't know what my expression must have looked like, but I assumed I looked like a love-struck fool. The heat in my cheeks was also a sign my entire face was scarlet.

"Did I interrupt something? I can leave if you need me to," Mary said, lightheartedly. Her lips stretched into a wide grin just before she winked at me.

She hadn't changed much since the last time I saw her. If I didn't know any better, I could swear she and Merrick were fraternal twins. Her blue eyes stood out starkly on her tanned and flawless face. She always kept her hair dark, but there were times when she was daring and put purple, blue, or pink in it. She was adventurous and beautiful, and from the look on her face, that hadn't changed either.

"Merrick was just telling me he was leaving," I said, grinning like an idiot. "It's good to see you again, Mary."

"Same to you, Grace. I've heard a lot about you lately."

"You have?"

Her mouth curved into another playful smile. "Lots." Stepping up to Merrick, she wrapped her arms around his neck. He leaned down to return the hug, looking awkward in the process.

"Good to see you little brother. I've only got tonight before I have another few days on flight." She stepped back and looked him over with a scrutinizing twist to her lips. "My God, you look nice tonight."

"I can clean up pretty well," Merrick replied, his voice light, but his expression somewhat guarded.

"You want to come with us, Grace?" Mary asked. "We're going to get some dinner and catch up. I'd love to hear what you've been doing over the years."

"Oh." I struggled to speak, my mind scrambling on how to reject the offer without sounding desperate to get away. "I, um, no, thank you. You two go and have a good time. I have some things I need to do tonight."

Call Keara and ask her what the hell was happening to me, for starters.

Merrick turned toward me, his brow furrowed and his lips turned down, but Mary saved me. "Another time then, for sure."

"Yeah, of course. Thanks," I smiled.

Mary watched me for a moment, her gaze curious if not completely confused. But she didn't push for anything else. I needed to get the attention off of me and onto her before I bolted out the door at a dead run.

"I'm sorry, I'm just curious. You said you have a few days on flight. What does that mean?"

"Oh, I'm a flight attendant. I have a few days off at a time and I go back tomorrow."

"That sounds exciting."

"Not really," she chuckled. "It's boring most of the time, but it can be fun with some of the people I work with. I get to see a lot of neat places, too."

"Don't let her fool you, Grace," Merrick cut in. "She loves every minute of it."

Mary laughed and smacked her brother on the chest. "Only because I get to meet rich businessmen that get a little too handsy."

"And how does Sam feel about that?"

"He hates it, but he's seen what they look like. Old and stinky. Plus, he knows I'll never leave him for another. He's too good to me."

"Yeah, well he better be or I'll have to kick his ass again."

Mary rolled her eyes and turned back to me. "So how much longer do you have to take care of this loser? He seems to be moving around just fine."

"Well, that's up to him, I guess," I replied, glancing up at Merrick. "He still has quite a bit of therapy to get through, but most of it will be on his own anyway."

Merrick squared his shoulders, another deep frown stretching down. "I thought you'd need to help me with the leg."

"I will, but you're getting around really well so full time care isn't going to be necessary. No reason to pay for something you don't need, right?"

He lowered his head and shifted on the crutch. "I guess."

Mary lifted herself up onto the counter, a perfectly plucked eyebrow lifting curiously. "Interesting."

"What?" Merrick asked.

"Nothing." Her smile was wicked, but more teasing than anything else. She turned to address me and there was no animosity or ulterior motive behind her next words. Just pure inquisitiveness. "Last I heard, you were with Jason Reed. You two still an item?"

I was too busy dealing with the shock of hearing Jason's name come out of Mary's mouth so suddenly, I totally missed Merrick's entire body flinching.

"Jason Reed? *That's* the Jason you told me about?" he asked, a growl in his voice. He'd gone from anxious to angry in one second flat.

"Um, we aren't together anymore. Broke up a long time ago," I said to Mary, ignoring Merrick.

"Oh, good. He's an asshole. If you two were still together, I was going to tell you to leave his ass and go after my brother here," she said with another wink, then smacked Merrick's shoulder. "He can be an asshole, too, but he'll eventually feel bad about it."

I chuckled right along with her, until I looked up to see Merrick's hardened expression. I couldn't tell if he was mad at *me* or something else. Whatever it was, I didn't want to be around him when he finally snapped. I was tired, emotionally and physically. And frankly, this whole conversation was getting the best of me.

Coward, I hissed in my mind.

"Calm down, Merrick," Mary sighed.

With that, I snagged my purse off the counter and waved goodbye to Mary. "I'll be here Monday, Merrick. Have a good night."

I didn't wait for a response. It was the first time I brushed him off so quickly.

When I reached the front door, I heard Mary finally speak. "Leave it alone, Merrick."

Whatever *it* was, it couldn't have been good.

Chapter Ten

Merrick

I was torn between the desire to go back to hiding from *everyone* and the need to climb out of this pit I found myself in.

Dinner with Mary was filled with her constant questioning about how I was feeling, what Grace was helping me with, and when I was going to stop being a 'big baby'. She didn't let up until I talked, which took a lot longer than she planned for.

I didn't blame her. I'd been acting like a child ever since I got back, treating her and everyone else like a burden. The same way I treated Mom like an annoyance.

"I'm working on it," I informed Mary.

"I can see that," she said on a sigh. "The question is why?"

"Does it matter?"

"I guess not. But maybe if you knew the reason why, it would help you understand the *how* a little better."

She had a point. I knew *one* of the reasons, but it scared the hell out of me. Just thinking about the last several weeks with Grace made me sigh and cringe at the same time.

I couldn't stand to have things done for me. Being in the military taught me to take care of myself, to be independent. I'd spent the better part of the last twelve years learning to survive in life or death situations and being trained to run *toward* the danger.

Now, it just felt like all of that was play time.

"I'll get through it. That's all I can do, right?"

By the time Mary brought me home, I was done talking and decided that thinking about the why would only hinder the how. Mary didn't know what she was talking about.

"I know things haven't changed, Mer, but we all hope you get through it," my sister said, her voice despondent. Then she left, going back to a life she enjoyed having.

But things *had* changed.

The pain was diminishing, making it easier to adjust. There was finally a light at the end of the tunnel and, angry or not, I was getting to the end. I was working at getting back to the old Merrick that Grace wanted.

Because *I* wanted *Grace*.

I wanted her more than I wanted to be pain free. Almost more than I wanted to see again.

The pull between us was so intense, focusing on anything else these days was completely pointless. She helped with my therapy, with cooking, with *everything*. And even though I hated it, I'm glad it was *her*.

She was there when I got frustrated, calming me down and reaching that part of me that was once filled with courage. The part of me I thought was still back in that miserable desert. She reminded me that the things which seemed *impossible*, were actually possible. I just needed to *want* it more than I wanted to *hate* it.

I hated a lot these days and I was tired. Tired of the anger and hopelessness. It drained me every single day.

There were also other changes.

Grace was quiet over the next couple weeks. Sure, we talked as much as we always did with an argument here and there, but only because I provoked her. She was just so damn sexy when she argued back. Her voice changed to this husky tone that made my chest tighten. The energy she radiated made every nerve in my body come alive. I promised to stop taunting her, but that was one promise I didn't think I'd keep for very long.

Plus, I'm pretty sure she enjoyed it as much as I did.

Grace asked about Mary and her husband, Sam. She asked about Mitch and, at my request, we even went to see him one day during the week. Leaving the house wasn't my favorite thing, but my brother was more important. The trial for the accident was quickly approaching, putting the whole family on edge since Mitch was still recovering. Even with her silence, Grace kept me grounded, which helped Mom keep her worries at bay. They didn't need me to lash out or lock myself up when it was still so fresh.

Keara and Josh came up in conversation quite a bit, too. Wedding plans were such a big deal to these women, but I didn't see the fun in it. Just a lot of stressing out about what was available and where it happened. It shouldn't matter *where* it happened, only that it *did* happen. Right?

We even argued about *that*. The same teasing and flirting as usual, but it just wasn't the same.

Grace distanced herself more each day, and no matter what I did to try and bring her back, she just wasn't the Grace from before. There were moments I told myself it was only in my head. Like the times she laughed at my lame jokes or when she kept encouraging me to try harder with therapy.

Those moments, she was the Grace I was falling for.

Then, there were the quiet times she seemed to be in another place entirely. Her voice grew timid, the smile was gone from her words. She stopped humming, stopped singing.

She was suffering.

From what? I had no idea. But I *know* pain. I know suffering better than a lot of people. It also didn't escape my notice that the suffering was just one of the connections Grace and I shared.

"What are you thinking about, Merrick?"

I sat up, breathing through the ache in my leg that came whenever we finished exercises. The end was coming fast. I wanted it. I wanted to move forward. But then what happens? Grace wouldn't be here any longer, and I was tempted to re-break my leg just to keep her.

You're a desperate fool.

"I'm thinking about what comes next," I said with a half shrug. "When my leg is ready to go, what will you do?"

She sighed, humming as she thought about her answer. The tingling from that small sound traveled through my chest and down my spine. *How is it possible for her to affect me like this?*

"Well, I'll find another grumpy guy to help take care of, won't I? One that likes to swear and throw things."

She was trying to lighten the mood, but I was being serious. If she wasn't here with me, who would she end up with?

"If I asked you to stay a little longer ..."

Her hand landed on my shoulder, her fingers squeezing gently. "You've got this, Merrick."

"That's not what I meant."

"I know what you meant. It doesn't change the fact that, eventually, you won't need me or your mother to help you get by. You'll see."

Maybe it was because I *wanted* to hear it, but she sounded disappointed. Of course, she misunderstood what I was trying to say.

"Grace–"

The shrill ring of my cell phone resonated throughout the room and, once again, the opportunity to talk to her was snatched away from me.

Her hand fell away from my shoulder and she answered the phone. I was going to break every phone in this house if I needed to, just so I could get a word in before I was too much of a coward to say them.

"Hello? Oh, hi Emma. I'm doing just fine. Yes, he's right here, just one moment."

The touch of her hand on mine forced me to draw in a long breath, bringing with it the sweet, inviting fragrance of Grace. If I could see, would I miss that completely? How many other things would I miss if sight took over?

She placed the phone in my fingers, but instead of pulling away, her touch lingered just a moment longer. Not long enough to satisfy me, but long enough to convince me to keep trying. To keep working at being the kind of man she could want. The kind of man she needed.

For now.

The knowledge of who her ex was, forced its way into my mind, and she took the tensing of my body as discomfort. Jason

Reed would have never deserved Grace and imagining how he must have treated her only made me angrier.

Grace cleared her throat and pulled away. "I'll be in the living room if you need me."

And I was back at square one. Nothing good came from anger anymore. Not here.

"Merrick? Hello?"

Lifting the phone to my ear, I resisted the urge to follow Grace. "Mom. I'm here."

"Hi, son. How are you today?"

"Fine."

Deep breaths.

"Okay, good. Well, your father and I were wondering if you wanted to come here for dinner. Mitch is moving around a bit and we thought it would be a good idea to have everyone here tonight. What do you think?"

I closed my eyes and took another deep breath. "That sounds great."

"Are you sure?"

I rolled my shoulders to release the tension pulsing in my neck and back. "Yeah, Mom. It's been a while since we've all been together."

"It has," she replied, unable to mask the excitement in her voice.

She wanted the family in one room, whole and happy. After the way I'd acted lately, I wasn't going to stop her from getting what she wanted.

"What time?"

"In a couple hours. You're welcome to invite Grace if you want."

And there it was. The gentle, hopeful push. I should take advantage of that suggestion, bring Grace with me and get her to see that I wasn't really an asshole all the time.

"I'll talk to her about it."

"Good. We'll see you around five then?"

"Yeah."

After our goodbyes, I dropped the phone to the bed and laid back down. I was tired. Tired of the work I had to do to get back to normal. Tired of not being myself.

Just tired.

It was pathetic. When had I become such a pussy? I used to be strong and intelligent. Not this whiny bastard that couldn't figure out what the hell he wanted.

The sound of footsteps outside my bedroom made me tense. My pulse raced and I couldn't take deep breaths anymore. I could almost smell that sweet vanilla scent coming off her skin. What would I give to press my nose to her neck and stay there for hours?

Almost anything.

"Do you mind if I leave early tonight, Merrick?"

God, that made everything hurt more. She wanted distance and I wanted ... what the hell *did* I want?

I hadn't been with anyone in a long time. Didn't even know *how* to be with anyone. With Grace, it would be uncomplicated. So easy to just let go of all the dark memories that haunted my mind. It would be so painless to find comfort in her.

"Merrick?"

I sat up and dropped my head forward. My mouth opened to say how much I needed her, but I forced other words instead. "If you need to leave early, that's fine. I'm going to my parents anyway."

"Oh good. I have plans with Keara and Josh. Kind of a small engagement celebration I guess. I just wanted to make sure you had some dinner."

Always worrying about me.

"Like I said before, Grace, you aren't my maid."

She didn't speak and I didn't hear her move. It was a standoff of sorts. Who was going to break that awful, awkward silence first?

"I guess I'll just be here with you tomorrow then," she muttered.

Fuck, I wanted her even more every time she did that. Never 'I'll *see* you tomorrow' or *'See* you next week'. It was always, 'I'll *be* here'.

Who does that? Who is so aware of a person that they change the way they say goodbye? Something so ingrained in their minds, just to make that person more comfortable.

"Goodbye, Merrick."

I nodded.

That's it.

A simple nod of acknowledgement. It was all I could do.

Moments later, the front door closed with a soft click, and Grace was gone.

"Let her go, Merrick. Just let her go."

"How you feeling, sweetie?"

Mom's hands tightened around my arm as she led me to the couch. There was no counting steps here and after bumping into the coffee table, it was obvious I'd hurt myself before finding a seat. As always, Mom came to the rescue.

"I'm good, Mom. Getting stronger every day."

"That's wonderful, son. Grace said you're making good progress. But I want to know how you are *feeling*."

I paused. How the hell was I supposed to answer *that* one? *I'm feeling like a sack of rotten potatoes. I'm feeling desperate for the woman that stays with me almost every day and taunts me with her voice and her touch. I'm feeling like there's no hope for a future with me, and there isn't a God damn thing I can do about it.*

Saying any of that would either make Mom upset or she'd take my life into her own hands and start pushing harder.

I could tell her that wanting Grace was the only thing that kept me from remembering all the shit. That she'd gotten through to me in ways no one else could.

"I feel good, Mom. A little tired, but good."

I settled into the couch cushions and set aside my crutches, waiting for her to push for more. She surprised me by just sighing and patting my shoulder. "Dinner will be ready in a minute."

"Thanks, Mom."

She kissed my cheek and her weight came off the cushion next to me. I closed my eyes and leaned back, resting my head on the back of the couch. This was the same couch that used to be in the living room of our old house. It felt the same and smelled the same, but I couldn't get a grasp on what it actually looked like.

Seconds later, someone else dropped to the couch, making me bounce off the cushion a good inch.

"Looks like you're almost back to normal. How much longer on the crutches?"

Micah.

"No idea. Don't really care. I'm just taking it one day at a time."

"Mmhmm, I bet you are."

I couldn't resist taking the bait. "What the hell is *that* supposed to mean?"

He hesitated. I could almost hear the wheels turning in his mind, picking what to say that would get a rise out of me but wouldn't make me go ballistic. "Made a move on Grace yet?"

It would feel really good to smack him on the back of the head right about now.

"I don't want to hear it, Micah."

"Why not?"

"Because."

"Because why?"

"Stop," I demanded. "We aren't kids anymore, man. I'm not going to argue with you."

Another pause where the only sounds were the voices coming from the kitchen.

"Guess you really *are* taking it one day at a time. It's good to see that you're not so full of rage anymore." His weight shifted back until he was right next to me. He cleared his throat and bumped my shoulder. "Mitch hates the crutches, too, if it makes you feel any better."

"It doesn't."

"You move better on them than he does. Poor guy keeps losing one and he won't let anyone help him either. How did you figure it out on your own with that hard head of yours?"

"Grace helped. She adjusted them so I could move easier."

"Is that right?"

I threw my head back and closed my eyes. He wasn't going to give it up.

"You want her right?" he inquired, almost too calmly.

"Doesn't matter."

"There's nothing wrong with that, Merrick. You can want someone. You can even move forward and *have* someone. Settle down with a family, get a job doing whatever you want. Hell, you could even take up knitting for all we care. But it's possible."

The air wasn't coming in smoothly anymore, my nose burning with the hard breaths I was pulling in and pushing out. If I opened my mouth, I would say something really stupid.

"Have you talked to her?"

"Why is this any of your business?" I snapped. "What makes you think any of that is what I really want?"

Micah's hand landed on my shoulder and stayed there until I could catch my breath. "Because it's what you wanted before, man, and it doesn't make you weak."

No. It doesn't make a man weak to want a future, but it makes him selfish when he had no future to give.

"Micah–"

"I've seen the way you are when she's close by. I see the way your face changes when someone says her name. Like a light turns on inside you and all the dark things you refuse to tell any of us about; they just fade away."

I held my breath, locking in the tautness of my jaw and gathering all the control I could possibly muster, just to stay silent.

"It's okay, Merrick. She sees it, too."

All I could do was sit there next to my little brother, blinking like a fool. "Excuse me?"

Micah sat forward with a huff. "I see her at the hospital on occasion, checking in. I've talked to her a couple times. You know, Grace and I used to be able to talk about a lot of things. When we were younger, I'd run into her all the time. But now, all she seems to focus on is you."

It wasn't the first time I'd heard this. According to my family, Grace Samuelson was very aware of me and maybe even had a crush on me back when we were younger. It actually surprised me. How? When I didn't even pay attention to her, how did she stay interested?

"She said she sees a change in you once in a while. Sees that light in your eyes. The same one that used to be there, back then."

"What else does she say about me?"

I knew he was smiling now, only making it more difficult to avoid smacking him in the head.

"Well, that's the problem. She's just like you these days. Keeps it all inside. But she can't hide it. Not really."

"Boys. Dinner's ready," Mom called.

We both stood and I maneuvered the crutches under my arms, bumping the coffee table in the process. Micah dropped his hand on my shoulder again, but instead of moving, we stood there in silence. Until I finally got the courage to say it.

"What was wrong with me back then, Micah? How did I not see her?"

He gave me a mirthless laugh. "You only saw what you wanted to see; what was right in front of you. We all did it, so don't feel bad." He slapped my shoulder and declared, "Maybe now's your chance to see the world differently."

I let out a harsh breath. "I *can't* see."

"No shit. You can't, but that doesn't mean you can't *try*."

Mom called for us again, this time a little impatiently. Micah's words didn't really hit me until later on, but when they did, I realized my brother was one of the smartest men I'd ever known.

We made our way to the dining room and my family waited while I got into my chair. Sam, Mary's husband, greeted me with a brief hug. I couldn't remember exactly what he looked like, but I'd always considered him a brother. He took care of my sister, that's what mattered.

Mitch patted me on the shoulder and cursed the inventor of crutches. We spoke quietly for a few minutes while Mom and Mary brought the food to the table.

"You look good, bro," Mitch said. "Sorry I bitched at you so much when you complained. I didn't realize how painful everything must have been. Not until now."

Mitch had been a trooper through this whole ordeal. Since the accident, he seemed calmer, a little more patient with everyone. The times I was able to visit with him, we'd actually grown a little closer. Another connection through suffering.

"It's good to be together," Dad said from the head of the table. "I don't know how long it's been, but it's nice to see all of your faces here tonight."

Mom sniffed and Dad whispered something to her that none of us could hear, not even me. It *was* good to be together, even if some of us were a little broken.

"Where're you two going?"

Dad had just informed all of us that he and Mom were leaving town the next day. I was the only one that seemed to care.

"Oh, just a short trip for a couple days," Dad replied. "Thought we would go see the Grand Canyon or something like that."

Or something like that?

Strange. Mom and Dad never went on a vacation during the week and they certainly never went without having a solid plan. It was very suspicious, but then again, it was none of my business what they did with their free time. I shrugged and dug into my food. They could go wherever they wanted. Mom needed a break anyway.

"You have an appointment when we get back. It's early on Friday with Dr. Samuelson," Mom reminded me.

I'd completely forgotten about the appointment. I hated going to the doctor, especially when it had to do with my eyes. That would explain why I hadn't been to him since I first got back.

"Is that necessary?" I asked.

"Yes, it is. You need regular exams, Merrick. You've skipped too many and I won't let you miss this one."

I'd somehow avoided seeing the eye doctor for the last several months. Grace's father wasn't happy about it, but he tried to be understanding. There were a lot of other things to worry about instead. Now, more than ever, I didn't want him checking my eyes.

"I'm blind, Mom. Regular exams won't change that."

Mom started to argue, but Dad stopped her. The two of them started talking quietly back and forth while the rest of us pretended not to listen.

Mary spoke up, her voice insistent. "Merrick, just go to the damn appointment. It's an hour tops out of your day."

Sam started to calm her. "Give him a break, babe."

"He doesn't need any more breaks. It's time to step up."

My older sister was getting more intolerant these days, but even though Mitch and Micah started arguing in my defense, she was right. It took absolutely nothing for me to go to an appointment. I knew what to expect and it wouldn't change anything.

And Grace's father was counting on me to be compliant. It was the least I could do.

"I'll go," I said loudly, silencing their rising voices. "I'll go, Mom. Jeff has gone out of his way to take care of me. I don't want to let him down."

Silence.

Mitch attempted to cover up his chuckle, but since he was sitting next to me, I heard it clear as day. My elbow found his side, only making him laugh harder.

"It's early in the morning. Before Grace comes over," Mom said. "He opened an earlier appointment just for us."

"That's fine."

"Will you be alright while we're gone?"

"Yes, Mom. Grace will be there."

I didn't realize what I'd said until the table was silent once more and I felt heat rise in my cheeks. Could I be any more transparent? The easy acceptance of needing someone to help me was certainly a surprise for my family, but it was more of a surprise for *me*.

The smile in Mitch's voice was unmistakable. "Grace will take good care of him, Mom. Don't you worry."

I swung my arm to the side and felt the impact of my hand against Mitch's side.

"Oomf! Hey, what the fuck was that for?"

"Language," Dad shouted.

This time, it was me that attempted to cover up the chuckle. Micah didn't even try. His booming laughter made it impossible to hold in my own.

"I swear you boys never change," Mary chimed in with her own laugh.

"I was just pointing out the obvious," Mitch added. "He's obviously in lo– *OW*! God damn it!"

"Mitchell, I won't tell you again," Dad said, a little less authoritative. He, too, was holding in the laughter.

"You all see it, don't you?" Mitch continued. "He's changed since Grace came into the picture."

"Shut it, Mitch. Leave the man alone," Micah ordered to my surprise.

For several minutes, only the sound of silverware scraping plates could be heard. I'd never wanted to run away more than I did right then. Mom's curiosity was almost palpable. I didn't need to see her to know she was probably shaking with it.

"She's a wonderful girl, Merrick."

"Yeah, she is."

"Have you thought about–"

"No."

"Why not?"

Not only was it the very worst time to bring up whether or not I ever thought about dating again, but it just couldn't happen.

"It's just not possible, Mom."

"I don't understand," she said. "You have as much right as anyone else to–"

"I said no. Just ... please. I don't want to talk about this."

"Okay, son," she mumbled.

I dropped my fork onto my plate and started to stand. The crutches crashed to the floor when I moved my chair and I struggled to find them. By the time they were positioned under my arms, I was ready to explode.

"I'm tired. Can someone please drive me home?"

I slowly moved out of the dining room, bumping into a wall on my way. It was a miracle I didn't do more damage. I couldn't focus on anything but getting the hell out of there just to avoid the conversation I knew was coming eventually.

Five minutes later, I was seated in the passenger seat of my father's truck, feeling that cold shiver run up and down my spine with every bump in the road.

I hated being on the road, period. It was so much worse knowing it was dark outside and not being able to see a damn thing. I gripped the handle on the door and timed my breaths, keeping them even and long. Another thing Grace taught me.

"Your mother just wants you to be happy, son."

I laid my head back on the seat and sighed, relaxing my hand slightly so the audible cracking of the door liner would stop. "I know, Dad. She just doesn't understand."

"What is there to understand?"

"I can't make Grace happy."

"Who the hell told you that was up to *you*?"

Focusing on the conversation was helping me avoid the thoughts about what was out on the road. I kept telling myself that I was in Morgan, Utah. There weren't bombs waiting for us at every corner. No dead animals lying on the road with explosives hidden inside.

"Who says she even wants me that way? She's my nurse. She's just doing her job," I stated.

"That's not the point, son."

"Then what is?"

"The fact that you've given up before you've even started," he barked, making me flinch in my seat. "It doesn't have to be Grace, although I'll tell you right now you won't ever do better than Grace Samuelson. It's that you keep thinking you're broken enough to be a burden when the truth is, you're still you. Just a little cracked."

"She deserves better, Dad. I've got issues that haven't even begun to die down. I can't even sleep at night without knocking something over. I'm angry. I'm tired. I don't have very much to give."

Dad sighed as he made a sharp turn. The truck bounced a little more than normal and I sat up straighter, every muscle in my body tightening. Waiting for the force of an explosion.

It never came.

The truck just rolled to a stop and Dad shut it down. "Grace was never the kind of girl to worry about something so superficial, Merrick," he explained. "She saw deeper than anyone else."

I turned my head and frowned. "What do you mean?"

"When you two were younger, that girl used to wait for you. To see you any chance she got," he chuckled. "She *saw* you, Merrick. Not the kid that was popular and played sports or had everyone in the palm of his hands. She saw the boy that felt and cared about more than himself. She saw the boy that eventually ended up joining the military because he wanted to protect his country."

She saw me. And what was I doing?

"She saw you all the time and you never saw her," he added, twisting the knife a little deeper.

"You're right."

"I'm always right, my boy, but I used to be like you kids. When I met your mother, I was terrified. What could I give a woman like that? I was just a kid with dreams that seemed further and further from my grasp. I was still in school and didn't have a plan. But it wasn't my decision."

I waited. He'd never told me any of this before. Mom and Dad always seemed to have their shit together better than anyone else. We all thought they just saw each other and that was it.

"She chose me, by some miracle, knowing I was just ... me. After we got married, I was just a banker. Still am. I give other people money, doesn't mean I have any of my own. But she stayed with me because that's what love is." He took a deep breath and blew it out in a rush. When he spoke again, he was smiling. "When she looked at me, she didn't see perfection or some big fancy love story. She saw someone who would protect her and fight for her. Someone who would love her in spite of any flaws she *thought* she had. It didn't matter what was in front of her, because I was standing behind her. That's how she knew I was the one."

"Dad ..."

"And you know what? None of that relies on a pair of eyes that don't work anymore. So, yes, Merrick. I'm right. You didn't see her before, but maybe now you finally do."

My heart raced and my hands started to sweat. The sharp knife in my chest started to retreat.

"The question is," he continued wearily. "What are you going to do about it? Sit back and watch life pass you by? Or are you going to take life by the balls like you always did?"

It wasn't in me to laugh at my father's words, no matter how out of place they were, but I still argued. "I've changed."

"No, you haven't. You're stronger because you had to be. Smarter because of the mistakes you made in the past. The sadness you've known, that only helps a man become happier because he learns to appreciate what he has. You haven't changed, you're just wiser because you've learned life."

His door groaned as he pushed it open with two last words said to me.

"Use it."

Chapter Eleven

Grace

Watching Keara and Josh together was like watching the middle of every romance movie ever made. The happy times, the love, the kissing, the touching ... it was *always* that way. Never before had it made me feel anything but happiness for them.

Tonight, I was jealous. I was lonely. I just wanted to close my eyes and pretend that Keara and Josh were me and ... anyone.

"Grace, did you hear me?"

I lifted my eyes and saw them both staring at me with searching eyes.

"Huh? I'm sorry, I wasn't really listening."

Keara reached across the small table and took my hand, her beautiful diamond glistening in the dim light of the restaurant. The two of them had invited me out for dinner and I'd accepted immediately. Anything to get some distance from Merrick. I wasn't really in the mood for celebrating, but I couldn't take the thunder from Keara. She'd waited for this for so long and I was truly happy for her.

"Are you okay, sweetie? You've been gloomy all night."

I shook my head and looked down at my plate of food. My steak was barely touched and my potatoes looked like there was an explosion. "I'm just tired."

Keara's gaze was on me, scrutinizing every movement I made. I didn't dare look up from the massacre on my plate.

"Josh, baby, will you do me a favor?" she suddenly asked.

"What do you need?" he asked.

"Call Christie for me, please. Tell her we need her and Jen tonight."

I barely opened my mouth to stop him when Keara stopped me. "Don't even think about it."

Josh's smile was wicked as he rubbed his hands together like a villain does right before he catches the good guy. Not that Josh was villainous, but he looked like he was enjoying my helplessness.

"Does that mean you might come home drunk?" he inquired, bouncing his brow at my best friend.

Keara rolled her eyes, but she couldn't stop the pink from rising in her cheeks. "Maybe."

Josh puffed out his chest and stood from the table, already dialing the number.

"Keara, I don't need an intervention, plus, tonight is *your* night."

She looked offended. "You know me better than that, Grace. If I was staging an intervention, you wouldn't know it was coming. This is a girl's night. You need it."

I kept my mouth shut because, like always, she was absolutely right. I needed to spend some time with the girls. I needed to get my mind off of Merrick and how intense my feelings for him had become. I could barely stand to be close to him anymore without feeling like I was going to burst.

I needed distance. I needed to get my head on straight before I did something stupid like tell him how much I wanted him. How the loneliness went away when I was with him.

"They're on their way to the house," Josh stated when he returned to the table. "I just got called in, so I'm heading to the station."

Keara's smile dropped for only a moment before she pulled it right back. She wanted to stay proud of Josh for what he did for work, but it still scared her. She didn't like being alone either.

We paid for dinner and climbed into Josh's truck. The drive to the station only took a few minutes and Josh leaned over to kiss Keara before waving goodbye.

"You two make me sick, you know that?"

Keara burst out laughing as she slid into the driver's seat. "Yeah, well, you'll have to suffer through it."

We drove for a minute before she drew in a long breath. "Do you mind if I stay with you tonight?"

"Of course I don't mind, Keara. Is everything okay?"

"Yeah, I just hate sleeping in that house without him. I don't like being alone."

"That makes two of us."

"At least you got your parents there with you. And Merrick. He's close enough that you could shout and he'd be right there."

Would he come? Would he at least try?

Yes, I think he would.

Keara pointed to the couch the second we walked into her house. "Sit. Stay."

I rolled my eyes and fell into the cushions, making myself comfortable while she wandered around the kitchen.

Voices outside signaled that Christie and Jen had arrived and before I could move, the front door flew open to reveal the two of them with beaming smiles on both of their faces.

"I believe we have been summoned," Jen smirked, gliding into the house and heading straight for the kitchen.

Christie shut the door and waddled over to the couch, almost falling on her butt as she sat down. "I so need this right now," she sighed.

"A couch?"

"No, a girl's night. Gary is driving me crazy."

"He is?"

She turned her head and lifted an eyebrow, her expression telling me I was in for a treat.

"Did you know that they have a book just for men on what to expect when your wife is pregnant?"

I shook my head.

"Well, they do. Who was the moron that wrote *that* book? They should call it *'How to Piss Your Wife Off When She's Pregnant and Hormonal'.* I swear to God, every word in that thing causes Gary to freak out."

I pulled my bottom lip between my teeth in an attempt to keep the laughter inside.

Christie adjusted her massive belly and got more comfortable. Then she let out a harsh breath. "He said he was having jaw pain, so we went to the dentist – a male dentist no less – and that idiot told Gary he has TMJ because of stress. And do you know what that dumbass dentist said next?"

I shook my head again and bit down harder on my lip.

"He said it's sympathy pain. *Sympathy* pain! Can you believe it? Gary is having sympathy pain with my pregnancy, so guess what he does? He goes and buys this big ass book for dads and reads the whole thing in two days."

"Oh God, is she talking about the book again?"

I turned to see Jen walking out of the kitchen with two glasses of wine in her hands. Two very *full* glasses of wine. She handed one to me and winked. "I told Mike if he even *thought* about reading that book, I'd leave him faster than a hooker leaves a hotel room."

"Yeah well, I can't leave Gary because I've only got a month left and I can barely wipe my own ass," Christie exclaimed.

Keara's howl of laughter came from the kitchen and I couldn't hold back the giggles. I held tight to my glass of wine, the liquid bouncing as I laughed.

"It's true!" Christie shouted.

We calmed and Jen sat on my other side, sprawled out. The three of us rested our heads on the back of the couch and gazed up at the ceiling. None of us moved until the smell of something delicious hit my nose, making my head pop up.

"Sushi," Jen informed me before taking a considerable gulp of her wine. "It's one of those nights."

"Oh, don't even get me started on the sushi," Christie fumed. "Gary tried to tell me I wasn't supposed to eat it. I can eat *some* of it, but nooooo!" She leered at my glass of wine and licked her lips. "I can handle giving up a few things. Not that. I love the man, but if he tries to stop me from eating sushi again, I'll punch him in the wiener schnitzel."

Jen was taking another gulp of wine as Christie ranted, but it didn't stay in her mouth very long. Wine sprayed all over the coffee table and the hilarity of the moment was so flawless, we all would have fallen over if it wasn't for the couch.

Keara's laughter only made it worse. She snorted, making the rest of us snort until laughter was no longer possible. It just turned into a struggle to breathe.

A few minutes later, Keara was cleaning up the coffee table, her lingering laughter making us all smile.

"I'll get more wine," she sang and pointed at Jen. "You get the sushi out here."

The next two hours were spent with lots of wine, even more sushi, newlywed-sex talk, a sappy movie that made the four of us tear up, and a reminder that even when I was alone, I wasn't.

These were the kind of friends a girl needed in her life. Desperately. The kind of friends that would punch a bitch in the face for saying a few mean words about the other. Finding them wouldn't have been possible any other way.

I spent a while staring at Christie's ever-growing belly, feeling the kicks and twists while Christie struggled to hold her bladder. I remembered that feeling. Like someone was sitting on my bladder. Well, I guess someone really was.

Jen kept pouring more wine and I could barely move by the time the movie was finished. Keara only had a glass or two and stopped before the movie even started so she could drive us back to my parents.

The night was still young, but Jen needed to get home to Mike, and Christie – who looked ready to pass out – was her ride home.

We said our goodbyes, promising to get together again soon. I cleaned up while Keara packed an overnight bag and by the time we got to my house, we were both struggling to keep our eyes open.

I discretely glanced over at Merrick's house and saw all the lights off. Not that he would have turned them on, but there was no way he would be back already. Not when Emma had all her kids there.

"Is Merrick home?" Keara sang, bumping me with her elbow.

I shook my head. "He's with his family tonight. I bet he'll stay the night there, actually. He especially hates being on the road at night."

Keara and I sprawled out on my bed and sighed.

I glanced at the clock and *9:30 PM* blinked back at me in bright, neon green digits.

"Wow, we're lame," I snorted.

"We're adults now. Nine thirty is like midnight on the worst day of my life," Keara mumbled into the pillow.

"You don't have bad days, do you?" I asked, attempting to run my fingers through the knots in my hair.

"Everyone has bad days, Grace. It's part of being human. Hell, it's part of being *alive*."

The lightness I had been feeling all night started to weigh down. Heavier and heavier until my chest couldn't rise and my shoulders ached from the burdens they carried.

"And if there are more bad days than good? What then?"

Keara turned on her side and gazed at me with her all knowing grey eyes. Her expression gave nothing away and a few seconds passed before I finally looked away.

"The bad prepares us for the good. Even when it doesn't feel like it ever goes away. We just have to keep pushing through it."

"How?"

"I don't know, sweetie. I just know that God will never give us more than we can handle. So whatever hardships stand in front of us, we just have to remember that we can make it through. One step at a time."

The tears fell before I could even blink, but Keara was there, wiping them away as I took a ragged breath. The enormity of what I went through ... it was too much. Maybe God hadn't read me right when he was dishing out the shit. Maybe he accidently gave me too much and didn't realize I'd try to fake my way through it until it killed me.

"Why?" I growled as the breaths stirred the anger inside of me. "Why her? Why take *her* away from me?"

Keara's eyes widened as they welled with tears. "I don't know, Grace," she whispered.

The twisting pain in my chest finally released, and with it, came the waves of desperation I'd felt in that hospital room and for many days after. It took my breath away. Over and over, it fractured through me, tearing apart all the pieces I thought I had put back together.

"Get it out, Grace. Let me carry some of it."

I sobbed into my pillow. Loud, ugly sobs that would crack my ribs if they were any more violent. It all came back, like a flood filling the empty roads in my mind, bringing with it all the things no one wanted to see.

"I wanted her, Keara. I wanted her more than anything."

"I know, Grace. I know you did."

Her fingers softly drifted through my hair and she waited. She waited for me to tear my broken heart out of my chest and show her all the cracks and missing pieces, the ones I couldn't hold together any longer. The ones that had died when I lost my baby.

"The pain ... it was like having my insides ripped out. I hadn't felt her move all day and all of a sudden it felt like a knife in my back." The pain was unbearable. I remembered it vividly; it was terrifying. "Jason didn't answer the phone so I drove to the hospital by myself."

Her fingers constricted, pressing into my scalp as anger swept through her. I knew she was angry, because *I* was angry.

"Every contraction was a struggle, like my insides didn't fit inside of me anymore and everything was trying to force its way out. I could hardly breathe and I couldn't control the car. I almost crashed a few times because they were getting so bad, so I drove slow. So fucking slow! I was scared of what it meant, so scared that I considered turning around and going back home," I admitted. "But I didn't know what was happening. I just thought she was coming early and the only thing I wanted to think about was that I was finally going to see her. To hold her."

I looked up to see Keara crying right along with me. If she'd been there, if I hadn't been such an awful friend, she would have driven me to the hospital. She would have helped me breathe through the pain. She would have gotten me there sooner and maybe – just maybe – things would have been different. She would have held my hand when the doctor told me to push and she would have cried with me when ...

"I held her in my arms, Keara. She was already gone, but I held her tiny body against my chest and she was beautiful. Warm and soft. And she was gone. My daughter, my baby girl. She was gone and all I could do was cry."

Keara's arms came around me and I buried my face in her shoulder, sucking in deep breaths before letting them out with more tears.

"I just cried for her. I didn't know what else to do. I was alone in a cold room surrounded by strangers. They didn't say a word to me. They just watched me lose her."

"Grace ..."

"Do you know what it's like to actually lose a piece of yourself?" I pulled away, my cheeks wet with the hot tears that I'd held back for so long. They said it was time to let her go. They yanked her out of my arms and that was it."

I lost it then. The racking sobs came all at once and the year of agony and loneliness seeped out of every pore in my skin. The heavy darkness I'd left behind had followed me every step of the way, waiting for this moment. Waiting to surround me again.

I don't remember what happened next. Just that I was tired and the ache from remembering that day was as strong as ever. But I had someone with me this time. Keara held onto me until I fell asleep and she stayed by my side until I woke in the morning.

I didn't dream. I didn't wake once throughout the night. My mind didn't let me come back to reality until I was ready.

And when I woke the next morning to see the sun shining through my open window, I felt different. I'd let some of it go and even though I still longed for my baby, the burden was a little lighter.

Chapter Twelve

Merrick

Grace lost her child.

I just couldn't wrap my mind around it.

I should have been worried about eavesdropping on such a private conversation. It was obvious Grace had never truly shared what she went through. Keara was her best friend. How did she never know the storm brewing in Grace's mind this whole time?

And for me to invade the moment she finally gave up a little of her burden; I really *was* an asshole.

I spent most of that night trying not to think about how it must have felt for her to lose her daughter. I didn't sleep. The need to be there for her, to comfort her, was just too strong.

Now it all made sense.

The suffering I could feel in Grace, the loneliness she tried to hide with everyone else. Maybe she'd let her guard down because I was just the blind man she was taking care of, but I knew it was another connection. Something meant for me. If anyone could understand that kind of pain ...

"Merrick? I'm here."

Grace's footsteps moved swiftly down the hallway and into the kitchen. I stayed seated at the table, keeping a neutral expression. Pity was the last thing she needed to see.

"Good morning. Sorry I'm late. Keara stayed the night since Josh got called in and I think I had a little too much wine."

Her voice was light, an obvious smile in her words. Was she faking it like she did so well, or did she truly feel better?

"Good morning," I mumbled, clearing my throat when the roughness surprised even me. "Don't worry about it."

"You look pretty beat. What time did you get home last night from your parent's?"

She moved into the chair across from me, and that sweet smell she owned, hit my nose. I drew in a long breath and savored it.

Don't be creepy.

Rubbing my sweating hands on my thighs, I cleared my throat again. What was the question? The time I got home. *Shit.* What time was it when she was talking to Keara?

"Umm, not sure. Late. I hit the sack almost immediately."

"How did it go?"

Dad's words slid through my mind. *Use it.* The things my father said to me were like a light switch, turning on something inside me. Fear was never allowed to guide my decisions. Not until recently. It was time to grab life by the balls again.

"It was really good," I smiled.

"Well, I hope you're ready for today. I found some new exercises I want you to try out. I think they'll help with that stiffness you've had in your thigh."

Stiffness. God, I'd played that off for the last week and thought she decided to give up on it. The stiffness wasn't in my thigh, but it was the only explanation I had to physically hide how much she affected me.

I just nodded my head and curled my lips into a grin. "Sounds great."

She didn't say anything for a full minute, then I heard her sigh and stand. "Have you eaten yet?"

"No, I wasn't really hungry."

"Well, I'm starving. I'm making pancakes and eggs. Oh, and bacon."

My stomach rumbled loudly, making her snicker.

"I bet you're hungry now, huh?"

I listened to her move around the kitchen, guessing exactly where she was every time she moved. It was a game we'd started playing a couple weeks before. Something to help me pass the time and keep me aware of everything around me.

I didn't realize it at the time, but the game helped ground me more than being able to walk. That feeling of helplessness lessened each day. My ability to stay alert to what was happening around me helped with the shakiness I'd experienced early on. I didn't feel like I was locked up in the dark anymore.

Grace moved again, her steps light. She was humming today.

"You seem cheery," I pointed out. "Stove."

"Right," she confirmed and moved a pan onto another burner. Those sounds were becoming more and more familiar to me. "I slept well for the first time in a long time. I feel a lot lighter today. Fresher."

"Good. Any particular reason?"

She moved again. "Not really."

"Sink."

The water turned on and I gave myself a mental pat on the back. That one was difficult since it was so close to the stove.

"Right. You're getting really good at this."

"I've learned to listen." *In more ways than one.*

Minutes passed and she shut the water off and moved again. "Counter."

"Which side?"

My mind flew through the categories of sound I had stored away. Distance, volume, whether or not it sounded like she was behind the counter by the fridge or in front of it, closer to the stove. "Fridge?"

"Ding, ding, ding! We have a winner."

I smiled and shook my head. "You're on one today. You *must* be feeling good."

"Why do you care so much about how I'm feeling?" she asked.

I shrugged my shoulders and tapped my fingers on the table, a nervous tick I'd somehow developed when I was around her. "No reason."

"Well, since you look exhausted, I'll let it go for now."

She moved across the kitchen and the sound of glass clinking together reached my ears. "Island."

"Right. So, tell me why you look like you didn't sleep a wink last night. Did you have a nightmare?"

Grace tried to get me to talk about my dreams; the ones that woke me so violently. She heard them. Hell, she nearly experienced them with how close we actually were to each other when we slept.

"Actually, I didn't sleep much at all."

"I thought you hit the sack when you got home."

"I did."

"Then why didn't you sleep?"

"I just didn't," I replied a little too harshly. My neck strained when I dropped my head forward. The guilt must have been plastered all over my face at this point, but she didn't acknowledge it.

She moved, her footsteps getting a little closer. "Where am I now, Merrick?"

My ears perked, sensitive to every movement of her clothes and the sound of her breathing. "Past the island."

"Mmhmm, and now?"

I swallowed, my fingers tapping a little faster on the smooth surface of the table. "Closer."

Her sweet vanilla scent lingered beneath the smell of the bacon and the pancakes she must have been carrying.

"And now?"

She was right beside me. Her warmth spread across my shoulder and neck, and my fingers suddenly froze. Without thinking, I lifted my arm and found hers, wrapping my fingers around her slender wrist. She set the plates down on the table and stayed there, not pulling away like I expected her to. Letting me touch her. Her breaths quickened as mine did, and it took all I had not to yank her against me.

Knowing my luck, we'd smack foreheads and that would end the moment completely.

"I didn't sleep, because I was thinking about you."

"About me?" she quaked.

"I was thinking about ..."

I stopped, trailing off and finally coming to my senses. Who cared *why* she was feeling happy today? She was having a good day.

I wasn't going to darken that by bringing up what I heard through that window.

"I was thinking about maybe going out today. Getting out of the house."

"You were?"

"Yeah, I want to go somewhere with you. Anywhere."

My fingers were still wrapped around her wrist and the pregnant pause made me release her.

"Okay. Let's do it."

I couldn't stop the dirty thoughts that came to my mind. A grin pulled my lips up, and I quirked an eyebrow.

"I mean– shit. Why does that always happen?" she grumbled.

I threw my head back and laughed. That deep laugh that works the stomach and rises up through the chest. The kind that makes all your worries disappear.

Grace couldn't hide anything from me these days. I knew, without a doubt, she wore her emotions on her sleeve. Her face must tell people everything.

Then how? How did no one know what she went through?

The nightmares Grace was always so worried about were nothing compared to the anguish she was feeling.

How did *I* not know?

Because Grace handled life with ... well, grace. She was strength and hope all in one, and even with the weight of loss so freshly on her shoulders, she found the ability to bring light to a man that could have cared less in the beginning.

A man that would blindly give her anything now.

"Where should we go?" she asked as we dug into our breakfast.

"Where do *you* like to go?"

"Well, anywhere I can think of is too far."

"Why?"

"You don't like being in the car, so I don't want to make you–"

I raised my hand in front of me and shook my head. "No. Anywhere. I can handle it today."

I took another bite of food, closing my eyes and chewing slowly. She really was an amazing cook. Pancakes weren't supposed to taste that good.

"Let's go to lunch then. There's an awesome sushi restaurant in Ogden. We can get it to go, then drive up the canyon. I know a place we can just sit and relax. Since it's getting kind of chilly outside, we'll need our jackets."

I'd never had sushi before, and the thought made my stomach turn. Raw fish just wasn't for me.

Didn't stop me.

Not today.

"Sounds like a plan."

I was scared. Terrified, in fact.

What was in the takeout box in front of me ... well, if I could see it, I know it would look suspicious.

"I don't think you could look anymore disgusted," Grace said with a laugh.

"I'm not sure that I was prepared for this. I normally don't eat raw fish."

"Well, what you've got there isn't raw. In fact, it's deep fried. You'll love it, I promise."

"If you say so."

I didn't want to make her think I was doing this just for her, even though I was. Never thought I'd be eating fish rolled in rice and seaweed, on a picnic bench, at a rest stop in the middle of a canyon. The sound of rushing water from the Weber River made the whole thing kind of ... peaceful.

I slowly rolled my fingers over the contents and discovered that the pieces were big enough to just pop one in my mouth.

Quick and easy, Merrick. Don't be a sissy.

Grace was watching me. I knew it because of the laugh she was clearly covering with her hand. I heard the tiny snort when I leaned down and sniffed the food.

"You think it's funny, Grace, but you didn't experience what I did overseas. Some of the food ... well, it was questionable," I informed her.

"I promise, what you're about to eat will not only awaken your taste buds, but you'll be begging me to get sushi every night from here on out. That, or you'll absolutely hate it. There's really no in between."

I drew in a long breath, letting it out slowly as I lifted the small piece of foreign food to my lips. "If I hate it, don't take it too personally."

She laughed again, only this time, she didn't hold it back. *God, you're beautiful.*

If her laughter sounded that breathtaking, I could only imagine. Did she toss her head back, raising her face to the sky, when she laughed? Did her eyes sparkle?

I shook my head and tossed the piece of sushi into my mouth, chewing slowly at first and waiting for the urge to spit it out.

"Holy shit!" I gasped, almost choking on the succulent rice as I did. "This is delicious."

The flavors bounced around, each one better than the last, and the subtle taste of the seaweed brought it all together. I reached for another piece while I continued to chew.

"Don't go too fast or it'll be gone before you even get a chance to enjoy it," Grace said, an apparent smile in her voice. "Believe me, I know."

"You like it that much?"

"Mmhmm," she replied, chewing her food and letting out a small moan that sent the blood in my head rushing downward. "Mmm, that was a good one, and yes, I love it. At first, it was just a special treat now and then, but over the years, it was the only thing I could really enjoy. Keara and I used to go crazy for it and Mom has a knack for ordering surprises *off* the menu."

"I get the hype now. It really is pretty good. Why haven't I ever tried it before?" I asked myself.

"Well, it's not really something you decide to just try one day. Everyone I know started eating it because someone told them how good it is and convinced them to go for it."

"I can understand that," I nodded.

We ate in silence after that, the cool air settling over us. Autumn was close. I fought back the disappointment I felt at not being able to see all the colors I'd taken for granted all these years.

I finished my food before her. Grace was right. I ate mine too fast and wanted more. She laughed and smacked my hand when I reached over to try and take some of hers. I couldn't be as stealthy without seeing where it was, but I still tried.

When we were finished, she gathered the containers and tossed them in a nearby garbage can. When she settled beside me on the picnic bench, I sat a little straighter and took slow breaths. Even with the undertone of near-autumn leaves, I could still smell that sugary scent. Like she spent her days baking cookies instead of helping a blind man get by.

She pressed a little closer, her thigh brushing mine. Then she shivered against my arm and let out a harsh breath.

"You cold?"

"A little. Guess I should have thought about that before we came here," she chuckled.

I felt the cool air against my cheeks, but the nearness of her didn't let me feel it anywhere else. I couldn't be near her and *not* feel like I was on fire.

Poor choice of words.

I did the only thing I could think of; I raised my arm and wrapped it around her shoulders, gently pulling her closer. God help me, but it felt right holding her like that. As if I was actually human again.

Grace didn't argue. In fact, she squeezed in even closer until she was nestled against my chest, shivering and sighing.

"You're really warm."

Tell me about it.

We sat at that picnic table for a few minutes longer, just listening to the river and breathing in the fresh air. I hadn't left the house much in the last few months. Hell, I'd only left the house to satisfy my mother under the threat of starvation or for doctor's appointments. I never went out just to go out. Never felt the need for fresh air until recently.

Until Grace.

She changed things for me.

Funny how one decision, one tiny thing, can set you on a completely different path.

I closed my eyes. The right one was aching more than usual, maybe from being outside, or maybe it was just the fact that I didn't sleep the night before.

"You ready to go?" Grace asked softly, resting her head against my shoulder.

"Not yet," I replied, my voice rough.

"You okay?"

I nodded and opened my eyes, feeling the pressure change with every blink. It was a good thing I had an appointment in a couple days. I was going to have to tell Jeff about this new development.

"Do you ever wonder how one decision can change everything?" I asked.

Grace sat up a little straighter and I felt her eyes on my face. "Umm, yeah. I guess so."

"I wonder how many things would change if I'd just made one different choice."

She was silent for a minute before she whispered, "I wish I would have done things differently."

"That makes two of us."

"The problem is that if things were different, the chances we would be here now ... well, we probably wouldn't be."

I drew in a long breath. That was the problem. Without all the decisions each of us had already made, nothing would be the same. The good things never come without the bad.

"You may not have joined the military and met those men that you love so much," she added.

I nodded, knowing she was right. "But I wouldn't be blind. I'd be able to see you."

"Would you?"

I turned my head and frowned as she pulled away a few inches, taking her warmth with her. "What does that mean?"

"I'm just wondering if we would even know each other at all."

We both pondered on that for a moment. She nudged me in the ribs with her elbow and laughed softly. "You might not have even lived in that house. Maybe you'd be living far away. Who knows? You wouldn't be a hero. Ryan might have died if it wasn't for you. I wouldn't have a job that I loved going to every day."

Of all the things she'd just said, that last one made my ears perk the most. "Do you mean it?"

"What? That I love my job? Of course I do. You may be grumpy most of the time, and sometimes I want to smother you with your own pillow, but you also make me laugh." Her warmth came closer to me and her cold hands cupped my face. "This is unprofessional, but you're my friend, Merrick. Life would be dull without you."

I started to smile, then she kissed my cheek. Her lips were cold and warm at the same time. The tingle they left on my skin made the exhaustion from lack of sleep simmer away.

"You're really warm, Merrick. Are you feeling okay?"

"I'm fine. Just fine," I sighed, a fuzziness starting to fill my head.

"We should go. Get out of this cold air."

I didn't want to leave. I wanted to stay at that picnic table with Grace Samuelson staying warm because of me. With Grace in *my* arms and sharing deep, life-changing thoughts with *me*.

Then my eye started to ache a little more and my head started to feel a little heavier. Grace guided me back to the car and I slumped in the passenger seat while we waited for the heat to push through the air vents.

"We shouldn't have stayed so long. I don't want you to get sick," she said breathlessly. For some reason, she'd had to help me a little more than usual, even with both crutches.

"I'm a grown man, Grace. Getting sick is something I can handle."

She sighed and I imagined she was shaking her head at me. Minutes later, we were on the road and the usual paranoia I experienced in a car was absent. I couldn't concentrate on anything, not even my breathing. My head just couldn't hold itself up, all my thoughts jumbled.

"Merrick! Merrick, we're back. I need you to help me, okay?"

It only could have been a few minutes. It had to be. But we'd already made the twenty-minute drive back to the house.

I couldn't remember a moment of it.

Grace sounded so far away or like she was under water. I opened my eyes, expecting to see her lovely face in front of mine. She wasn't there, not even a glimpse of her. The ache in my head, however, was different. It almost felt like a bright light was shining in my eye, making me flinch and squeeze them shut.

Strange. That hadn't happened to me before.

A tiny arm slipped behind me and pressed against my back. My legs felt like heavy bags of sand, barely pushing them out the door of the car.

"Merrick, stay with me for just a little longer. Let's get you inside first."

What is she talking about? And why is it so hard to keep my head up?

"One step at a time," she grunted.

My feet moved, but only a few inches. It took forever before I finally dropped onto my bed with Grace falling on top of me. The crutches clattered to the floor, making me flinch.

"God, you're a big guy."

"Just stay right here," I all but begged. My voice felt scratchy and I barely heard the words myself.

"I need to get you something for this fever, Mer. You're burning up and I don't know what's wrong."

"I'm fine, Grace." I pulled myself up to sitting and reached out to find her arm. I wrapped my fingers around her fragile wrist and tugged gently. "Just tired. I'm so tired and I just want you to stay here with me."

"Merrick ..."

The urge to beg more was so strong, but I finally caught up to the way I was behaving and shook my head to clear the cobwebs. "Okay. It's okay. You go ahead."

Her hands landed on my face, moving around as she felt the heat of my skin. "Damn it! This came on so fast. You're scaring me, Merrick."

"Don't be scared, Grace. I'm here. I'm okay."

"You're not okay. I can barely understand you. Your words are slurring and your voice sounds like sandpaper."

Her hands dropped to my neck before leaving me completely. I felt that loss. It was the same empty feeling I had the day I came home from Iraq and my men didn't.

Their faces flashed in front of my eyes, or the eyes I *used* to have.

It came on so sudden, there was no way to stop it. I saw them laughing and joking around. Ryan was laughing like a hyena, the way he always did, and it only made the rest of them laugh harder. He was always the jokester of the bunch. Pulling pranks on anyone and everyone he could get to.

His brown eyes reminded me of a dog's eyes. He hated when I told him that, but it was true. Big, round, and curious. He looked too young to be a part of that world, but he was there all the same. His obsidian-black hair shined in the sunlight. He always overdid it on the hair gel.

"Gotta always be picture worthy for my girl. She wants to see me looking as sexy as I will when I get back."

Eric Crawford, our driver, was trying to smack Ryan in the back of the head while Darius Worden, our medic, shook his head, pretending it wasn't funny anymore. Those two couldn't be more opposite. Eric was the palest of white, with blonde hair and blue eyes. The poor kid got sunburned sitting inside his CHU, which was basically a box big enough to sleep in.

Darius had dark, caramel-colored skin and dark, brown eyes. He called himself *'the flavor'*.

"I'm the only one here that has spice."

They were all there. My brothers. I could finally see them and my lips stretched into a smile.

"You boys look like you've been on vacation," I called.

Ryan turned to look at me while the other two gave me the finger.

"You've seen better days," Ryan smirked.

"Merrick. Who are you talking to?"

Their faces swirled into nothing, and the darkness I'd seen for so long shut them out completely.

"Grace?"

Her hand caressed my face as she slipped something into my mouth. "It's a thermometer. Keep it under your tongue."

My chest weighed a thousand pounds and getting a good breath was difficult.

"Something's wrong, Grace."

"I know, Mer. I'm here."

She hummed for me while I fought to get comfortable. My clothes were stuck to my damp skin. Grace helped me remove my shirt and pants, leaving me in my underwear. Normally, I'd be concerned with whether or not I was sporting another erection for her.

Not this time.

My body wasn't cooperating with my mind and my head felt like it did *that* day.

"Shhh, rest. I'm not leaving."

I must have been mumbling *something* because Grace kept trying to calm me down.

Then the nightmare began, but it was no longer my brothers in that MRAP. It was Grace. Her dark hair drifted over her shoulder, and although her face was fuzzy, I knew without a doubt it was her. Instead of Eric at the wheel, it was Grace driving that truck and before I could take a breath, the force of impact from the EFP hit just as hard as I remembered.

"No!"

The driver's side disintegrated and the burning started in my skin, a raspy sizzle mixed with the screams from my men.

I crawled out of the truck, like I always did. My vision grew fuzzy and dark as I pulled Ryan off the side of the truck and dragged him to safety. All the while, my mind was on Grace. She'd disappeared when the EFP hit and I couldn't decide if it had ripped her out of the truck or if ...

I looked back at the fiery hunk of metal and saw her. Long white dress, strands of hair sweeping across her face as the breeze blew by. She was beautiful. So bright and vivid with the dark smoke surrounding her.

"Grace! Over here, baby! Run!"

I screamed for her, begged her to get away from the truck, knowing those bastards were about to blanket it with bullets.

"Please!"

But she didn't move. She just smiled at me, and I knew then that I'd lost her. The flames engulfed her and burned away the material of her dress before exploding around her.

Then she was gone and the pain started. The darkness closed in. I turned to find the rest of my men and, through the fog, all I saw was blood, fire, and sand.

Suddenly, it didn't matter what I saw. Because I'd lost her. I'd lost the one person I should have protected with my own life.

I laid there, alone in the sand with the sun burning down on me. The sound of bullets whizzing over my head didn't startle me like I remembered. I was numb to everything but the fire.

A cold hand swept over my face, cupping my cheek before trailing up to my forehead. The coolness of that touch banished the burning in my body, like a euphoria I'd never felt before. Like an instant relief from the pain.

Then nothing ... until it started all over again.

Chapter Thirteen

Grace

Merrick was getting worse.

His fever wouldn't break, and it was difficult to keep him still and resting. He was too strong and the things he must have been seeing were just too intense.

I sat by his bed all night long, unsure of whether or not I was making it worse by not taking him to the doctor. I had no way of even getting him to the car with both of our parents out of town. My only option was to call Micah who told me to monitor Merrick's temperature and try to keep him hydrated until he could come.

"The hospital is the last place he needs to be right now, Grace. Same with an ambulance. He'll be more comfortable at home."

"But Micah, he's getting–"

"I know. But it's Merrick. He's stubborn. I'll be there soon, just keep me posted. If you're really worried, you can try to bring him in."

"No. I barely got him into bed. There's no way I could get him to the front door let alone inside my car, all while keeping him comfortable," I declared.

We decided to wait until morning. I could still try to break his fever in the night and stay by his side until it did.

My mind raced as I tried to think of the possible causes. It wasn't the sushi. It hit too quickly to be the food. It was chilly outside, but not so much that it would have caused him to get sick like that. His fever was high, but not high enough to take serious action.

Not yet.

At this point, I don't think anything could stop what was happening in his head.

"Grace, I can't."

I opened my eyes at the sound of his voice. He'd been saying things all night that didn't make any sense, calling for me over and over. I leaned over to look at him, his eyes still closed, brows furrowed together. The sadness on his handsome face almost did me in.

Touching him seemed to help. His face, his neck. It calmed him a little more each time; brought him back from wherever his head was. All the while, he mumbled things about Ryan, about his men, and even the pain.

Burning.

He was living the explosion all over again, and I couldn't stop it.

"I'm here, Merrick." I placed a cool washcloth over his head and stroked his cheek. He was still hot, still cringing from pain, and his skin was dry. Not a drop of sweat. That's what scared me the most.

"I can't do it. I can't watch it." He tossed and turned a little more while I cooled his face.

"Shh, you're here, Mer. You're here with me." I moved to sit beside his hip, leaning over him until I could control his erratic movements a little more. His eyes were closed and his mouth set into a hard line. I ran the cool cloth over his neck and down across his collar bones. Harsh breaths caused his chest to quickly rise and fall, making it hard for him to speak. I placed my hand over his heart, attempting to calm him.

"I can't, Grace. I can't watch it."

"Watch what, Merrick?"

"I can't watch you burn again. It'll kill me this time."

"Shh, Merrick. I'm not burning. I'm right here at the side of your bed. We're in your room and there's no danger near us."

"No," he insisted and shook his head, cringing from more pain. "It's not real. It can't be real. You aren't supposed to be here."

He was having another hallucination. How many times would he have to re-live everything before his mind finally decided he'd had enough. This was nothing like the nightmares I overheard at night. This was real to him. The fever was making it real.

"Merrick, I'm right here and you're right here with me. Nowhere else but here." I prayed the words would penetrate the darkness engulfing him. They pulled him out of it before, but this was different. "Come back to me."

He tossed some more, almost knocking me off the bed. I kept my hand over his heart and spoke quietly while he struggled to relax.

"You want me to sing?" I asked, my voice quavering from the tears that threatened to fall. "I'll sing, Merrick."

He groaned and turned his head. When his eyes opened, I sucked in a sharp breath. Those light blue eyes were glossy from the fever. The strength it must have taken him to open them, was clearly overwhelming. But that wasn't what made my heart thud to a stop. Merrick opened his eyes and looked right at me, as if he could actually see me sitting beside him. Those beautiful, piercing eyes focused on my face and his body stilled.

Just as quickly as it happened, that focus was gone. His eyelids shut and he groaned again.

"I can't watch it, but I can't look away," he whispered.

I bent forward and slid my hand up to cup his cheek. Merrick sighed and the agony on his face softened.

"I'm here," I said.

His breaths evened out when I started to sing *'First Day of My Life'* by *Bright Eyes.* The words telling him that right then, in that very moment … it *was* the first day of my life. It was the start of something I hadn't seen coming.

The feel of Merrick sinking into the bed was a relief. He was finally sleeping, finally calming down enough to rest. I kept singing softly. A lullaby I'd sing all night long if it kept him happy.

"I really do think I was blind before I met you," I whispered to him. Taking a moment to really absorb the honest truth about that very sentence.

I didn't know where I was before. I didn't really know *who* I was. Not before Merrick. As I continued to sing, I told him the reality of what I *actually* knew. "I *do* know where I want to go, Merrick."

I took a deep breath and kept humming as I started to stand, but I didn't get very far. Merrick's hand found my wrist, startling me for a moment until I looked back and saw his eyes opened. This time, they weren't focused, just empty.

"Stay," he said, roughly. "Please, stay with me."

"I'm not going anywhere."

He pulled me back to sit on the bed, but just when I started to settle in next to his hip, he pulled me farther. I found myself lying next to him, his arm pressed against my lower back and his face buried in my neck.

It was surprisingly comfortable to have him pressed against me, even when he was burning up with fever. He settled in and sighed, holding me close.

"It's safe here," he muttered against my skin. "Right here. It's peaceful. Even though I can't see you, I feel you."

My nose started to sting. I closed my eyes to hold back the moisture filling them. If it was safety he needed, it was safety I'd give him. Any way I could.

Because I was in love with Merrick Thatcher.

I was in love with *all* of him. Even the parts he thought were broken. He was strong even when he didn't think he was, brave when he was scared. He was kind even when he was angry with life, and he made me laugh more often than not these days.

Merrick had his issues, but he faced them head on without realizing it. That made me love him even more.

The sudden realization took my breath away and the movement in my chest made Merrick come closer. He was plastered against me, his arms circling my waist tight enough that I wouldn't be able to pull away if I wanted to.

But I didn't want to.

I found my breath a moment later and continued the song, telling him that I was glad I didn't die before I had the chance to really meet him. That I could go anywhere with him and I knew I'd be happy.

"I guess we *will* just have to wait and see ..." I whispered to him.

I started to drift, the stress of the last few hours catching up to me. I was too comfortable to keep my eyes open. So while Merrick's breaths tickled my skin, I hummed until sleep claimed me.

I woke that next morning to find myself still pressed against Merrick, only it was *me* plastered to *his* chest. It was warm. Too warm with his fever. I carefully climbed out of the bed, checking his temperature once more before leaving the room to let him sleep.

I found Micah in the living room, spread out on the couch with his phone on his chest. He woke when I walked into the room.

"How is he?" he asked, sitting up and rubbing his eyes.

"His fever dropped a little. He's finally getting some rest," I replied through a yawn.

"Good news. As long as it continues to drop, he'll be just fine."

I nodded, looking down at the floor and trying to get my bearings.

"You okay, Grace?"

"I'm fine. Did you call your parents?"

Micah sighed and looked at his cell phone. "I did. Mom freaked, but I think I convinced her that we had it under control. She agreed that there was no reason to come back early."

"Where are they?"

Micah just shrugged, seemingly unconcerned about it.

I found it odd that my parents had left town the same day Emma and Nathan did, but there was really no reason to be suspicious. They could do whatever they wanted. Even though the way my parents had left *was* questionable.

Mom avoided talking about where they were going, saying they just needed to get away for a few days. Dad just shrugged and said he was doing whatever Mom wanted him to do.

When I asked Keara about it, she informed me that it was a mystery to everyone at the clinic as well. She'd just been told to reschedule patients and close until Dad got back.

Once Merrick showed signs of a fever while we were sitting at that rest stop, I'd forgotten all about our parents and focused on him. I was his homecare nurse after all. It was my job.

The fear that overwhelmed me just happened to come with it.

Micah came and went throughout the day, checking on us when he wasn't sleeping or back at the hospital. Merrick woke a couple times, mumbling about being thirsty and trying to figure out where he was. His mind hadn't caught up with his body yet, but once we got him settled, he went back to sleep.

I was exhausted by the time Micah brought dinner.

"You should go home and get some rest," he suggested as we ate the pizza he insisted on bringing.

I was able to wake Merrick long enough to help him eat a bowl of soup before he passed out again, but I still felt guilty for eating a delicious pizza while he was in bed. Alone.

"I'm fine," I said around another bite.

"No, Grace. You aren't. You look like you've been to hell and back."

"Why thank you, Micah Thatcher. When did you become such a charmer?"

He chuckled and shook his head. "I learned everything I know from that man in there," he smirked, pointing toward Merrick's room.

"Well, then. You seriously have your work cut out for you," I stated around a slow yawn.

"Seems his charms work pretty well these days."

My head popped up as I choked down the chunk of crust I'd just started chewing on. "What do you mean?"

Micah shrugged and wiped his hands on a napkin before gulping down half his beer. "It means it worked on *you*, so I have hope."

"What worked on me?"

"Don't deny it, Grace. I see right through you."

"See what?" I asked, innocently.

"You're in love with my brother."

My eyes widened, my heart thudding to a stop before I kicked it back into gear with a deep breath and a swig of beer. I avoided his stare. "Why do you say that?"

"Because it's the truth. Only someone in love with my brother would have lasted this long with his grumpy ass. Only someone in love with Merrick would be the one to snap him out of the shit he's been dealing with."

"I haven't snapped him out of anything."

"You have."

I shook my head and suddenly my appetite was gone. The exhaustion I was fighting hit me hard. I dropped what was left of my slice of pizza onto the plate and sat back in my chair.

"Grace," Micah said, somberly. "I don't know if you know this, but Merrick is stubborn."

I snorted, "Ha! You think?"

He smiled at me and added, "Everyone knows that man has a head harder than granite, but everyone also knows that you've got a heart softer than feathers. You two fit together, and if seeing is believing, I think I believe."

I opened my mouth to speak, but nothing came out because I had no idea what to say. Denying it would only disappoint me because Micah was right.

Like I discovered the night before, I was deeply in love with Merrick and I only fell further every day. But what about him?

"Merrick has too much going on in his life to think about–"

"Really?" Micah cut in. "You really think he's that blind?"

"I ... I don't know."

His brows drew together and the corners of his mouth turned down. "Neither one of you sees yourself very clearly, huh? That's too bad and also really sad. Maybe you both need a wake-up call."

"Micah."

"Do you love my brother?"

"Micah."

"Do. You. Love. My brother?"

My eyes closed while my heart lifted. "Yes."

"Good." He waited for me to open my eyes before demanding, "Don't stop."

He folded into another slice of pizza and that was that. The conversation was over and I couldn't think of anything else to talk about.

I rolled the idea of Merrick and me around in my head. Merrick had said things that made me think he felt *something* for me, but it was obvious he didn't think he was capable of those feelings. Yesterday was the first time he acted like he finally had things figured out. Like his injuries didn't make decisions for him anymore.

The whole day had been lighter, until his fever started. Even then, Merrick had come to a conclusion. It was obvious to me at the time, but I hadn't really thought about it until that short conversation with Micah.

Merrick wanted to live again and I was going to make sure he did.

I was dreaming.

I had to be dreaming because Merrick was gazing at me with that meaningful look on his face. The one he got when he talked about his family or when he talked to me about ... well, me. His eyes blazed with hunger as he did a slow burn down my body and back up. Then I was in his arms and he was kissing me and my whole body felt warm and tingly.

"Grace."

I pulled away and smiled.

"Grace."

Dream Merrick wasn't the one saying my name, even though it sounded exactly like him. His lips weren't moving, but he *was* smiling at me and I all but melted in his arms anyway.

"I hate to do this, but you need to wake up, Grace."

My eyes popped open to find Merrick sitting on the bed, facing me. The smirk on his face was suspicious, but damn, he was so sexy.

"Sorry, I'm awake now," I said, stretching my arms above my head. The pain in my neck and back was a clear indication that Merrick's desk chair was *not* a good sleeping chair.

"That's unfortunate," he chuckled.

"Excuse me?"

"You seemed to be enjoying whatever you were dreaming about."

I froze. *Oh shit.* "Ummm."

He laughed and shook his head. "Whatever it was, it was driving me crazy. I had to wake you."

I couldn't tell if it was an annoyed crazy he was talking about or the kind of crazy I felt every day from being over aroused.

God, please be the latter.

"Sorry?"

"Don't be," he muttered hoarsely.

Okay so maybe it *was* the latter.

Then again, his voice was probably rough from sleep. Then I finally noticed that he was dressed and his face was bright and awake. He'd been up and moving for a while, apparently.

"So, I don't really remember much, but I know I've been out for at least a day," he stated. "You haven't been here the whole time, have you?"

I nodded absently, not realizing that he couldn't see me until I'd already felt like a moron. "I have. I didn't want to leave you alone and Micah had a night shift last night, so he couldn't stay."

"Micah was here?" he asked, a little panic in his voice.

"Yes."

"Oh, umm, what did he have to say?"

A whole lot, but I'm not telling.

"Not much. We just kept an eye on your temperature and he brought food."

"Oh. Okay. Good."

Odd.

"Are you hungry?" I asked, standing to move in front of him. I was just barely above eye level with him when I reached up to feel his forehead. He was still a little warm, but his fever was almost completely gone.

Instead of answering me, he lifted his hands to put them on my waist, pulling in a deep breath. His eyes closed and I couldn't resist combing my fingers through his hair. I didn't even realize what I was doing until he softly groaned.

"Grace ..."

His breath was minty and I closed my mouth, hoping mine didn't smell awful.

"That feels good," he mumbled.

"I'm glad you're feeling better," I said, a little breathlessly.

His eyes stayed closed as I kept running my fingers through his hair, over his forehead, and down his cheek. The prickle from his shadow of a beard was rough against my fingertips.

"Can I touch you?" he asked, roughly.

"You are."

"No. Not the way I want to."

My pulse started to race, my breaths quickening. "How do you want to?"

Those strong hands pressed firmly into my waist and tugged me forward until I was standing between Merrick's legs. I couldn't pull my eyes away from his face. He looked so peaceful with his eyes closed. Then his lips parted on a sigh.

"Any way. Every way."

His breath tickled my chin and the room was suddenly on fire. I raked my fingers through his hair until I was cupping the back of his head. *What am I doing?* The grip around my waist tightened, his thumbs starting to move in circles around my stomach. I rested my other hand on his shoulder to keep my balance. Otherwise, I would have fallen over from the dizziness invading my head.

"Okay," I stuttered.

Those big, strong hands left my waist and lifted so slowly until they ever so gently cupped my face. I closed my eyes, soaking in the feel of his warm skin against mine. His eyes stared straight ahead, as if he were staring at my lips. I knew he wasn't seeing them, but my breath still quaked with each inhale.

His thumbs drifted over my cheeks, lingering there a moment before moving up to my eyes. His touch was gentle and hesitant, but determined. He wanted to see me any way he could, and this was the only way.

Our breathing was the only sound other than the hint of a slight sizzle from the electricity in the air around us. It felt like the room would burst into flames. Then the sound of the front door opening zapped it all away.

"Grace? You still here?"

Micah.

Merrick sighed and dropped his hands to his lap as I took a step back. "My family has the worst timing," he growled.

A nervous giggle bubbled up my throat as I took another step back, trying to catch my breath and calm the butterflies in my stomach.

Micah walked into the room and came to an abrupt stop when he saw us. A slow smile stretched across his face, and he winked at me, leisurely backing up into the hall. With a tip of his head he let me know he'd be in the kitchen before he quietly walked away.

I turned back to Merrick, whose eyes were pointed right at me, a wistful expression on his handsome face.

I couldn't believe it. He actually wanted me. But knowing that just wasn't enough.

"Why?" I asked.

"Hmm?"

"Why me?"

He hesitated and my stomach rolled with frustration.

"I don't know, Grace," he whispered and lowered his head. "But I really don't care about the why anymore."

But *I* did. I didn't want him to start something with me just because I was the only one around. I didn't want to pour my heart out to the man without knowing he wanted this, too. Without him knowing *why* he wanted this.

After the heartache I went through before, I had to be sure. Jason stayed with me because of the baby, even though he would have eventually walked away anyway. I know that now. What would be the reason for Merrick to stay with me? Because he couldn't see anyway?

No.

It just wasn't enough.

"I'll start some breakfast," I said, deadpan.

"Grace."

I refused to look at him, knowing the expression he was giving me would break me. "I'll meet you in the kitchen."

Then I walked away. It was the only way to protect my heart when the slightest shake would shatter it.

Chapter Fourteen

Merrick

I'd messed up somehow.

Before I even started, I'd fucked something up with Grace and I had no clue what it was.

Why me?

Did she really even *need* to ask that? Why *not* her?

She was a diamond in the rough. A woman like Grace is hard to find, I know that now. My fears about not being enough for her suddenly stopped being important. I just wanted her any way I could get her and I was going to do my damndest to make her happy, if she'd have me.

She'd taken care of me when she could have left me with my brother or anyone else. She stayed.

It shouldn't have surprised me how deep my feelings for her had become. It wasn't because she was just there, it was because she was everywhere.

I couldn't stop thinking about her and I didn't want to. She brought me peace without even trying.

"Looks like you're back to normal," my sister remarked when I stumbled into the kitchen later that night.

"Why are you here?"

"Well, hello to you, too." I didn't need to see her to know that whatever expression was on Mary's face, it was filled with sarcasm. "Micah had another shift and Grace asked me to come."

"She did?"

Mary sighed long and loud, just to make a point. "Yeah, she did. She was here for almost three whole days with barely any sleep, no thanks to you two idiots. I don't know why nobody called me, but whatever. You honestly think she'd just ditch you at the first sign of you feeling better?"

I carefully found my way to the table as she spoke, counting my steps as I rocked on my crutches and put more weight on my left leg. Every day I was stronger, but today felt like I'd taken ten steps back. In more ways than one.

"I guess not," I answered, settling into a chair. My head was still fuzzy, but I needed to be up and moving as much as possible. It chased away whatever this was.

"Well, she wouldn't. She's exhausted and still worried about you. I wouldn't be surprised if she was already asleep, though."

"What time is it?"

"Seven o'clock. You've been hiding in your room for a few hours."

After an awkward breakfast, I had retreated to my room, falling asleep for a couple hours until Grace woke me in the afternoon. We didn't talk much. Not with Micah sticking around most of the day. I didn't get a chance to ask Grace what I did wrong.

"Did she seem upset when she left?" I asked my sister, a little too transparently.

"No, just tired. A little quiet."

I nodded, thinking of that short conversation from this morning. Searching for any reason why Grace might be upset because of what I said.

"What happened this morning, Merrick? Micah told me you two looked pretty deep into something when he showed up and then suddenly, neither one of you was speaking to the other."

"I honestly don't know."

Another silent moment passed before Mary knocked on the table, getting my full attention. "Well? You going to tell me what the conversation was at least?"

I bowed my head and raked a hand through my hair, remembering how good it felt when it was Grace's hand. "She asked me a question and I guess I gave the wrong answer," I mumbled.

"And what was the question?"

"Why do you care?"

"Umm, was that the question or are you being a dumbass again?"

"Mary."

"Merrick."

"God, you can be really annoying these days."

There was a smile in her voice when she said, "I know."

I leaned forward and rested my arms on the table, smoothing my fingers over the hard surface and feeling some of the scratches made over the years. Why couldn't I be that sensitive to what Grace needed? Touch, smell, hearing ... it all came so much easier, but I still had no idea how to talk.

"Why me?"

"Excuse me?"

I sighed, suddenly embarrassed that I was relying on my sister to help me figure out how to speak to a woman. "She asked, *'Why me?'*."

"And?"

"And ... I said I didn't know and that I didn't care about the why."

"Hmm, that's interesting," she muttered.

"Why do you say that?" I asked, hoping she had answers for me I knew I'd never figure out on my own.

"Do you know what happened to her? With her ex?"

I nodded, remembering the conversation she'd had with Keara a few nights earlier. I still didn't know what to think about it. "The asshole left her after ... she lost her baby."

I expected surprise from Mary, but instead, she seemed to be all too aware of Grace's past. "Jason cheated on her a lot," she informed me. "Why she was with him, well, she's too good of a person. When he got her pregnant, he promised he'd stick around for the baby. Then, when the baby was gone, he was gone, too."

"How do you know all of this?"

"I listen to the gossip around the neighborhood sometimes," she said, a small chuckle following that little bit of information.

"People talk. Some of them knew Jason and some of them have seen him since he left Grace. They put the pieces together. I just overheard them."

"How is this supposed to help me?" I growled. "It just pisses me off that she went through that."

"Well, if you paid attention to those small facts, you might understand the very important question Grace asked you in the first place. He didn't have a reason to stay anymore."

I felt like a child being reprimanded. I was too angry about what happened to Grace to really understand what it did to her. "So, he left her as soon as the only reason he stayed was gone," I stated.

Mary's chair screeched across the floor when she stood. "What does that tell you?" she asked.

Her footsteps moved to the fridge, leaving me to think. I heard her gasp before she shut the door. "God, I'm starving," she groaned.

"Help yourself."

"I certainly will. So?"

"It tells me Jason Reed is still the asshole he always was," I grumbled. I knew I should have kicked his ass back in high school. He was always playing the girls I knew, making them hate all of us anyway.

A few beeps on the microwave and then Mary was back at the table. "That's the obvious part. You think that might have had an effect on Grace?"

"Of course it did. I can already tell that she tries to hide it, but it's there. She didn't deserve that."

The microwave beeped and the smell of pizza filled the kitchen. Mary moved around the room for a minute before placing a plate in front of me. Then it finally hit me.

Why me?

"I want her for *her*. Not any other reason."

"So you *do* know why then," she said.

"There really isn't a *why*. It just *is*. I can't picture myself without her anymore. I don't want to." I thought of all the things I discovered about Grace since she started coming over. All the things I couldn't get out of my mind. "She's kind and compassionate, but she has a spark when she needs it." I smiled. There were a lot of arguments we'd had that ended with me needing a cold shower.

"She's smart and funny. She's beautiful in every way that matters and even though I know she's beautiful on the outside, I don't care. And not because I can't see her. Every time she walks into the room, I feel her. Everywhere. Not seeing her ... it sucks, but I don't have to see her to know I'm in love with her."

Mary cleared her throat. "That's a pretty good answer. Why didn't you go with that?"

"Because I'm an idiot."

"No, you're not. You're just a man."

I gave a bitter laugh. "That doesn't really help."

"No, but it's necessary," she chuckled. "She wants you, too, Mer. She just wants to protect herself from another heart break."

"How do you know all of this?"

"I'm a woman," she said, as if that was supposed to answer all questions in the known universe. "Remember that and you'll be just fine."

I pushed away from the table, suddenly needing to fix things before Grace had a chance to think about it too much. And she *would* think about it.

"Where you going?" Mary asked when I stood and fumbled with my crutches.

"I'm going to talk to her."

"You should really let her sleep."

"I know, but this can't wait. She needs to know."

"Okay, okay," Mary said. Nobody realized that I knew exactly when someone was smiling when they spoke. Voices changed with expressions. It was one thing I learned early on and only got better at recognizing. My sister included.

I started for the front door, miscounting my steps and accidentally bumping into the wall a couple times.

"You've got two options," Mary called behind me. "I can take you over there or you can attempt it by yourself."

I stopped, panting for breath from the adrenaline coursing through my veins. I had no idea how to get to Grace's house. It wasn't far, but it had been too long since I'd seen the surroundings.

"Will you tell me where to go?" I pleaded.

Her footsteps started up the hallway and stopped beside me. "Of course, little bro." Another smile.

We made it out the front door and the nervousness suddenly overwhelmed me. Rejection. It sucked and it was always a risk.

Don't be a coward. You've been through hell, what's a little rejection going to do?

"Turn left and move slow," Mary directed. "When you hit concrete again, that's the sidewalk leading to the porch. Turn left and follow it to the door. Two steps, I think, is all there is."

"Thanks, Mary."

Her hand touched my cheek, patting softly. "Don't screw it up. Just be honest. That's all she wants."

I nodded. "I will."

"Good luck."

Then she was gone and I was alone, outside, for the first time in months, no more ready for this mission than I was weeks ago.

I stood at Grace's door for a good five minutes before I finally reached out and knocked. My heart pounded in my throat, my hands sweating, but I finally figured out what I needed to say to her.

The sound of the deadbolt twisting, reached my ears before the door creaked open.

"Merrick?"

"Grace." I cleared my throat and tried for a lighthearted tone that sounded more droll than anything else. "How are you?"

"Umm, fine. What are you doing here?"

Good so far. "I needed to talk to you."

"About?" She sounded apprehensive.

She had nothing to be afraid of because it was *my* entire self-worth she held in her hands. *That's stupid, Merrick. Be a man.*

"You asked me a question earlier and I'd like to tell you the answer."

"Merrick, I don't think–"

"Please, Grace. Just give me a few minutes and if you want me to leave after, I'll go."

I held my breath, waiting for her to tell me to take a hike. She didn't and my relief almost made me fall over on my crutches.

"Come on in," she relented. It almost put me out of my misery, but there was so much more to say.

I rocked forward on my crutches and stepped into the house. Grace shut the door and guided me over to the couch.

"Do you want anything?" she offered.

Just you.

"No. Thank you."

To my surprise, she sat next to me, making the cushion sink beside me as her leg brushed up against mine. The room was suddenly stifling.

I tugged on my shirt collar and swallowed the fear down. Way down. "Thanks for letting me in. I was expecting you to shut the door in my face. I deserve it," I said, forcing a weak smile.

"Merrick—"

"Sorry. I just, I'm really nervous."

"You are?"

I chuckled and dropped my head forward. Honesty would go a lot farther in this situation. "Yeah, for some reason I feel like if I could see your face, I'd know if you were mad or not. I can't tell right now and it's killing me."

"I'm not mad," she denied soothingly, then placed her hand on my arm.

"Good."

Several tense seconds passed as I gathered what courage I could find. Never in my life had I been this on edge. Not even on the plane to Iraq. That was child's play compared to this.

"What did you want to tell me?"

I swallowed thickly and drew in a long breath. Her hand slid down my arm and wrapped around my fingers when I started tapping my leg. I wanted to just blurt it out right then and there, but I had some explaining to do.

"I was in charge of my men," I began. "First Lieutenant. My team relied on me to know what to do at all times and they trusted me. I always felt like I let them down, even knowing I had no control over what happened. It's just something I can't fight hard enough."

It's also the very thing that kept me going those first weeks of hell, after the attack. Thinking about my men was all I had and seeing them in my head, over and over again, was the only way I could cope. It kept me grounded in a strange sort of way.

Grace squeezed my hand tightly, her soft skin engulfing mine. I lifted our hands and pressed my lips to the back of hers. It was instinct. Pure, natural instinct to touch her like that. Her gasp made me close my eyes, but she didn't pull away. I pressed my nose to her skin and inhaled that sweet smell of hers.

"You're so soft," I whispered, mostly to myself, and kissed her hand again. It took a few long moments to finally drop them back to my thigh, then I forced myself to get back on track.

"I was in the Army National Guard. We were brought in to train the Iraqi military, teach them how to do things right so we could get out of there. It wasn't the most ... vigorous job, according to few, but it was important. I wasn't sneaking into buildings or capturing prisoners, but I was doing something that would hopefully end the need for those men to even be there doing that shit.

"We'd travel to small bases to train, sometimes spending ten days at a time there. We were surrounded by Iraqi soldiers and we'd spend the nights smack dab in the middle of the compound."

I took a deep breath, remembering how nervous I was that first night I stayed on a foreign base. It wasn't active, but it was still dangerous. Men are capable of anything when it comes to their beliefs and protecting their families.

"A lot of those guys were really great. They were just like us. Kids protecting their country, or at least trying to by doing what they were told. Then there were some who hated us and just wanted us gone. I get it. I'd feel the same way, but it wouldn't change anything. We were still there and they still hated us. Just had to do my job and move on, all the while hoping nothing got too violent.

"I'd heard about the teams that ran into a rogue a time or two. No one can weed out the bad ones until it's too late. That kept us alert, but how do you control something like that? You can't," I scoffed, still wishing it were different. "Some of them would try to infiltrate the trainers. They'd squeeze themselves in until they were established nice and tight, then they'd turn the gun on us because they believed it was their destiny. What they were *supposed* to do."

Even now, I could feel the bitterness in hearing the stories. I wanted justice for men I never met.

"It happened, but not so often that it gave us reason to stop. We had a job to do whether they liked us or not."

I recalled the faces of some of the Iraqi men I had to trust, at least temporarily. They were funny and crazy; innocent. They just wanted it over, too. Living in a country that had some hard times – just like any other – came with its struggles. It wasn't their fault. Some parts of war *can* be civil. That's why it's possible to eventually end it without more losses than necessary. It's just that humans always failed at the civil part.

"It wasn't all training and tiptoeing around each other. There were times where we went days just doing paperwork." I paused, a sick amusement making me snicker. "I loved those days. Writing a report about the mission progress or someone I didn't think belonged was easier than holding a gun. I didn't want to be out there risking my neck and I didn't want to have to kill. No man does."

It was so much simpler to spend the day in an office writing the same things over and over, counting the numbers for supplies, listing names and dates. I would have done anything to stay in that office every day, even if I was bored out of my mind half the time. Paperwork didn't have an expiration.

"Then there were days we had free time. We'd hit the gym in the morning, eat, take inventory on our gear, and spend the rest of it trying to stay cool. Relaxing. There was always a little bit of normal, but it wasn't ever enough."

"What kinds of things did you do?" Grace inquired, her small voice penetrating my memories.

I shrugged. "Anything really. Video games, reading, whatever we felt like that we had at our disposal."

"I didn't realize you had all that over there."

I gave a half shrug, "Not many people do."

It was an attempt to center ourselves before we had to roll out to another compound. Before we had to see the destruction on the streets as we drove by.

It was a countdown.

"Ryan spent a lot of his free days making lists. Lists about what he needed for the nursery, what Miranda was craving, or what the doctor said at her last appointment. He'd spend hours staring at the ultrasound pictures she sent him," I mused, grinning because we all knew he was obsessed with it no matter how much he actually tried to hide it. "Then, when he finally felt some peace about what was going on back home, he'd join us for a movie or a barbeque. I didn't realize it at the time, but I was jealous of that. The ability to forget where he was and focus on home ... I wanted that."

"I'm sure it was difficult," Grace whispered. "I can't imagine what it would be like not knowing what was happening back home."

I was so wrapped up in trying to stay alert and ready that I forgot to worry about normal things. After a while, you forget about sports teams and scores when you're in the middle of the desert surrounded by people that really don't like you being there. Any moment could become your last. There isn't time to truly care about the next game. You try because it's what you're supposed to do, but it's rarely real.

It's still an odd feeling to just forget. But eventually you realize that all the luxuries back home need to *stay* home. You don't really need them anymore. Not out there.

"It gets frustrating," I continued. "Sometimes, you forget the reasons *why* you went there in the first place. It's hot on a good day. When it rains, you end up covered to the hip with muck and mud. It's not the most beautiful terrain, especially on base. Everything is covered in dirt and sand, and even the sky looks like it's just dust sweeping back and forth. Blue skies were rare. You tend to miss those little things that people back home don't ever think about."

I released Grace's hand and rubbed my palms over the tops of my thighs. I was starting to feel all those doubts again. The ones that made me angry in the first place. The uncontrollable things.

"No one knows what goes through the mind of each man out there. It's no longer a job that feeds your family or pays for school," I told her, knowing I spoke for ninety nine percent of the men out there. "I was done. Sick of the smells, the air, the purpose. Why should I stay and risk my life for people who wanted me dead anyway? For what? To teach a few men something they might use against me?"

I raked my fingers through my hair and drew in a long, cleansing breath. Grace needed to hear it all. She needed to know that the damaged man in front of her wasn't empty. I still had so much to give and I wanted to give it to *her*.

"I was there for my brothers and that was it. Not for the money, not for the pride." I shook my head and spoke the truth. "I was there for the man at my side. The one with his loaded gun ready to fire to protect me. I was there to protect *him*."

I remembered that day so clearly. The day I knew I finally found the right reasons for being there.

Grace waited. I didn't know what she was doing with her hands and I couldn't see her face, but she was listening to every word that left my mouth, like she always did. That's what made me keep going.

"So, I opened the door to my CHU – the box I called home – and I prepared myself to hate another day, but to *live it* because Ryan depended on me to live it. They all depended on me to live it just like I depended on them, running on empty or not." Deep breath in and out. "Then I looked down, and I saw this flower."

I paused, searching for the right words and seeing that marvel in my mind. As soon as I did, I felt the heat. That dry desert sun and the breeze that only made it worse. I felt the sand that was stuck between my fingers and toes. Not the smooth, cool sand at a beach. Not that. This was the kind that felt like dusted chalk. Lifeless. Stuck to everything until the color beneath it was lost.

"It was just a weed. Something that only grows in the dry and blistering heat of the desert, in the dust and sand. And this flower ... it was the first color I'd seen in months other than brown. I can still see it in my mind so perfectly. White. So white that it was the very absence of color, but to me, it was vivid.

"The leaves were covered in dust, until you couldn't even see the green and this flower, it was just there. Surrounded by nothing."

It was a fucking miracle.

I grinned. "And I thought, that's what it's all about. Finding the beauty in the ugly, the good in the bad, the light in the dark. This one tiny thing; it was for me. It was a reminder that life doesn't have to be clean and perfect to be beautiful."

I closed my eyes and the image locked in. That small, insignificant flower held my world on its petals. A fragile world on a delicate surface.

"I left the base that day and when I came back, it was gone. Shriveled up and already dead. Even something meant to grow in the worst of conditions, couldn't survive a life there. Because the life we get is precious. There one second and gone the next. But that flower – that flawless white flower – was the only thing I could see in the dust." I swallowed past the thick lump that had formed in my throat and pressed on. "Life should be that way. Somehow, I forgot what that meant to me."

Grace had no idea how close I came to forgetting completely. A man can only take so much before that life gets the best of him. I didn't want to be saved, but she'd done it before I could blink. She'd cared about me enough to be a light in my dark, brittle world.

I leaned back on the couch and turned my face to the ceiling. "I've been through hell, seen shit you could only dream of in your nightmares, and I've gone up against men three times my size. You'd think I would be prepared for anything, but I'm not. I'm still scared of the dark and the monsters that lurk there." I took a deep breath and forced myself to say the words I truly felt. "You're the only light I can see, Grace, and for a man who still feels the need to hide under his blankets at night, you're a fucking miracle."

Grace was holding her breath. I could tell from the complete silence beside me. I hesitantly reached over and fumbled around to find her hand again. When I had my fingers wrapped around hers, I pulled them up to my lips again, almost desperate for the feel of her.

"You asked me, why you," I muttered against her skin.

She tensed and exhaled.

"It's you because, I may be broken and damaged, but with you, I've never felt more complete."

To my disappointment, she pulled her hand away, but the panic was short-lived. She cupped my cheek, turning my face toward hers. For the millionth time, I wished that her face would appear in front of my eyes. Just once.

"Merrick. You're not broken. A little scratched up, maybe," she pointed out. "But sometimes, scratches make things beautiful."

I grasped her small hand in mine and turned my head to kiss her palm. She whimpered when I pulled my lips away, the sound sending lightning through my veins.

With a weak tug, she pulled my hands forward, guiding them closer until I was cupping her face.

"Do you still want to see me?"

"More than anything," I confessed.

Her skin was so soft, like velvet or silk. I was scared that if I wasn't gentle enough, I would hurt her. My fingers weren't as rough as they used to be, but they weren't worthy of touching her beautiful skin.

Didn't stop me.

I drifted over her cheeks, her jaw, her chin, feeling every feature and painting that perfect picture my eyes strained to see so desperately. I wanted to touch her lips, but I'd save those for last. They'd take the breath right out of me, no doubt.

Shifting forward, I combed my fingers through her hair and discovered it was longer than I pictured in my mind. The strands slid between my fingers like silk; exquisite.

She took a shaky breath.

"Is this okay?" I asked, my voice rough.

"Yes," she whispered back.

With trembling hands, I slid my fingers over her ears, registering the feel of a piercing in the cartilage at the top of her left ear. God, I loved that. For some reason, that piercing was so sexy to me.

I glided my fingers down her jaw once more and pressed my thumbs inward until I touched her nose. It was so petite. Smirking, I lightly tapped the end of it. "You were right. This nose is small, but it sure is straight."

She giggled, letting out a harsh breath. "Am I what you imagined?"

I moved my thumb between her eyebrows and felt the soft worry lines on her forehead. "Better, Grace. So much better and that's saying something. You're beautiful."

Her cheeks moved under my hands. A smile.

I couldn't resist. I had to know what that smile looked like, what it felt like. I dropped my hands until the tips of my fingers found those full, soft lips. Her smile pulled back in, but I couldn't bring myself to be disappointed.

There would be many more opportunities to make her smile and I sure as hell would take every single one of them.

I tugged on her bottom lip with my thumb, the urge to taste that lip, stronger than ever before. Her breath slid over my fingers while I memorized the feel of it.

"I want to kiss you."

I held my breath, waiting for her permission and not caring if I got it. After all this time, nothing was going to stop me from tasting

Grace. Just one little taste of her. That's all. I needed it more than I needed that breath.

"Yes," she sighed.

I didn't pause, I didn't even think. I leaned in, slow and steady, hoping I wouldn't miss and knowing I just didn't care anymore. Our noses touched and I wondered if her eyes were closed.

It was in that moment, just before our lips touched, that I knew without a doubt in my mind I would do anything for her. I would *be* anyone for her. But I didn't have to, because she already accepted me the way I was.

Her lips finally pressed against mine and heat exploded inside me. For the first time ever, it wasn't just a kiss.

It was *everything*.

Everything my wrecked soul could possibly ask for.

I held her face between my hands, keeping her right where I wanted her as I deepened the kiss. Those lips parted, inviting me in, and I finally got to taste her.

Cookies. How did someone taste like cookies?

A low moan left her mouth when her tongue tangled with mine. I couldn't take it anymore. I pulled her closer, locking my lips with hers and snaking my arms around her waist.

She buried her hands in my hair, holding me against her, taking the kiss to a completely new level. Slow and steady. I felt her every movement, heard every breath that escaped her. The slower the kiss, the faster my heart beat against my chest.

"Merrick ..."

Hearing my name leave her mouth was like listening to her sing. What surrounded us, just disappeared.

"We need to slow down, Merrick."

God, I didn't want to. I wanted to lay her out in front of me and explore every soft inch of her. But the man I wanted to be for her, wouldn't let me. So I slowly pulled away, keeping her close.

"Okay," I breathed.

She leaned in to press her lips to mine again, holding my face between her hands. "That was ..."

"Yeah."

"I never ..."

"Yeah."

Those were the last words spoken for a good hour. I leaned back on the couch and Grace planted herself in my arms with her head on my shoulder. Counting the number of times I kissed her forehead or her hair, was impossible.

She didn't complain and I didn't question her need to slow things down. I'd give her whatever she needed at whatever pace she needed it. As long as I could stay right there beside her.

It was peace. Plain and simple.

"It's getting late," she said with a sleepy sigh.

"It is."

"I wouldn't mind staying here all night, Merrick, but I have to work early tomorrow," she informed me, a smile in her tired voice.

I chuckled. "Well, we can't have you showing up late to work, can we?"

Her head shook back and forth against my shoulder, bouncing with silent laughter.

"Would you mind helping me to the door?"

Her head lifted as she pushed up to stand. "Of course."

I stumbled to the door on my crutches, the stiffness in my injured leg making it more of an effort than usual.

"I'll be at the house when you get back from your appointment."

That's right. I had to meet with Dr. Samuelson, bright and early. If only the reason was for Grace instead of my eyes.

She opened the door. I reached out and found her hip, tugging her against me. My leg wasn't the only part of my body that was stiff. Feeling Grace pressed against me was almost as good as kissing her.

She lifted onto her toes and kissed me. Hard. Passionate. I almost tossed my crutches aside to push her against the first wall we stumbled into, but as quickly as it started, she pulled away.

"Goodnight, Merrick."

"Goodnight, Grace."

I left that house with the taste of her still on my lips and the hope of more.

Chapter Fifteen

Grace

I was in so much trouble.

If Merrick could kiss like that, what else could he do?

Sleep was out of the question, but I still rose the next day, feeling refreshed and – for lack of a better word – giddy. Merrick Thatcher had kissed me like a starving man. If I hadn't experienced it myself, I never would have believed it.

I wandered around the house for a while after Mom and Dad left for work. They got back really late after Merrick had gone home, fortunately. My unusually cheery behavior sent Mom's spidey senses into a frenzy, but Dad seemed really preoccupied. Neither one of them asked.

I threw in some laundry while I waited for Merrick to get home from his appointment. It felt like high school all over again. Me, constantly checking outside while I waited for a car to pull into his driveway, just to get a glimpse of him. This time was different, though. This time, Merrick actually knew I was there.

My phone rang and his name popped up on the screen. My stomach fluttered as I answered. "How did it go?"

He chuckled, that deep sound resonating through the phone. "Good morning, Grace."

And when the man said my name ...

"Good morning," I replied breathlessly. "How did it go?"

"Your dad is thorough. He should have been a private investigator."

I could only imagine. He cared about Merrick almost as much as he cared about me. "Well, why wouldn't he be thorough? You *are* a friend of the family."

"Hmm, I guess I am."

"So? Everything is normal?"

"That depends on your definition of normal. I still can't see." He sighed and cleared his throat. "I'll tell you everything when I get back. Mom wants me to come with her to get some supplies, so we'll be another thirty minutes or so."

"Sounds good."

"Will you be there when I get back?"

He asked the question as if he didn't already know the answer. He was just as unsure as I was about this new thing between us. "You know I will," I said, a beaming smile stretching my lips.

"Good. See you soon."

I spent the next forty-five minutes trying to keep my mind on anything else but Merrick. It was impossible. The things he said to me the night before, what he went through; it all seemed surreal. I couldn't imagine living that. Feeling like every day could be your last. No wonder he struggled so much to control his anger. It's not simple to go from one extreme to another.

And to be told that I made a difference for him. Well, what woman doesn't want to hear that? I just hoped it was the *right* difference.

My phone rang again. This time, Keara's name flashed across the screen. "Barbeque on Sunday. My place. You're bringing Merrick."

"Well, good morning to you, too, Keara."

"Yeah, yeah. Good morning, yada yada. Will you bring him or not?"

"Umm. I think so."

"You think so?"

"I'll ask him."

"Okay, good. Then what's with the hesitation?"

"Well ..."

Would he even want to come with me? Leaving the house earlier that week was one thing, but spending time with other people seemed to be a stretch.

Keara gasped and I squeezed my eyes shut. She knew.

"You tell me what's going on, right this minute, sister. Is there a new development? Did something happen between you two?" She spoke so fast, I could barely keep up.

"What makes you think something happened?" I asked, innocently.

"Don't give me that. I know you too well, Grace Samuelson. When you have a secret, you get all nervous and your voice changes to this high-pitched I'm-so-innocent-it's-sad tone. Now, spill it."

I drew in a long breath, but my ears perked at the sound of a car pulling in next door. "I need to go, but I'll tell you this. Merrick is a much better kisser than we ever dreamed of."

Keara gasped again. "Are you ... did he ..."

"I have to go. I'll call you later and I'll ask Merrick if he wants to come to the barbeque."

"Wait!"

"Bye."

I hung up and shoved my phone in my purse. She was going to kill me.

Walking outside, I saw Emma carrying groceries into the house. I picked up the last of them from the back seat of her car and hauled them inside. When I reached the kitchen, Merrick was sitting at the counter with a grin on his face.

"Thank you, Grace," Emma said, taking the bags from my hands.

"No problem. That's the last of it."

"Good. This boy seems to be in one of his ravenous moods. You'll have to make sure you make a little extra for dinner tonight in case he wants a late snack."

"Got it."

Merrick shook his head. "I'm right here. You don't have to talk about me like I'm not here."

"I'm not, sweetheart," Emma said sweetly. "I just know anytime I talk to you about these things, you aren't paying attention."

"I pay attention," Merrick argued.

"Not when Grace is in the room."

I felt heat rise in my cheeks as Merrick shrugged. "She's distracting."

"Mmhmm, I'm sure she is."

I wanted the floor to swallow me up. Did he tell his mom? I'd probably lose this job if she found out.

"I'll let you two finish up," Emma said and grabbed her purse off the counter. "I've got to get to the hospital and finish these interviews."

She kissed Merrick on the cheek and said her goodbyes. The second the front door shut, Merrick was out of his chair, balancing on one crutch.

"Get over here," he said, that gruff voice sending shivers down my spine.

I wouldn't have been able to stop myself from going to him if I wanted to. The pull between us was just too strong.

I walked toward him, his outstretched hand waiting for me. When I finally put my hand in his, he pulled me against him. He moved his crutch to lean against the counter, and when that other hand cupped my chin, I found it difficult to swallow.

Those blue eyes of his looked like they were seeing right through me. His lips curled up into a smirk when he heard my breath catch.

"I've been waiting for this for hours," he whispered, then crushed his mouth to mine.

This kiss didn't even compare to the night before. It was so much more. I felt it in my toes and fingertips. Merrick consumed me with his kiss, tangling his tongue with mine and keeping me right where he wanted me.

When both of us needed a breath, he pulled back, resting his forehead against mine.

"I can't stop thinking about you."

"Same here," I panted.

"Is it wrong that I just want to kiss you all day?"

This made me giggle. "No, because I want the same thing. But we can't. You have therapy to do and you have to tell me what happened this morning. Did you tell my dad about the fever?"

He nodded, tugging on my bottom lip with his thumb. It was so natural to let him. "I did. But I honestly wouldn't have had to with Mom there. She was all over it."

"Good," I said, spreading my fingers over his chest. "You can't ignore anything."

He lifted his hand to my hair and combed his fingers through it, a thoughtful expression on his face. "I know, baby. I won't."

There's no explaining how it felt to be called that. I melted right there. If I didn't get this day going soon, I'd end up doing exactly what he wanted. What we *both* wanted.

"Come on," I said, grabbing his hand and pulling him with me.

He left his crutch by the counter and limped along beside me. He was putting more weight on his leg and the improvement was remarkable. I was anxious to see what his doctor would say.

"Please tell me you're taking me to my bed," he pleaded.

I smiled. "I am. But it's only so we can get your therapy over with today."

He groaned, but stayed with me, entwining his fingers with mine. Holding hands wasn't supposed to be so exciting, but it was with Merrick. His capable hands had held weapons and fought enemies. To feel that kind of power wrapped around me was marvelous.

When I sat him on his bed, he grabbed my hips and brought me between his legs. "You sure you don't want to make out for a while?"

It was awfully tempting, especially when he looked so hopeful. But his recovery was more important than my desperation for his touch.

"We've got work to do, then I promise we can relax for a bit."

He smirked, bouncing his eyebrows up and down. "I like the sound of that."

I laughed and shook my head. "You're impossible."

"You like it."

"Shut up and give me your leg."

"Oh, she's bossy. You've been holding out on me, Grace Samuelson."

The heat in my face was overwhelming. This was the Merrick I knew so long ago. Playful and happy. Always trying to make someone laugh.

I slowly lifted his leg and started the movements we had been doing for a good week. When I turned the effort over to him, he was lifting his leg higher than ever before and he didn't look as strained as he usually did.

"Looks like it's *you* that's been holding out on me, Merrick Thatcher. Where did this determination come from?

He grunted as he dropped his leg for a short rest. "I don't know what you're talking about."

The smirk on his face was a dead giveaway.

"Oh my God. You *have* been holding back. Why?"

"Maybe I wanted your hands on me more than I wanted to walk on this thing. So, I might have faked it a bit."

I didn't know what to say to that. It excited me and worried me all at once. There was no question Merrick wanted to be back to one-hundred percent. He complained about it endlessly in the beginning. I wanted him to progress, but knowing he sacrificed a little of that just to be close to me was a turn-on.

If that made me pathetic, then I was a hot, pathetic mess.

"What are you thinking, Grace?"

I watched him complete another rep before, lifting his pant leg to check the scars over his shin. He wasn't near as self-conscious about it as he used to be, but I still felt his muscles tense when I touched the raised skin with my fingers.

"Any pain today?"

"Not there."

I glanced up to see the hungry expression he was sending my way. "Then where?" I whispered.

"Tell me what you're thinking about and I'll let you kiss it better."

I rolled my eyes, ignoring his panty-dropping smile, but I was too aroused not to play along. "I was thinking about what could possibly make you hold back from your progress just so I could touch you more."

His smile faded and in its place was a baffled frown. "Are you serious?"

I shrugged, "It's a valid inquiry."

I pulled his pant leg down and moved to his side, lifting his shirt and shifting his pants to check the scars at his hip. He sat up and grasped my hand.

"Are we done with exercises for today?"

"Umm, no, but if you need a break then–"

"Good."

With that, he yanked me down beside him until I was sprawled out on his chest.

"What are you doing? Be careful, Merrick."

"Grace, I'm a grown man. I know what causes me pain and what doesn't, and you, babe, are causing me pain."

I lifted up onto my elbow and tried to climb off the bed, but he wouldn't let me.

"Not that kind of pain, although, where your leg is at could be considered blissful pain."

I looked down at my leg, nestled between both of his and pressing up against his left thigh. "Oh."

"Yeah, oh."

I tried to move away again, but he wasn't having it.

"You stay right here or you'll end up on your back, and I promise you, once I get started, you won't want me to stop, and I *won't* be stopping."

Hottest thing I've ever heard.

I played with that idea a little in my head and Merrick started laughing, drawing my gaze. He was so handsome. His jaw, even covered in stubble, looked strong and defined. His Adam's apple bounced as he laughed and never before had I ever wanted to kiss that part of a man until now.

"God, Grace. You have no idea how incredibly sexy you are. I can practically hear the thoughts running through your head and it's driving me crazy."

"It is?"

"Yes. You do that a lot."

"Do what?"

"Drive me crazy."

"How?"

He sighed, tucking me against his side as he sat back against the headboard. It was comfortable being pressed up against him with his arm around my shoulders. I didn't want to move away, even if I really should.

"Well, your smile for one thing."

"Excuse me?"

He chuckled, kissing my forehead and inhaling deeply. Every minute that passed made me fall for him a little more. This silly side of Merrick sent warmth stretching through my chest. His smile was real and striking. A smile that made a girl shiver when it was directed at her.

"I hear it all the time," he shrugged.

"You hear me smile?"

"Of course I do." When I didn't say anything, he added, "I guess it's not something people really think about much until they need to. I do because there's no other way for me to read people."

"So, you know when I'm smiling and when I'm not."

He nodded. "I'm best at hearing *you*. It's beautiful because you smile so much, even when you don't want to. But I know the difference between your fake smile and the real one. The real one ... well, let's just say it gets me going."

I shook my head, a dry laugh leaving my mouth. "You wouldn't feel that way if you could see me. I might smile a lot, but I'm not your usual type."

His arm constricted when he sat up straighter. "And what would you say is my usual type."

"I don't know," I pondered with a frown. "Not me. Maybe someone like Keara or Jen. They're so outgoing and pretty. Skinny and flawless."

"You think I want flawless," he stated, a deep line forming between his brows.

I sighed. I'd already screwed this up because I couldn't just take a damn compliment these days. His history didn't really lend a hand either. I'd seen the girls he spent his time with back in the day. Why would that change now?

"I don't know, Merrick."

"Listen. Don't get me wrong, I'm sure Keara is wonderful and I know Jen is great. To be such good friends of yours, they would have to be. But let me make myself clear. I don't want a flawless woman. I don't want *them* and I don't want someone that's plastic and fake all the time. Maybe when I was younger, I went for that kind of thing because I didn't know any better. To be frank, my dick guided me everywhere."

"I'm not saying–"

"I know," he cut in, kissing my forehead again to soften the interruption. "I just want you to understand that things have changed for me. Not just since you've been here, but before that. I know in my gut that you're beautiful because I feel it every time you're near me. I know you have one of the biggest hearts out of all the women in this town, and I *know* you've experienced more suffering than many could claim. I see it. I see *you*, Grace."

He was getting too close to the fragile cracks I'd been keeping hidden, but no one had ever said anything like that to me. It was hard to keep him out, especially when I was in uncharted territory here.

"And you didn't deserve what you went through," he added, tenderly.

I sat up, feeling my chest crack a little more. The vulnerability I fought back every day, came roaring through me. "What do you mean?" I asked, my voice unsteady.

Merrick kept his arm around me, following me up, not letting me get any farther away from him than I already was. "It means that if anyone can understand what you went through, it might be me. At least, I'll *try* to understand."

"I don't know what you're talking about, Merrick. I think maybe–"

"I wouldn't have walked away, Grace. Not like he did."

My breath caught in my lungs, burning. Dizziness swam through my head and I shut my eyes to focus on the deep breath I needed so badly.

He knew.

"I would have held you for days, as long as it took for both of us to feel whole again. I would have done anything to comfort you and let you know it would be okay," he declared.

The stinging started in my nose until just breathing in and out hurt. My vision went blurry as moisture filled my eyes. "I ... I don't ..."

"I overheard you and Keara talking the other night. I'm sorry I didn't say anything, I just didn't want you to think I was a creep."

I took a deep breath, blowing it out slowly in an attempt to control the sobs rising in my chest. Why did it have to hurt so bad no matter how much time passed? I was stronger because of it, but the wound still felt so fresh.

"I didn't even choose a name for her," I whispered, the dam cracked a little more and my heartache started to seep out of walls that only weakened over time.

They say time heals all wounds, and maybe it does. But some wounds get re-opened too often. They're poked and prodded until it's time to close them again. The problem is, most of the time, whatever stitched them up just wasn't strong enough.

Merrick pulled me to his side as he leaned back in the bed. His lips pressed against my hair as I curled into myself. "I couldn't give her a name when all I felt was pain. I wanted it to be special, but the only thing I could think of was how short the time was that I got to hold her."

I could barely hear my own voice, but I knew Merrick heard my soft whispers. It was so quiet in the room, as if the world around us stopped everything for this moment. The moment I finally faced what I only briefly touched on before.

"She was supposed to be my saving grace. She was supposed to change everything for me. Even if Jason left anyway, she was going to be the one person I fought for. The one person that made me want to keep going."

Merrick tightened his hold around me while my body trembled with the need to cry. "But then she was gone," he said against my hair, speaking the words that had already tumbled through my head.

I squeezed my eyes shut, trying to picture her again. That small tuft of dark brown hair on the top of her soft head. The dimple she had in her chin, even when she was so still. The birthmark on her shoulder, same as mine. The images had faded over the last year, but I could still see her and feel her.

"She didn't need a name, because she was you," he muttered. "A Grace the world just wasn't ready for."

I nodded, knowing in my heart that God was holding my baby in his arms and taking care of her tiny spirit.

"Where is she now?"

I swallowed, remembering the need to scream when I was asked what I wanted to do with the body. By that time, Mom was already with me and she made all the arrangements. "She's buried in the North Morgan Cemetery. I haven't gone to see her yet, but I need to. No matter how much time passes, it still hurts as much as it did then. But I know now that just because she's gone, doesn't mean she didn't change my life. I'm a better person because of her. I've felt unconditional love."

I took a few deep breaths and turned to face Merrick whose expression hit me deep. That connection we had to each other wasn't just from a lifetime of acquaintance; it was from months of tragedy circling around in our minds and peeking out every corner.

We both felt broken and scattered, but we wanted to hold the other together more than we wanted to fix ourselves. And maybe that was wrong, but for now, it was all we had to give each other.

It was helping.

Merrick was being tortured by the memory of those men lost in battle and he would feel that for a long time.

"Just because they're gone, Merrick, doesn't mean they didn't change lives."

He nodded and pressed his lips together in a tight line. "They died heroes. I won't take that away from them," he stated.

Silence surrounded us as we let the thoughts of our pasts drift away. It wasn't a long discussion about our feelings or the things we just couldn't get through, but it was one perfect, unbreakable stitch tied in place.

We stayed on that bed for a couple hours, holding each other, kissing, laughing. He explained what he told my father about his eye and that Dad said he would look into what it could mean. He'd been experiencing sensitivity more and more each day for short periods of time. I didn't know what it meant, but I knew it was something he didn't want to think about. Not yet.

Our conversation quickly moved to lighter things. Family, old friends, likes and dislikes. Merrick surprised me. He was rough and intimidating, but he could be playful when he wanted to be. What surprised me, was how easy it actually was to talk to him. He listened.

When he asked me what I planned to do in the future, I had an unfortunate realization. "I don't know what my future holds, but I do know I need to be released from my job."

Merrick looked surprised, but understanding. "So, is it because I chased you off or because you can't keep your hands out of my pants?"

I laughed, rolling my eyes because of course it would come down to *that*.

"I'm serious," he chuckled. "If it's because you hate the job, then I'll do better. But if it's a conflict of interest, I totally understand. I don't want you risking your job because you can't keep your lips off of me."

"Oh really? And who says I can't resist?" I teased.

He puffed out his chest and smirked, "Please. You've been groping me since the beginning."

I smacked his stomach and he turned to kiss me. What started out as teasing, quickly turned into passion. He kissed me slowly, savoring every movement of our lips. I was a dizzy, panting mess by the time he pulled away, only to drag me up against him from chest to toes.

I don't remember falling asleep. Only that I was too comfortable to keep my eyes open. A tortured sound woke me, making my eyes pop open to evening light shining through the window. I heard the sound again and my heart started pounding. Merrick's arm tightened around me to the point of pain and I had to use all of my strength to push him away enough to unravel myself. He was covered in sweat, his breathing erratic.

"Merrick."

His head turned back and forth, and his hands balled into fists. This is what it looked like. Watching him feel what happened, without a fever or anything else forcing his body to fight it. This was all his mind.

Not like that night of the fireworks when I found him shaking with fear. This wasn't something that tricked his mind into thinking he was in danger. This was living it all over again.

"Merrick."

"Ryan," he mumbled. His entire body shifted toward me, almost knocking me off the bed.

I leaned over him and tried to hold his head still. "Merrick. You're dreaming. Wake up, Mer. It's just a dream. You're here with me."

I repeated the mantra several times with no result. If anything, his jerky movements only got stronger.

"Ryan, cover," he groaned. "Where are you?"

His arms lifted to cover his crumpled face. The sounds he made, were frightening. I couldn't pull him out of this. Only he could.

I stayed over him, ignoring the ache from his arms bumping into mine. Then, I sang, hoping whatever darkness he found himself in, he would have the strength to climb out and come back to me.

The words of the song, *'An Attempt to Tip the Scales'* by *Bright Eyes*, seemed a little harsh for that moment, but it was the reality of life. Suffering doesn't stop by just waving your hand and hoping. It comes back whenever it wants to, when we least expect it. We just have to focus on the details that are the most important. The ones that are *worth* seeing. We push through it, making an attempt to balance the pain with the beauty.

As I sang, Merrick slowly started to still. Whether that was because of me, or because the nightmare was ending, I didn't know. I wasn't going to stop until he was calmed down, though, so I sat back against the headboard and tried to pull him into my side. His arm came away from his face and rested across my hips, but his eyes were still closed.

"Grace?"

"I'm here, Mer."

He turned his face into my stomach and his arm tightened around me, pressing into my back with his fist, just to hold on.

"Shh, I've got you. You're here with me. Nowhere else but here."

It was in that moment his shoulders started to quake. I felt every bit of loss I'd experienced, shift around to make room for his. Because if anyone was going to take a piece of that burden, it was going to be me.

Chapter Sixteen

Merrick

I tried to steady my breathing, counting through each breath like I practiced so many times before. It didn't help. I couldn't hold it back anymore. The flood of fear, pain, and grief was just too powerful to deflect.

Grace let me bury my face against her stomach. A safer place than where I'd been. Her fingers combed through my hair while she hummed, attempting to calm me. I clung to her like a child to his mother. Like a lost man clings to the memory of home.

Grace was my home.

Her hands moved down my neck to my shoulders, lightly drifting her fingers back and forth as I counted breaths.

I didn't even realize I'd fallen asleep when the dream hit, so fast. One minute, I was safe, wrapped around Grace, and the next ... I squeezed my eyes shut tightly, but the things I saw were still there. If only I could be blind in sleep, too. My mind just wouldn't let me forget.

Grace didn't speak. Her hums softened and her hands stilled, but she didn't push for anything.

Breathe in. Breathe out.

"Merrick?"

I wanted to stay right there, with a clear mind; only Grace to worry about and worship. The images didn't go away, though. The only way to free my mind from all the shit, was to get it out in the open. Like she did.

"It was just another standard day, as far as standard went," I started, swallowing the lump in my throat and resting my cheek against Grace's stomach. "We rolled out like any other morning after our PCCs and PCIs."

She leaned forward and kissed the top of my head, unknowingly giving me the comfort I needed, to tell her what happened.

"It was just another day."

Mom and Dad didn't even know. I'd never been capable of telling *anyone*. So, when it all came to the surface, there was no way to hold it back. Not when it had been eating at me every single day.

"The trip usually took a couple hours depending on what we ran into. I was in the passenger seat as commander, Eric was driving, and Ryan was gunner. Just like always. Darius was talking about some chick that started writing him a couple months before, and the rest of us were just laughing along. As if that was the only worry we had."

It was the first red flag I should have seen. If you get too relaxed, shit happens. Every. Single. Time.

"Eric hit the brakes, hard, and we all shut our mouths. It was Darius who asked what the hell was going on because it wasn't an expected stop. I called in to the rest of the convoy to hold until we straightened it out. And Eric." *Deep breath in.* "He just looked at me. No words. I remember his skin was so pale, even more than normal, like he'd seen a ghost. I'll never forget what that kind of fear looks like. He'd seen it before the rest of us even had a chance. He always saw trouble first, that's why he was the driver."

Grace's fingers came back to my hair and I shut my eyes, the soothing touch helping me ground myself. My voice felt like sandpaper, every breath taking a massive effort.

"Everything happened so damn fast, Grace. I saw the fear on Eric's face a split second before that reflection shined in my eyes and I knew. It was a signal. I didn't even get a full breath in before the impact."

"What was it?" Grace asked softly.

"An EFP. Explosively Formed Projectile. It's just an inverted copper plate in a fucking can, with explosives. The design is what makes it so deadly. A molten kinetic missile. It hit the driver's side perfectly and Eric was just ... gone. That thing burned through everything. I thought I was dead. No way I survived that giant, fiery hole in the front of an armored vehicle. But I did and I felt the burning more than the damage to my side." I dropped a hand down to my ribs, remembering the burn spreading over my skin. "I didn't even know my leg was broken, not until I found Ryan hanging over the side of the MRAP. By then, the adrenaline was flowing so fast, I could have been hit again and never have felt a thing.

"I dragged Ryan for fifty feet with my broken hand. I had to shove my fingers under his vest and use whatever strength I had left in my arm. They'd already started firing. Every hit against my vest knocked me down. But I had to get Ryan out of there. It was the only thought I could process. *'He's gotta see his daughter'.*"

I remembered the pain finally registering the second we collapsed behind the second truck. Once I was down, there was no getting back up. I tried and maybe that's what frustrates me most. I tried, but I couldn't. The dust in the air from bullets hitting the earth all around us, the heat from the flames, the screams; I wanted to fix it. But I couldn't.

"I planned to go back for Darius, but he was already gone and the MRAP lit up like the Fourth of July," I explained to her, my voice strained, re-living the despair I'd felt in that moment.

Grace breathed with me, rubbing my shoulders once more to release the tension that overwhelmed me. Her fingers never left me.

"You wouldn't think there's a sound when metal melts, but there is. It's a sizzle at first, then a loud groaning screech, like a giant just reached down and slowly crushed everything with his fingers. Then it all collapses in on itself. I heard the roar of flames mixed with the medevac lines being called out. I heard them so clearly and saw the panic on some of the faces around me and I knew. There was a chance we weren't going to be saved."

"You could still see at that point?"

I nodded. "The last thing I saw was the fire and Ryan, bloody and unconscious. Then it all went dark. I saw just enough to feel the end coming. Just enough to feel how useless I was."

"Merrick."

"I know. I know it's wrong, but it's the truth."

She slid down the bed until the warm puffs of her breath touched my cheek. Cupping my face, she kissed me, soft and slow. It didn't come close to the passionate kisses we shared before falling asleep, but it was just as powerful.

"It's okay, Merrick. It's okay to feel weak and vulnerable sometimes."

I started to shake my head, but she kissed me again and took my mind somewhere else.

"It makes us stronger," she declared, pressing her forehead to mine. "It prepares us for what's coming."

"And what's coming?"

"More. But we don't let it break us completely. We fight through it, even when we feel the end. We cry and scream and get angry, but we don't give up."

I swallowed, feeling a warmth rise up in my chest as she spoke. "How did I not see you before, Grace?"

Instead of answering, she kissed me again, but it was me that took over. I didn't want an answer and I didn't want to talk anymore. I just wanted her.

I traced her lips with my tongue, urging her to open for me, and she did. She arched her back, pressing her warm, soft body against mine. I rolled on top of her, balancing on my elbows so I wouldn't crush her and pressing my knee between her legs. It hurt, but I didn't care. It was worth the pain.

I slid my hand down her side, over her hip to the back of her thigh, lifting her leg to wrap around my hip. Grace whimpered and started to rock back and forth, pressing harder against my knee. I broke away from her lips with a groan and kissed my way down to her neck, burying my face there as I tasted her. She continued to move against my knee, her breaths quicker the closer she came to release.

It was the sexiest thing I ever experienced; Grace using me to pleasure herself. I wanted more.

Moving my hand back up over her ass, I grinded my hips against her. I wanted inside that tight body, but she was too far gone and I didn't want to stop. She was close. No way I'd take that away from her.

She wrapped her arms around my shoulders, moving faster. The uninhibited moan that left her mouth, made me dizzy with arousal. I was hard as steel and pressed against her stomach. How long had it been for me? Too long. I wasn't going to last.

I kept my knee right where she wanted it and lifted onto my arms. I wanted to watch her, to see her come on my leg. I wanted to see if her face flushed scarlet and what her lips looked like when she cried out. But I couldn't. Not with my eyes.

So, I slowly moved my hand up her body, cupping her breast briefly to feel it fill my hand. Perfect. When I found my way to her neck, I wrapped my fingers around her, feeling her raspy breaths pull in and out.

"Merrick," she whispered. "I'm going to–"

"I want to feel it, Grace." I pushed my knee forward a little more, her breath catching as her hips lifted.

"Yes."

I glided my fingers, as gently as I could, up her neck, over her chin, finding her lips. Her hot breath fanned my fingers, and her lips opened wider as I traced them. I pressed my knee forward even more and her hands gripped the back of my shirt when she cried out.

That soft skin heated against my fingers and I couldn't stop my grin. I closed my eyes and pictured her cheeks, a dusty rose color. They had to be. Every muscle in her body tightened, then released, wave after wave making her gasp.

A growl rippled up my chest when she came, electricity slithered up my spine. I couldn't stop it, didn't want to. I came hard, collapsing on top of Grace once it was over.

Her arms wrapped around my shoulders as she breathed with me, taking my weight. I finally shifted to the side and buried my face in her neck, inhaling that sweet scent of her, now mixed with mine.

We laid there for a long time. Fully clothed, quiet, and unmoving.

Safe.

"They're here!"

I heard the voice, loud and clear, as we passed through the gate at Keara's house on Sunday afternoon. I held Grace's hand as she quietly guided me across the grass. No crutches today. Almost six weeks on them was enough for me. I was still limping, but the pain was minimal. A cool autumn breeze slid over me and the smell of grilled meat reached my nose.

The last barbeque I'd been to was in Iraq, with the smoldering desert sun beating down on me. The meat was overcooked and the only sides available at the time were beans and canned potatoes. Enjoying an afternoon like that didn't come easy. Not when all of our ears were listening for that crackling whistle from an incoming mortar.

Obviously, a barbeque in a friend's backyard, smack dab in the middle of Morgan, Utah, would be a lot nicer. Peaceful.

So, I tried to relax. Ignoring the misplaced worry that a part of me just didn't want to release. The part that waited for the peace to be taken away. Any minute now.

"Breathe," Grace whispered, pressing closer to my side.

She understood now. All those emotions and frustrations I experienced whenever we left the house, were very near the surface. Sometimes they were impossible to hold back.

"Welcome, Merrick," a male voice greeted.

Grace stopped, but kept her hand in mine. It was frustrating, not being able to get a good look at the people in that backyard, but I trusted Grace.

This wasn't the desert. These weren't enemies.

"Merrick, this is Josh and Keara," Grace chimed, squeezing my fingers.

I held out my other hand and waited for someone to take it. "Nice to finally meet you. I remember you, back in the day, Josh." A firm grip slowly bobbed my hand up and down.

"So glad you're here," Josh said before releasing the handshake. "It's been a long time."

I dropped my arm, but it was snatched up by a tiny hand and tugged forward.

"Oh my God. I can't believe Merrick Thatcher is at my house."

Keara. No doubt.

"Hey now," Josh grumbled.

"It's fine, sweetie. He's taken anyway," Keara giggled, holding my hand a little longer than what was considered normal.

"She's impossible," Josh mumbled when Keara finally released me.

Grace pressed closer to my side and I lifted my arm to wrap it around her shoulders. She slid right into place and wrapped her arm around my waist. "I *am* taken, but it's nice to finally meet you, Keara." I stated.

"Good. Don't be a dick and we'll get along just swimmingly."

My laugh came so suddenly, reaching deep in my gut. No wonder Grace loved her friend so much. She was very entertaining.

"I promise to not be a dick," I smiled, winking awkwardly since I had no idea if my eyes were even pointed at her.

She hummed another giggle anyway. "Then have a seat. The burgers are almost ready."

"Thanks, Keara," I nodded.

Her sigh held a hint of awe. "Merrick Thatcher."

I guess Grace was telling the truth when she told me about her and Keara having a crush on me so many years ago. I smiled, giving her the one that made Grace hold her breath. Keara didn't disappoint.

"Okay, Casanova, come sit with me," Grace chuckled, pulling me to the side and helping me into a chair.

Once I was settled in, I felt like I could focus on everything else. Grace introduced me to Gary and Christie, then Michael and Jen. All of them said they were excited to finally meet me and they were glad to see me doing well.

It was surprising.

I expected more hesitation than I got, especially when I knew damn well my scars weren't pretty. They had to have questions, but all of them seemed to want to know about *me*, not what happened.

At last, I was able to completely relax by the time we started eating. The conversation turned to the Colson brothers and what they had all been up to. Grace and the other women talked about wedding shit while Josh told me about his training to be a paramedic.

He told me he knew a few medics who served in Iraq at the same time as me. Turns out, the world is a lot smaller than I imagined.

Two of the men on the same convoy, were good friends of his. They returned home recently and, instead of the anxiousness I usually felt thinking about that day, it was pride. Pride in the men that fought with me and honor to have served beside them.

That was a new one. Something I figured I lost when I came home injured.

"We'll have to get together with them sometime whenever you're up for it," Josh suggested.

"Sounds good," I replied, genuinely.

Grace's hand landed on my thigh and I sat up straighter. She hadn't left my side the whole afternoon, and every brush of her arm or touch of her hand sent my blood racing.

After that moment in my room, I couldn't keep my hands off of her. We didn't discuss what happened and we didn't need to. No awkwardness followed and, if anything, it only made me want her more.

"So, Merrick," Keara remarked. "What are you going to do when you're healed up?"

"What do you mean?"

"Well, do you need to finish up some schooling? Or are you going to find a job at the base?"

I'd never even thought about that. Grace and I had talked about what we wanted, but the biggest thing was whether or not I wanted to travel or master Braille.

The job I had before my deployment was no longer an option. Hell, a lot of jobs were no longer an option. It was just another thing I'd given up on without even thinking about it.

"I have no idea," I said, a little hesitantly.

"Well, I'm sure they've got jobs at the base you can do."

"I don't know."

"Why not?"

Grace's hand moved to mine. "Have you thought about what you're going to do?"

I shook my head. "Being blind has its drawbacks."

"I get it," Grace smiled. "Doesn't mean it has to stop you."

I pondered that conversation the rest of the day. Was it possible to get a job and somehow provide for myself? Taking one day at a time, didn't really leave a lot of room for planning. Plus, I'd accepted that whatever future I could give to Grace, it wouldn't be extravagant, but I'd make up for it by being the kind of man she could be proud of. Any way I could.

Maybe I didn't have to just *accept* it. Maybe I was wrong. Just maybe, I could embrace it.

"You've been quiet," Grace declared as we pulled into the driveway later that evening. "Did I say something wrong?"

"No, not at all," I reassured her. "If anything, you and Keara made me think."

"About what?" She turned the ignition off and waited.

"About what the future holds. I never thought about a job or what I could still do. It just wasn't a possibility."

"And?"

I sighed, reaching across the console to find her hand. "And I'm looking forward to it."

I knew she was smiling, but she lifted my hand to her face anyway. I felt her lips stretching up, then she kissed my fingers. "Good."

We made our way inside my house, and the sexual tension I'd felt all day, came to a head. We were alone and I was suddenly eager to have a repeat of Friday.

I am a man after all.

Grace shut the front door behind us and I stopped fighting it. I could hear her surprise when I backed her up against the door. Her hands lifted to my chest, her breath whooshing out when I stepped closer and roughly pressed our bodies together. I felt her hands come around my neck as I leaned in to kiss her.

She curled her fingers in my hair, pulling me closer as our lips moved together. I pressed my hands into the cold wood at either side of her head and deepened the kiss. She arched her back, pressing into me like she always did, setting my skin on fire.

"Fuck, Grace. I want you so bad right now."

Her whimper slid against my lips, then she threw her head back as I licked and nipped at the soft skin of her neck. I could stay there forever, tasting Grace while she was wrapped around me. I snaked my arms around her waist and lifted her off the ground, feeling a twinge in my leg and not caring in the slightest.

"Merrick, wait."

Her breathless voice barely registered in my mind, but I found the strength to stop. "What is it?"

"I don't want you to hurt yourself."

"Believe me, it's worth the pain," I growled and dove in for another taste of her neck, making a path down to her exposed collar bone.

"Oh, God."

"You can call me Merrick," I mumbled, biting gently at her skin.

She let out a breathy laugh and pulled away as much as she could with the door pressed against her back. "Merrick, we can't."

I sighed, setting her feet on the floor and giving her neck one last kiss. "I forget the reason," I admitted.

"I'm still your nurse and even though I wasn't on duty today, I don't want to risk–"

"Got it. I understand," I cut in. "So, you're fired."

"Excuse me?"

"I just fired you."

"You can't– "

"Oh, I think I can."

"Merrick."

"Grace."

She made a frustrated sound which only made me smile. She was so damn sexy when she was aggravated and there was even a tiny stomp from her foot.

I pressed my forehead to hers, kissing the tip of her nose.

"I'll call the hospital tomorrow morning and ask for an official release," she said.

I couldn't resist. "I can give you an official release right here and it will only take a few minutes."

She laughed, throwing her head back enough for me to dive back in for more. She loved when I kissed her neck. I couldn't get enough of it.

"Please, Merrick."

I shifted on my feet and adjusted my pants. "Okay. I'll stop, but it's causing me a lot of pain."

"Where?" she asked, looking down at my leg.

"Not there. And not the bad kind of pain either." I stuck my bottom lip out in a playful pout and she pulled it between her lips and bit down. She knew exactly what that was doing to me, but before I could do anything about it, she pressed her hands against my chest and gently pushed me away.

"Goodnight, Merrick," she said breathlessly. Then she was gone; out the door before I could make the switch from one brain to the other.

I raked my fingers through my hair and painfully walked to my room a few minutes later.

What hit me then, wasn't sexual frustration. Though, I was feeling a lot of that. And it wasn't disappointment, either, even if my hard on *was* feeling *that*.

It was pure and utter happiness. A resolution.

I loved Grace and I wasn't going to wait any longer to tell her.

Chapter Seventeen

Grace

Why did I insist that I would be able to sleep?

I glanced at the clock for the thousandth time in just a few hours.

12:30 AM.

My entire body still felt Merrick pressed against it. Every inch of my skin was still tingling from his touch. I was desperate for *something*. Anything.

I stared up at the dark ceiling of my room, debating on whether or not I was completely crazy or just stupid.

Stupid.

I'd just walked away from the sexiest man I'd ever known. One who was ready to give me what I wanted without needing to ask for it. And for what? Because I thought it was a risk to my job.

Who does that?

Apparently, I do. And now, I was suffering the consequences.

The truth was, I was nervous. The last time I'd been with a man, I was several weeks pregnant and he was an asshole. Merrick would be different, but damn if I couldn't just let go and do it already.

Silently cracking my window open the second I walked into my room, I had listened to Merrick move around. Of course, I didn't hear much, but I saw his shadow. Those shoulders, broad and strong. His chest, so hard and muscular. I knew he undressed to go to bed and his body was mouthwatering.

It was torture, knowing he was almost naked and so close.

Closing my eyes, I moved my hand beneath the sheets and lightly glided my fingers down my stomach. Maybe if I could find a small release, I'd be able to sleep. I didn't realize I was practically panting until I heard Merrick's voice come through my window.

"You're not allowed to touch yourself, Grace," he growled. "Not tonight."

I let out a frustrated groan, pulling my hand out of the sheets. I didn't need to ask how he knew. It was obvious I couldn't control myself. "Why not?"

"Because *I* want it."

I closed my eyes, arching my back off the bed and squeezing my legs together. It only made it worse.

"Is it strange that I can still feel your skin under my fingers?" he asked, roughly. "I'd be climbing through your window right now if I could."

"What would you do?" I asked, breathlessly.

"Mmmm," he rumbled. "I'd kiss you first, until you were dizzy, just like you make me feel."

I exhaled slowly, already feeling the blood rushing down my body.

"Then I'd spend a long time learning every inch of your skin. I'd touch you everywhere, taste you everywhere. Then, when you were ready, soaking wet and begging for it, I'd pin you to the bed and shove my cock inside of you. I'd make you come over and over again. All night."

I was out of my bed before he'd finished the last two words, slamming the window closed before scurrying out of my bedroom. I made it into the hallway and tiptoed to the foyer.

I wasn't going to wait any longer.

As soon as the front door clicked shut, I all but ran across the front yard, barefoot and in nothing but my boy short panties and a thin spaghetti strap shirt. I made it to Merrick's front door in a matter of seconds. Breathless and aroused.

He was waiting for me.

The door swung open, revealing Merrick in nothing but his boxer briefs, that perfect V at his hips and those powerful legs keeping him steady. Hunger overtook his face and a massive bulge tented between his legs. I swallowed thickly as I stepped inside, just inches from him.

"I can feel you without even touching you, you know that?" he whispered. "Every nerve in my body goes on alert when you're near me."

I let out a harsh breath, heat rising in my cheeks, and suddenly, the door slammed shut and he was on me. Holding my face in his hands and kissing me ravenously. I briefly worried about his leg when his hands dropped to my ass and lifted me off the ground. He didn't flinch with discomfort. If anything, he looked more relieved than pained. I wrapped my legs around his waist and my back hit the door once more.

"Christ. What are you wearing?" he sputtered as his fingers slid to the hem of my boy shorts and underneath.

The grip of his rough fingers on my bare skin forced me to bite my lip to keep from crying out. He pressed his hard stomach between my legs and took my lips in another greedy kiss. I'd been wet for hours. No doubt he could feel it, but it didn't stop me from rocking against him, searching for the right pressure.

He grunted against my lips, pressing me harder into the door to pin me with his hips. When I was steady, he slid his hands up my sides, taking my tiny shirt up with them. The cool air hit my skin and his hot fingers left a trail of goose bumps behind. My nipples ached the closer he came to them and finally, with a harsh breath, he cupped my bare breasts in his massive hands.

"Fucking perfect."

"Please, Merrick," I begged. For what? I didn't know.

Anything.

Everything.

I whimpered as his hands left my breasts to tear my shirt over my head. Both of us moaned with relief once we pressed together, skin to skin. My sensitive nipples slid against his chest, making me wild. I gripped onto his shoulders, feeling the scarring beneath my right hand. He didn't flinch anymore when I touched him. The scars didn't matter to either one of us.

"Hold onto me, baby."

I wrapped my hands around his neck and held on tight. He turned, a determined look on his face while he counted his steps. We both laughed when we bumped into a wall, but within seconds, we were in his room and he was dropping to sit on the bed with me straddling him.

All laughter died out when he pulled my hips forward, a gasp leaving my lips at the feel of his hardness pressing against me. Then his hands returned to my breasts, slowly finding their way. The anticipation of his touch made me shift forward, offering myself up to him. When his head dropped to my chest, I held my breath, crying out as his lips wrapped around my nipple.

His hands never stopped moving. He found every rib, every dip and curve. He was everywhere. I took my turn, scratching my finger nails across his back, feeling that ripple of muscle when I did.

When his hand came to a stop, directly over my heart, he leaned back. We were both panting, frantic for more.

"Can I have this?" he asked, pressing his hand against my chest and making me pause.

Happiness, pure and simple, overwhelmed me.

My heart.

The muscle in his jaw twitched and worry clouded his features. The uncertainty behind that look almost broke the very thing he was asking for.

"You already have it, Merrick."

He sighed with relief, kissed me fully, then circled his arms around my waist. Our chests were crushed together when he stood, pausing halfway to adjust his leg.

"Be careful."

"Don't worry, baby. I've got you. I can't fall with you in my arms. It's just not possible."

My heart skipped a beat. I didn't think that kind of thing really happened, but for the space of a full heart beat, everything inside of me stopped.

This couldn't be real. Nothing about this could possibly be real.

Merrick turned, staying steady on his leg, and laid me down on his bed. He shifted on top of me, adjusting his leg so he could settle between mine. He took both of my arms in his hands and firmly planted them above my head. When he was sure I wouldn't move them, he started slowly gliding his fingers back down to my ribs.

"Grace, I want you to have better. I know you *deserve* better, but I want you too much to let you go. It's worth the risk. Being able to love you is worth anything."

My eyes filled with moisture as I gazed up at him, seeing the sincerity on his face and wishing that he could see how happy he made me. His eyes were pointed down, as if he was looking slightly over my shoulder, but he was seeing me in his own way. I knew that now.

He brought his hand back to my heart and drew in a long breath. "If this is mine, I swear to you, I'll take care of it."

"I know, Mer."

I lifted my legs to wrap them around his hips again and he bent forward, holding his weight up with his left hand next to my head. The arm was practically back to normal, only giving him problems when he overused it. I turned my head to kiss his wrist. The hand over my heart came up to my face, sliding lightly over my lips, my nose, my eyes.

"I'm going to take my time, Grace. Being this close to you, touching you this way, is worth savoring."

He started slow.

The kisses that covered my face made me feel beautiful. The kisses he seared into my neck, made me feel safe. Then his fingers drifted over me, sliding back and forth over dips I didn't think were all that interesting.

Merrick found them fascinating.

"You have the softest skin," he whispered with a grin. "And you smell like sugar."

I closed my eyes as he circled my breasts.

"These feel beautiful. They fit so flawlessly in my hands."

My eyes rolled back into my head when he bent forward to take one in his mouth. He flicked my hardened nipple with his tongue, then lifted my breast to kiss the skin underneath. The skin that is only touched by the wire of a bra.

Oh God.

It was a sensation I'd never felt before. Merrick noticed. He took his time, just like he promised and his hands followed every kiss. Every bite. He counted my ribs, pushing my hands back up above my head when they came down on instinct.

"Leave them, Grace. I'm not done."

I giggled when he started over, tickling me in the most delirious way. By the time he made it to my navel, I was a mess. All I could do was breathe.

Touch is so powerful. The anticipation is potent.

He kissed the skin above my panties, spending a full minute running his mouth back and forth from one hip to the other. I released a harsh breath when his fingers finally curled under the material and slowly peeled them down, brushing against my sensitive skin.

The rumble in his chest could be felt at my toes. *This is what pure bliss feels like.*

"Bare?" he gasped.

My eyes popped open, and I lifted my head to see his face hovering above me, those shoulders straining with the effort it was taking him to hold still. "Is that–"

"The sexiest thing ever? Umm, yeah," he growled.

My response flew out the window when his lips pressed against that bare skin. Screw my job. I wasn't giving this up for anything.

"Merrick ..."

He lifted up on his knees so quickly, I was afraid he was stopping. Then he tore my panties down my legs and tossed them aside. His eyes were closed and I wondered at the disappointment he must feel not being able to see what he was doing.

I was completely off base, however, because he looked more aroused then I *felt*. Which is saying something.

"I have to see you," he stuttered.

I was only confused for a split second. Then his hands slid up the inside of my legs, so slowly, sinking behind my knees to lift and spread them open.

I knew what he meant then. I could barely catch my breath, just thinking about it.

The cool air touching my hot flesh made me shiver, but it was quickly replaced with a full-body tremble. How could someone have so much power with just a simple touch?

I gasped when his hand cupped me, putting just the right amount of pressure exactly where I needed it. It was only a moment, then his fingers drifted up and down, back and forth. Finding every inch of flesh he couldn't see. Seeing me in his own way.

Then those gentle fingers delved into my slick flesh and my hips shot off the bed.

"You're soaked, baby."

"Aaah," I gasped.

He refused to surrender, driving me to the edge before bringing me back. He circled that tiny bundle of nerves, over and over, until I was on the verge of screaming. He relented, but it wasn't his fingers that gave me relief. If you can even call it that.

I opened my eyes, only to see his head lower slightly before his hot lips wrapped around that swollen bud. His finger slid inside of me, curling up enough to make me see stars. I closed my eyes again, too turned on to really watch, my body rippling with pleasure. His low, gruff moan made it all the more gratifying, vibrating against me as he sucked, hard.

"Christ. You even taste like sugar," he whispered against my skin before removing his finger, only to add another.

After the slow build he had instigated and the constant need for just a little more, my body wasn't turning back. It was when he lifted one of my legs to rest on his shoulder, that I felt the tightening begin. He put his mouth on me again and it was over.

My body ignited and he held me *right there*, taking me further into the blaze. Spurring on the sparks of pleasure until they faded into hot embers.

I couldn't move, couldn't even open my eyes.

He kissed the inside of my thighs, breathing harshly, but patiently waiting for me to come back down.

"That was beautiful," he said, resting his cheek against my thigh.

Words wouldn't come, so I just hummed a sigh in agreement. *Exquisite*.

He slid up my body, kissing a path up the center of my chest, then lingering at my neck. He loved it there and I'd be lying if I said it wasn't my favorite place for him to be. Well, *one* of my favorite places.

I brought my hands to the back of his head, curling my fingers to hold on. He found my lips and kissed me, slow yet powerful. Like the curl of a wave just before it breaks into a rage of energy.

All day, I had felt that energy. Whenever I was beside him, all of his attention was on me. *Seeing* me like no one else did. He had looked like a man who knew that what he wanted, was right in front of him. He was just deciding how to take it.

Now, he was taking it. And I was more than willing to give it.

"Grace," he mumbled against my lips. "I want you to know something."

"Okay."

He lifted up, taking some of his weight off my chest. I watched him swallow and lick his lips nervously, that firm jaw twitching a little before he spoke. "I'm in love with you."

My fingers constricted as happiness surged through me, bringing energy to every limb and a curl to my lips.

"I've loved you since the beginning, I think," he explained, speaking slowly and intently. "You're everything I could ever want and so much more."

I cupped his face, tracing his cheek with my thumb and feeling the scar that ran across it. He was beautiful. Exquisite in every way. I moved my thumb to trace his lips. "I love you, too, Merrick."

It was a spark. It had to be. Something in his eyes that drew my attention.

Then, he blinked, and it was gone. But his smile was devastating enough to distract me.

He kissed me hard, sliding a hand down to my thigh. My mind briefly registered the need for protection when he slowly slid his boxer briefs off, but it was quickly swiped away. We were both clean. I'd read his chart and he knew he could trust me. That's why neither one of us hesitated when he positioned himself at my center.

We moved against each other, both of us pausing at the first touch and reveling in the relief of finally being there.

He pulled his hips back a little, pressing his forehead to mine. Then, he slowly surged forward, stretching me enough that I had to hold my breath to take him. He stopped, pulling back only to pitch forward once more, a groan leaving him until he was fully seated inside of me.

We stayed right there. Unmoving. The fullness overwhelming me.

His breaths fanned my face and I already felt the build. It was impossible, but that's what Merrick did to me. He awakened everything by doing nothing.

I lifted my hips to force him deeper and that was the push he needed to let go of his control. He took me hard, deep. His hands were everywhere, then planted at the sides of my head. He pushed his hips forward, forcing me up the bed, inch by inch. I met every thrust with one of my own, driving him on. Driving us both to the edge.

"Grace."

He was close, but so was I.

I felt him swell inside of me, finding places he hadn't yet reached. "Yes."

The build was quicker. A rush of liquid heat searing my veins until finally ...

I shouted his name, unable to hold it back. He swallowed my cries when he crushed his lips to mine, and he kept thrusting. In and out. Drawing out the pleasure for both of us.

A final thrust and his weight fell on top of me, his arms trembling when he tried to hold himself up. I embraced him and took all of it, because it's what I wanted.

"I love you," he whispered in my ear.

I closed my eyes and felt a hot tear slide down my temple.

This ... *this* was bliss.

Chapter Eighteen

Merrick

I knew it wasn't a dream before I even came fully awake.

The warm, soft body pressed up against me, was real. For the last five mornings, she'd been *absolutely* real. And here with me.

Her parents had a lot to say about that, but it wasn't the time. Grace had stayed with me every night that week. It still wasn't enough.

She'd gotten another job in the hospital. Instead of the actual homecare nursing, she was given a coordinating position until the patients they had scheduled for the near future, were ready. It required her whole day, but she enjoyed it and the people she worked with. Plus, she came home to me every evening.

I made some phone calls when I wasn't doing my exercises or practicing Braille. The base nearby had a few civilian positions they were excited about having me try out. One of them included counseling with other wounded soldiers and getting involved with the Special Operations Warrior Foundation that had helped my family when I was injured.

I was more than happy to be a part of it. They had funded the way for my parents to travel to Germany to see me, so I was gratefully indebted to their cause. A lot of other men needed help and so did their families. I would start the next week out getting to know them and training on what would be required of me.

In just a matter of days, the struggles from the past few months went from obstacles to stepping stones. Instead of looking down, I was finally looking forward.

All the while, Grace was with me. Encouraging me to take a chance. For the first time since I lost my sight, I felt like I wasn't a burden. I knew I could do anything, even blind.

The only thing I wanted it back for, was to see Grace. To see her smile and laugh. To see the twinkle in her eyes when she teased me. To see her body arch off the bed when I made love to her.

Her hand came to my chest and she sighed, still sleeping but staying close to me like I wanted. Even in the middle of the night I reached for her. It helped me sleep. The nightmares were still there, but waking to feel her next to me made the panic swiftly ebb. It brought light to that darkness and instead of feeling like I was about to lose my mind, I took control of it.

Most of the time, I pulled her against me and made love to her until the storm passed. She asked me about it one morning and informed me that she was more than happy to be my outlet. As each day passed, I could sense the peace lingering more and more.

What had felt like a cage, suddenly turned into ultimate freedom.

I knew it was because of Grace, but I also knew that I'd worked my ass off to get there.

"Mmm, why are you awake, babe?" Grace mumbled.

I curled my arm around her shoulder, pulling her on top of me a little more. Her legs straddled my hips and she settled in with her nose pressed to my throat.

I loved the feel of her skin against mine. It's why I made the no-clothing-in-bed rule that first morning together when she had nothing to change into but those scraps of material she showed up in.

She agreed that it was a very strict rule that should never be broken.

"Just thinking about you," I said against her hair.

"And what were you thinking?"

"That I've got a hard issue that needs to be hammered out with you," I smirked.

Her chuckle vibrated against my chest, then she lifted onto her hands. I felt her stretch her back when I latched onto her hips. She shifted on my lap, discovering the issue I was talking about.

"I like to take care of rising issues immediately," she teased.

I sat up quickly, making her yelp with surprise. Once my back was pressed against the head board, I lifted my hips and pulled her down roughly. She gasped, but kept moving against me.

She was already so wet, and feeling her slide over me sent me quickly to the point of no return. I bent my head and found her breast, licking my way to her nipple and pulling it between my lips. She clutched my head against her chest and lifted on her knees. I positioned myself at her entrance and helped her slowly sink down, engulfing me in her slick heat.

"You feel so fucking good," I muttered against her skin. "Take me hard, baby."

She did exactly what I asked. She went wild on top of me, taking control only to give it back when it became too much. I kept my grip on her hips and helped her keep a rhythm that drove us both over the edge.

She whispered my name when she came. It swiftly sent me spiraling with her.

We clung to each other for several minutes, slowing our breaths as I explored her body for the hundredth time.

I knew every inch of her. The places to touch that would make her sigh, the dips and curves that I had discovered; they were all ingrained in my memory.

I still wanted the sight of her. I wanted to know the exact color of her skin. I wanted to see the goose bumps I felt rise whenever I touched her.

But my imagination was vivid.

That would have to be enough, for now.

I was dreaming of Grace.

I didn't even know we had fallen asleep again, but Grace was riding me, her breasts swaying from her thrusts. I could imagine what she looked like above me and I could only see it in sleep. It's funny that I would truly rather touch that skin than see it.

Grace opened her mouth to cry out, her face blurry in my subconscious, but the only sound I could hear was the shrill ringing of my phone. I opened my eyes and flinched. There was still nothing, but my right eye ached, reminding me of the sensation of going from dark to light.

Grace was tucked in my arms, her face pressed to my chest and her hand over my heart again. The phone continued to ring, but she didn't move a muscle.

I must have wore her out this morning, I smiled to myself.

Shifting slowly, I carefully let her fall away from me. Her sigh was so sexy and I already felt the stir between my legs.

But the phone kept ringing.

I felt around on the nightstand and finally found the annoying plastic square. Flipping it open, I brought it to my ear. "Yeah."

"Merrick? It's Jeff."

That woke me completely. "Dr. Samuelson?"

"Yes. I'm sorry I woke you. I, um, thought Grace might answer the phone."

"Oh, no I got to it first."

Awkward.

"I'll cut right to the chase, then. I need you to come in sometime today."

I frowned, a little ball of anxiety forming in my stomach. "But I was just there a week ago."

"I know, but this is important."

I sat up, being careful not to jostle Grace too much. "What's going on, sir?"

"It would really be much easier if you came in so I could talk to you. I can contact Emma if you need me to."

"That won't be necessary, but I'd really like to know what's going on. You're making me nervous."

Jeff sighed and a rustling sound came through the phone before the sound of a door shutting. "I think I figured it out, son. After finding out what you're experiencing, I made some calls. There's a real possibility that your right eye can be corrected."

My entire body stiffened and my heart thumped wildly. "Excuse me?"

"This is why I need you to come in. I can answer any questions you have."

I might be able to see.

The idea seemed completely foreign to me. This had to be a crazy, sick twist in my dream. I scratched my fingernails over my head, tugging on my hair until pain registered.

Not a dream.

"Sir."

"I know, Merrick. Don't think. Just come in and we'll talk."

I nodded, mostly for myself. Making the decision so I wouldn't be able to back out. "I'll be there within an hour."

"Good. I'll push back the rest of my patients."

I closed the phone and raked my fingers through my hair again. My shoulders were trembling. My lungs were burning. What was happening?

And what the hell could correct my right eye? My left eye was toast, I knew that and I'd accepted it, but to see out of one eye ... it was so much better than nothing.

I opened my phone and pressed the button to call Mom. I spoke quietly, not wanting to wake Grace yet. Not until I could focus.

"Mom."

I didn't intend for my voice to quiver and she picked up on it. Nothing got past Mom. Not even when it got past me.

"What is it, sweetie? Is everything okay? Oh, God, is it Grace?"

"Yeah. I mean, no. Everything's fine. Umm, I need to get to Dr. Samuelson's. Would you mind driving me?"

"What's going on, Mer?"

I cleared my throat and shook my head. "I don't know yet, but he said he has some answers for me."

Mom didn't need to ask any questions. "I'll be there in ten minutes. Let me call in and get someone to cover for me first."

I closed my phone and set it on the nightstand. It took a few minutes to calm my racing heart. Grace still hadn't stirred.

I turned, reaching around to find her hand. Her slim fingers were heavy with sleep. I leaned over her and dragged my nose down her cheek, over her jaw, and down her neck, kissing her there. Tasting her as I slid my other hand over her waist.

"Mmm, five more minutes," she said sleepily, moving closer to me. Like a magnet. It was the same pull I felt for her.

"I have to go, baby."

She stilled. "You do?"

"Yeah, your dad just called."

I imagine her expression was a little surprised. "What? He did? What's going on?" She sat up, forcing me back so we wouldn't knock heads.

I kissed her forehead and threaded my fingers through her hair. I hated lying to her, but I didn't want her to have any false hope. Not until I knew exactly what was happening. "I don't know. But I'll find out and let you know. Okay?"

"Okay. I'm helping Keara with some wedding stuff today. She took the day off. Maybe I'll head over there a little early."

"Go back to sleep for a bit. She'll be there when you wake," I whispered, kissing her nose. "I'm just going to get dressed and head out when my mother gets here."

"Do you want something to eat?"

"No, I'm only hungry for one thing, but I can't have it right now or I'll never leave this house."

She giggled when I moved my hand under the sheet and slid my hand between her thighs. I was being completely serious.

"Be good," she gasped, contradicting her words when she lifted her hips.

"I'm always good, baby." I kissed her hard, hoping that this pit in my stomach wasn't the warning I assumed it was.

"What are you saying?"

Jeff sighed and cleared his throat, the squeak of his chair breaking through the silence in the room. It forced hair on the back of my neck to stand on end. This didn't feel real and I couldn't discern between curiosity and a disturbing alertness.

I'd just been told that Grace's father had never given up on finding a way to help my eyes. In fact, that little trip our parents made was a joint effort in finding more answers.

"I'm saying that, with surgery, there's a good chance you'll be able to see out of your right eye. Maybe not perfectly, but it's something."

Surgery. One more surgery could possibly change everything.

No. Don't hold your breath. Not yet.

"How did this happen?"

Jeff shifted in his chair with another squeak, then spoke. "That fever of yours must have made everything more sensitive. Thank God for it. The fact that you were having light sensitivity at all was the first clue."

"And the surgery?" I asked, knowing it wasn't going to be a simple one.

"Well, I'd need to make a few observations. It would pretty much be a normal cataract surgery with a few minor alterations. It's a risk, but it won't make things worse if that's what you're wondering."

"Does that mean this might be something that could eventually come back on its own?"

"No, if anything, it would only become more painful until you need surgery to correct it anyway. At least, that's my theory."

"Merrick," Mom whispered, resting her hand on my shoulder. "It's a chance. This is an easy decision."

"Is it?" I snapped, tightening my jaw to keep from saying anything worse. "I don't think so, Mom. It's hope. We all know what hope can become when the outcome doesn't end up being what we wanted."

"Son, what have you got to lose?"

Nothing.

Everything.

I had finally accepted that I was never going to be the same. I was a different man now. I had plans and expectations for myself. Blind.

This last few months was spent fighting the nightmares. Fighting the stress that invaded my mind. And now, when I finally figured out how to deal, this happened.

What if getting my sight back changed me? What if I had to face it all over again? Seeing it in my mind was one thing, but being able to see the scars and the results of what happened to me, would be another.

"Can I think about it?" I asked, ignoring the tension coming off of my mother.

"Of course," Jeff answered politely. "You take your time, son."

I stood and turned to the doorway, or what I *thought* was the doorway. Turns out it was just a wall. Mom was right behind me and helped me out of the building without saying another word.

What could she say that she hadn't already?

"Do you want to go to lunch?" she asked when we got settled in the car.

"No, thank you. I just want to go home."

"Is Grace waiting for you?"

I shook my head. She'd be well into wedding planning by now, but I'd be fine on my own. Just like she always told me I would be. And I'd finally gotten to the point where I agreed with her.

The drive was too long. Longer than it should have been because I needed to be alone. I don't even remember thinking about what was out on the road. I didn't care anymore.

I might get my sight back.

The thought made me nauseous, which only infuriated me. I should be happy about this. I shouldn't have to think about it.

Why then?

Because things had changed and I didn't want those changes to suddenly escape me.

Mom helped me inside the house and started to say goodbye, but I stopped her.

"Please, don't tell Grace."

"Why not?"

"Because. I need some time."

"Sweetie– "

"Mom, please. I don't want to give her false hope. Not until I've figured this out."

She cupped my face and kissed my cheek. "Okay, son. I'll leave it up to you."

"Thank you."

"Don't thank me yet," she replied. A pat on my chest and a tug on my shirt to straighten it, was the next thing I felt. Taking care of me like she always did. "I'll call you later. Keep your phone on you, okay?"

"I will, but before you go, will you do me a favor?" I stammered, struggling with the decisions I was making in my mind.

"Of course."

"Will you call someone for me? I don't know the number, but it's written down somewhere in my room."

"Ryan?"

I nodded, not surprised that she knew exactly what I needed to do. It was her phone he had called so many times before, trying to reach me.

I heard Mom fumble around in her purse, then the beep of her phone. She dialed the number in mine. "Just press send," she said, then hugged me tightly and left.

I found my way to the kitchen and sat down at the table. This was a long overdue conversation and I had a lot to say.

I pressed send, my hands shaking as I did, unsure if my best friend would even talk to me anymore. But I needed to try. I needed to set some things right so I could center myself in everything else.

"Hello?"

"Ryan?"

"Yeah, may I ask who's calling?"

I took a deep breath, clearing my throat so it didn't crack. "It's Merrick."

Silence.

I could only imagine what was going through his mind. I had ignored every attempt he made to contact me in the beginning, until he just stopped trying. The last time I spoke to him was in that hospital room in Germany, just minutes after I received a silver star for whatever it was the military thought I did. I hadn't hesitated to demand that he leave the room. The regret came immediately after, but I fought it.

That's how far gone I actually was at the time. I wanted nothing to do with the man I'd risked my life to save.

"Merrick. Wow, this is a surprise."

"Yeah, I know. I'm sorry about that."

"Sorry? Man, you have no reason to be sorry," he insisted. "It's totally fucked. I get it."

I wasn't the only one that had lost something in that attack. Ryan lost one of his hands and had multiple surgeries on the other, an attempt to fix his shattered fingers. The rest of his injuries were mainly superficial, with very few major burns. He also couldn't hear out of one of his ears. I didn't doubt he considered it just an inconvenience, but I knew what it was like to be missing a part of yourself.

"I don't expect you to say a damn thing, Merrick, because what can we say to each other?" he added.

"Still."

He chuckled. "Then, apology accepted. Just don't ignore me anymore and I'll forget all about it."

I shook my head, grinning because that's just who Ryan was. A forgiving fool that cared too much about me.

"I won't."

"Thank you, Merrick. For saving my life. For being strong enough to do it. I'm alive because of you."

"Ryan–"

"No, let me finish," he demanded before breathing deeply. "Miranda has her husband because of you. Charlotte has her father. There's nothing in the world you could possibly do that would stop me from being your friend. You name it, Merrick. I'm there."

There was nothing to say. We understood each other and I wasn't going to fight him.

"So," he hedged for us both, neither of us wanting to get too emotional. "Tell me how things are going. You adapting?"

I combed my fingers through my hair, remembering how long it actually took me to stop being so angry. It probably wasn't as long as others because I had one thing they didn't.

"I'm getting there, with help."

"You talking to the base counselor?"

"Not anymore. Someone better." I closed my eyes and thought of Grace.

"You met someone, didn't you?"

"Yeah. I did."

"Well, I want to meet her. If she's the one that got through your thick skull, she must be special."

I laughed. "She's pretty special."

We talked about my recovery and the therapy I did. He told me about the trouble he'd run into with his injuries and how Miranda didn't let him whine much about it.

"She's so busy with Charlotte all the time that my complaining is more like white noise," he said with a short laugh.

"You enjoying fatherhood?"

"God, yes. Every minute. I wasn't able to hold her much until recently, because of the hands. But man, hearing that little girl cry ... it's the most beautiful sound in the world."

"I bet Miranda feels differently."

He laughed, reminding me of all the times we spent doing just that. I'd had friends when I was younger, but none of them were as loyal or admirable as Ryan Warner. The man just had a way about him that could lock you in for life. There was never a bad hair on his head.

"So? Anything else you want to tell me?" he asked, bluntly.

He also knew how to get information. It was one of the skills Captain Bowman admired in our training.

"I've got a decision to make and for the life of me, I can't figure out why it's so hard."

"I'm all ears. Well, kind of."

I told him what I'd discovered only an hour earlier. Then, I told him what I was afraid of. He understood the effort it had taken to get where I was. It was a relief to know I wasn't being a complete dimwit.

"Listen up, Merrick. Just because I can't hear out of both ears, doesn't mean I can't hear. It doesn't lessen the experience, just makes me appreciate it all the more. You get your sight back in one eye, it won't change a damn thing, except what you see."

Well, when he put it that way ...

"I don't think I can go through it again. I've got plans, a life. Finally, I have a life that I can appreciate."

"I get it. I really do. But what happens after that?"

"I don't know."

"So, what do you really want? If you have plans, shouldn't you know?"

The only thing I really knew, was that I wanted Grace in my life. Forever. The short time we'd had together, changed more than seeing ever would. I also wanted that life to mean something.

"Here's an idea. How about you come down to Mona for a visit," Ryan suggested. "It's only a few hours from you. Take a breather. Give that Grace a kiss and tell her you need a minute. Come see Charlotte, have some beers, eat some junk."

"That sounds really good."

"Do you need me to come get you?"

"No," I said, shaking my head and feeling a little more relaxed. "I'll call Micah and see if he's got some time to give me a ride."

Ryan chuckled. "Good, because I want to meet that boy. Find out if he's really as smart as you say."

"Oh, he is. Believe me," I grinned. He'd proved it to me way too many times to think otherwise.

We made a few arrangements before saying goodbye. I called Micah and he agreed to drive me to Mona when he finished his shift.

I had two hours to think. Two hours to decide what to tell Grace.

I thought the decision to join the military was daunting. Thinking about telling the woman I loved that I might see again wasn't the scary part. The possibility that it might not happen; that's what terrified me. I tried so hard to push away the hope, but it was there all the same.

Me? I could find a way to handle it. But I didn't want Grace to even have to.

So, I made the dumbest decision I'd ever made. I'm a man after all. I get a few of those in a lifetime, don't I?

Chapter Nineteen

Grace

The weekend passed with only a few calls from Merrick. Mostly 'good morning' and 'good night', but I was grateful for them anyway.

He kept it short and sweet, telling me he'd see me soon and not to worry. He asked how the new job was going, told me a little about Ryan, Miranda, and little Charlotte, then told me to have a good day or sleep well.

I was ecstatic he had finally decided to see Ryan. When he called me Friday afternoon to tell me, I couldn't encourage him more. Keara stood behind me jumping up and down with happiness, too. That's how important we thought this was for him. Plus, she was just as invested in this relationship as I was.

Or so she told me.

"It's Merrick Thatcher, Grace. Don't get me wrong, Josh is my world and I love him to death, but Merrick Thatcher! If anyone deserves you, it's him."

I'd stayed so busy helping her with wedding plans, I didn't even think about how *not* seeing Merrick would actually feel. It was like a piece of me was missing while he was gone. And not because I had gotten so used to spending time with him.

Merrick was keeping something from me and I couldn't figure out what it was.

I knew it had something to do with what he discussed with my father, but no matter how many times I asked Dad to tell me what was going on, he wouldn't. He said not to worry about it and that Merrick needed to handle it on his own.

That scared me more than anything.

He could do anything on his own, but I knew what he went through and how easy it was to fall back to the dark he lived in after the attack. I also couldn't fight the feeling that it was all coming to an end. Like it did before.

Merrick wasn't Jason. But I was still me. I still had doubts no matter how hard I fought them.

Sitting at my desk in the hospital, I dropped my head in my hands. I was running on very little sleep and it was starting to get to me. Working on a Sunday was the only thing I could do to keep my mind occupied, but it was useless anyway. My mind wandered more in this small office than it did at home.

"Grace?"

I looked up to find Micah standing in the doorway with an anxious look on his face.

"Hi, Micah."

"You look horrible," he commented with a disbelieving shake of his head.

"Thank you, I feel just wonderful," I retorted, very sarcastically.

"He say anything yet?"

I shook my head and looked back down at the paperwork covering my desk. Micah came by the night Merrick left, and it was obvious from his behavior that night, he knew something I didn't. "Not a word. I know something's going on, Micah. Is it something I did? Is he hiding from *me*?"

"No. He isn't." Micah walked up to my desk and sat in the uncomfortable metal chair in front of it. He looked me directly in the eyes and firmly stated, "No way."

"Then what's going on? If it's stupid of me to feel this way, just tell me."

He sighed and rubbed a hand down his face. Micah looked a lot like his older brother, but his features were much softer. The same blue eyes shined back at me and I ached for Merrick even more. *What the hell is wrong with you, Grace?*

"He's with Ryan. They're probably spending all this time catching up. Merrick had a lot to make up for, so I'm sure he's doing what he can."

"You're probably right. I just can't help but feel like he's keeping something from me."

He nodded with a frown, then shrugged, as if he couldn't decide *what* he thought. "He'll be back by tomorrow. I'm sure of it."

"Mitch's trial is tomorrow, right?"

"Yeah. No way he'd miss that."

I sighed. Micah was right, as usual. I'd see Merrick tomorrow. "How is he getting home?"

"Ryan will bring him."

I looked back down at my desk, deciding to just go home and try to get some rest.

When I stood and lifted my purse to my shoulder, I met Micah's inscrutable gaze. Whatever it was he knew, he certainly wasn't going to tell me. I would just have to find out from Merrick himself, when he got back.

I didn't like the secrets or the evasiveness, but whatever Merrick needed from me, I would give it. Whatever it was, I was ready.

I woke early the next morning, the sound of Merrick's voice pulling me from sleep.

It reminded me of my first day back. The day I heard Merrick for the first time in years. He had been so angry that day, hurt and frustrated.

Today was different. His voice was softer, more anxious than angry, and his mother wasn't begging him to let her help.

Based on the conversation, neither one of them realized the window was open. They weren't in his bedroom, but they were speaking loud enough for me to make out what they were saying.

"Yeah, Mom. I'll tell her. Tonight."

"Good, because I can't just keep dodging the subject. I see her at work almost every day and she knows something is going on, son."

"Did you make a decision?" his father asked.

"I think so," Merrick replied.

"And?"

Silence.

The ball that had been in my stomach all weekend, expanded, and all of my worries came to a head.

Merrick *was* hiding something from me. They all were.

It hurt to think he couldn't trust me enough to talk to me. That after the turn in our relationship, he still felt the need to keep things from me. If his parents were urging him to say something, then it had to be big.

I sat up in my bed and pulled in a deep breath, calming the tightness in my stomach. "Think about this, Grace," I whispered to myself.

A decision.

Merrick had to make a decision about something and it was clearly a difficult one. I refused to consider that it had anything to do with me. I couldn't let myself go down that path. And if it did – if this was about me and Merrick – then I'd face that when the time came.

Tonight, apparently.

No. This was about Merrick. This was about something important to him and he was hesitant to let me in on it. So, I needed to give him the space he required to figure things out on his own. I couldn't solve everything for him and I knew he didn't want me to.

I had to trust *him*.

I got myself ready for the day, resisting the urge to go over there and demand they tell me what was happening. I was going to find out soon enough.

"Good morning, dear."

Mom was sitting at the counter with her giant cup of coffee in front of her and a new book.

"Good morning."

"It's nice to see you looking a little more rested," she said, her lips twisting into a wry smile.

"I still feel like I need another week," I replied, fighting to keep my shoulders straight and my eyes opened.

"Are you working today?"

"I am, but not until a little later."

"Then why are you up so early?" she asked, as if she didn't already know.

"Couldn't sleep anymore."

"Yes, well, love will do that to you."

I dropped my head forward and avoided eye contact. Mom hadn't been surprised when I told her about Merrick. In fact, she almost looked triumphant when she found out we were together. The hour she spent on the phone with Emma, afterward, was the only clue I needed to discover that they both hoped for Merrick and I to get together from the beginning.

Although, me spending my nights there wasn't really in their original plans. Merrick didn't care and had told them so. "We've both been through enough to figure out what we want," he'd said. "And to take it."

Dad was a little more hesitant to accept the relationship, but he came around when Merrick came over for dinner that last night I was with him.

"Merrick's a good man," Dad said, pulling me aside later that night. "I'm glad you're happy, Grace. I'm still your dad, though. I'll always feel that no man is worthy of you, but if anyone comes close, it's Merrick Thatcher."

It was exactly what I needed to hear at the time.

I was planning on moving out of my parents home as soon as possible. The idea was always in the plans. Once I found my feet, I would move on. Now that I had, I wanted to get myself together and be the independent woman I always wanted to be.

It's one of the things I did while Merrick was gone all weekend. Keara knew the landlord of some apartments in town and after getting a good look at them, I made the decision and submitted my deposit. All weekend, I'd been anxious to tell Merrick.

Now? I didn't know what to do.

"Is Merrick back?" Mom asked, sipping her coffee and pretending to read her book when, in reality, she was reading my every gesture and expression.

"He is," I sputtered. "I'm sure they're heading out soon. The trial starts today."

"Well, that should resolve awfully quick, don't you think? The guy who hit Mitch won't make it past the judge."

I nodded in agreement and opened the fridge to find something for breakfast. I wasn't even hungry, but I had to do *something*. There was a knock at the door and Mom stood to answer it.

"By the way, Merrick called late last night," she informed me. I whipped around to see the smirk on her face.

"He did?"

"You left your phone on the counter and you were already asleep. He said not to wake you."

"What else did he say?" I practically begged, searching the kitchen for my phone so I could see for myself that he had truly called.

Mom walked away with a chuckle.

"Mom! What did he say?"

I heard her open the door and my shoulders slumped as I fought the urge to stomp my foot. I loved the woman, but sometimes she was evil.

Two pairs of footsteps came closer to the kitchen. Slow and steady.

"You look so handsome," Mom said, an obvious smile in her voice.

Merrick was right. You *could* hear it sometimes.

"Thank you, ma'am."

Merrick.

I took in a sharp breath and froze in front of the open fridge. He was here.

"You call me Alaina, young man. I don't want to be ma'am to anyone."

They both turned the corner and Mom winked at me while I stood there, blinking in confusion. "Grace, there's someone here to see you," she chimed.

My mouth hung open, my eyes feeling like they were going to pop out of my head. I didn't expect to see him today. Not yet. I knew how he felt about me, but after the weekend, and overhearing that conversation with his parents, I just couldn't be sure.

"Does she look surprised?" Merrick asked my mother.

"Oh, surprised is an understatement," Mom laughed. "I'll leave you two alone. I've got to get to the library."

She grabbed her purse off the counter and walked up to me, clasping my shoulders in her hands. "It's going to be okay, dear," she whispered, then kissed my cheek and walked away.

A long moment passed in silence as Merrick and I stood in the kitchen, both of us obviously feeling awkward.

I shut the door to the fridge and stepped closer to him. I missed him like crazy. Those blue eyes, that shaggy hair, the scruff on his face that he only recently managed to make even. He was wearing a suit and looked so sexy. Those wide shoulders filled the jacket in a way no one else could. His hands hung at his side, curled into fists, like he was holding back just as much as I was. I had to hold my breath to keep from running to him.

He was gone two days, Grace. Get a grip.

"Hi, baby," Merrick whispered, gutturally.

I released a happy sob and he reached for me as I moved into his arms. I pressed my nose to his chest and inhaled, smelling that spicy cologne he rarely used. The one that made me dizzy with arousal.

"Damn. I missed you, Grace," he growled, his arms wrapping around me so tightly, it was hard to take a full breath. "Two fucking days and I about went insane." One of his hands moved to the back of my head and he curled his fingers in my hair, gently tugging my head back.

I saw the heat of desire on his face a second before he crushed his lips to mine. It was a kiss to dominate all the other kisses. Distance certainly does make the heart grow fonder. That, or it makes a person insanely desperate.

When we both needed air, he broke the kiss and pressed his forehead to mine.

I moved my hands up and down his arms, feeling the cords of muscle, the strength of what was wrapped around me. "I missed you, too, Merrick."

"I hated being away from you," he informed me. "I don't want to do that again, but it was good to talk to Ryan and fix things."

"How is he?" I stuttered, feeling like a jerk for not really caring what the answer was at that moment.

His shoulders lifted in a shrug. "He's good. Now, kiss me again."

My laugh was swallowed by his mouth and his tongue sliding against mine. He still had a hold of my hair and tugged again to move my head to the side to deepen the kiss. My arms went around his neck as I lifted onto my toes.

The reason for my anxiety was promptly forgotten. I couldn't even remember why I was so worried about him in the first place.

Merrick's chest rumbled when I pressed myself against him. "God, I feel like I've been a starving man for the last two days. Next time, you're coming with me."

"I won't argue with that," I grinned, cupping his face between my hands and lifting to kiss his closed eyes.

He threaded his fingers through my hair and kissed my forehead. "You sure you can't come today?" he pleaded with a pout.

"I'm sorry. I'm covering for Cindy today. She has to take her son to some competition in Salt Lake. I don't want to make her miss it."

He nodded and bent down to kiss my neck. "I'll deal with it. We're having a family dinner tonight. You and your parents are invited."

"I'll be there and I'm sure Mom and Dad would love to come."

"Good. It's at my place." He kissed me again and lowered a hand to grip my ass and give it a firm squeeze. "I've got to get going. They're waiting for me outside."

"Okay," I said breathlessly.

"I'll see you tonight, baby."

"Okay."

He chuckled and took my hand in his, allowing me to lead him outside. Emma was waiting by the car. The conversation I shamelessly listened to this morning, floated back into my memory.

Damn him for making me forget everything.

"Will we see you tonight, Grace?" Emma asked cheerily.

"Of course," I replied, suddenly feeling a little bit awkward, knowing they were all hiding something from me.

Tonight, I kept telling myself.

Merrick gave me another quick kiss and climbed into the car.

I stood on the sidewalk and watched them drive away, the pit in my stomach telling me that if I wasn't careful, things could go very wrong.

There were ten of us sitting around the table, eating and laughing. For once, not worrying about anything but the present.

After the trial – which ended fairly quickly once the judge saw pictures and blood work – Emma and Nathan stopped at a barbeque joint in town and provided dinner for all of us. Mom and Dad were closer to them than I had assumed.

Watching them talk like familiar friends made me wonder how much I'd actually missed over the last few years.

Mitch provided the entertainment by being his usual carefree self and Mary kept her brothers in check when she wasn't laughing hysterically from their antics.

Sam, Mary's husband, fit right in with the rest of them. He made it a point to tell me that once I was a part of this family, there was no getting out. He'd meant it playfully, but I was more nervous about the suggestion than the actual warning.

Mitch spoke briefly about the trial, filling me and my parents in on the details. It was sad to think that such a horrible accident caused weeks of pain and the justice took just as long. He didn't seem overly upset about it, though. The carefree, younger version of both Merrick and Micah wouldn't let something like that – and I quote – 'kill his vibe'.

Micah started arguing with Sam about which one of them would make a better lawyer. I couldn't help but laugh when Mary stated that both of them would be just awful.

Dinner was long since over and I could have stayed there for hours, laughing and chatting with all of them. That is, until Merrick's hand slid up my leg and between my thighs, hidden underneath the table.

I had to slap his hand away a few times, which did nothing but spur him on.

I'd never seen him smile as much as he did at dinner. His blindness didn't change the way his family interacted with him and I clearly saw the peace he felt being surrounded by all of us.

It was pretty late by the time everyone started to trickle out of the house. Emma wanted to stay behind and help clean up, but there wasn't much to clean except a few plates. I told her to go home and I would take care of it.

She hesitated, looking between me and Merrick before she relented. "Thank you for taking such good care of my boy, Grace. I knew you were someone special. Just stick with him, okay?"

I found the request extremely odd, especially for someone like Emma Thatcher. Knowing it had something to do with what I overheard that morning, I let it go.

"I'm not planning on going anywhere, Emma," I confessed, then absently added, "Not unless Merrick wants me to."

She glanced over my shoulder and I followed her gaze. Merrick was standing behind me when I spoke and he didn't look too happy about what he heard.

"What makes you think that would ever happen?" he grumbled.

Emma smiled sweetly, but her voice was saturated with sarcasm, clearly scolding her son when she said, "I just can't imagine what would make her think that, Merrick. Sounds like you two need to clear some things up."

That made his mouth snap shut and I couldn't have loved the woman more.

We said our goodbyes, then it was just me and Merrick. I was nervous. I didn't know when it would happen, but I knew something would.

I started scrubbing the dishes and humming to myself, trying to maintain the contentment of the night. A minute later, Merrick's arms came around my waist, startling me.

"You're stealthy."

"Of course I am. I'm like a cat."

I smiled, loving the feel of his arms around me. He kissed my neck, sending tingles down my spine. His hands moved to my hips and he pressed his hardness against me.

The plate in my hand went tumbling into the sink and I closed my eyes. I never thought it was even possible to feel like this.

Loving someone so much and feeling such passion for them that it makes everything else fade.

Merrick continued to kiss my neck, licking and nipping while turning me into a heaping pile of mush.

"I need you, Grace. I need to feel you, be inside of you."

He pressed against me again, making me moan and press back.

"Fuck, I can't wait."

He spun me around, crushing his lips to mine and spreading his fingers over my ass. He dug in and lifted me to wrap around his hips. Stepping to the side, he roughly dropped me onto the counter. My fingers found the waistband of his jeans just beneath that hard stomach. I curled my fingers inside while his hands roamed my body, kneading in those places that drove me wild.

I couldn't get enough of him, not when everything about him exuded strength. His chest, his stomach, that V at his hips. The scars that covered his left side did nothing but make me want him more. When his hands covered my breasts, I didn't hold back the whimper, wanting more but not sure how to get it.

"You need me, too, Grace?" he said, gruffly. "I'll take care of you. I promise."

His hands dropped to my thighs, sliding inward until he touched my center, massaging me until my hips thrust wildly against his hand. I fumbled with the button on his jeans and suddenly I was on my feet again, unsteady and panting. He made quick work of my shirt and pants, then lifted me back to the counter, removing my panties in the process. His hand came back to where I needed it most and when his fingers found my center, I cried out. "Merrick, please."

He pushed a finger inside of me, setting my skin on fire while he dropped his lips to my chest.

"So wet for me."

Seconds later, he was positioning himself and surging forward.

It was like finally coming home. This connection was like nothing else in the world. Of that, I was completely sure.

"Do you have any idea what you do to me?" Merrick rumbled in my ear. He drew me closer to the edge of the counter, sinking deeper. When he was fully seated inside me, he stopped. "Tell me you know," he whispered.

I knew. I knew he loved me. I felt it every day. Those days without him, however, made me doubt.

"Merrick."

He dropped his face to my neck. "You have to know, Grace. I can't do this without you, so you have to make sure you know."

I closed my eyes, a sigh leaving my lips when he pushed forward. His tongue slid over my skin and it didn't matter *what* I knew, I wouldn't have been able to tell him anyway.

"Do I need to show you again?" he demanded.

He started to retreat. My eyes popped open in a panic while my legs tightened around him, refusing to let him leave my body. He was too strong. Suddenly, he stepped back from the counter and took me with him. The second my feet hit the floor, he spun me away from him.

A hand pressed at the center of my back, pushing my chest down to the counter while his other hand pulled my hips back. I lost my breath, heat claiming my cheeks when that hand sank between my legs. Back and forth, he touched me with a purpose.

"Oh, God."

"I enjoy showing you, baby, but I need you to really understand."

Understand what?

I couldn't concentrate on what he was saying. Not when his talented fingers kept me on the edge. Without warning, he pulled his hand away.

"No."

"I can't wait," Merrick confessed, then slammed into me from behind.

"Yes!" I shouted.

He took me hard against the counter, supporting me with a hand cupped over my breast, controlling every movement.

It didn't take long at all. He'd barely gotten started when I threw my head back and cried out his name. His answering gasp told me he was right behind me. "Grace."

He spread himself over my back, kissing my neck tenderly while we both caught our breath.

"I love you," he breathed. "Don't forget that."

We eventually ended up in bed, me sprawled out over Merrick's chest while he quietly caressed my skin. It didn't take long before he slid down the bed and circled his arms around my waist. I closed my eyes as he tucked his face against my neck, giving me a quick kiss before settling in.

"I could stay here forever, you know that? Right here," he sighed, nuzzling my neck.

I reached over and combed my fingers through his thick hair, feeling the vibration from that delighted hum against my skin. "It would get awfully boring, wouldn't it?"

He shook his head, pulling me impossibly closer. "No. It's safe here. No decisions to be made, no stress or worry. Just safe."

His breath tickled my skin, sending a shiver over my body. He burrowed in deeper. I wanted to stop time. Just stay right in that moment and forget the rest. He was right. It *was* safe.

But my curiosity wouldn't let it go. "Will you talk to me now, Merrick? I know something's going on."

He sighed and kissed the sensitive spot where my neck and shoulder meet. When he pulled back, I slid down to eye level with him. Those bright blue eyes took my breath away. Even broken, they were one of the most striking things about him.

"I'm sorry, Grace. I was confused and scared, I didn't want to bring that on you," he began. "Everything happened all at once and it just overwhelmed me. There were things I needed to take care of before I made a decision and one of them was seeing Ryan."

"I understand, Merrick. I was worried about you, though."

"I know, baby. But you've got to realize that worrying about me won't make things easier for either one of us."

"You're right," I whispered, chagrined. I was disappointed in myself for not trusting him enough. He loved me.

"Doesn't mean I shouldn't have talked to you, though, and I'm sorry for that," he reassured.

"Does that mean you're going to finally tell me?"

He rolled onto his back, bringing me with him. His hold around me was tighter than normal, almost like he was scared I might run away. That didn't help my already frayed nerves.

"Your dad had some surprising news for me."

"Are you okay? Is it bad?"

He chuckled, kissing the top of my head. "Not bad, just unexpected." He drew in a long breath, tickling the top of my head when he blew it out. "He said there's a chance I might be able to see again."

"What?" I exclaimed, pushing myself to sit up so I could see his face. I wasn't expecting that at all. "Really? How?"

He raised his hand to my face, fumbling for a second until he was cupping my jaw. "My left eye is hopeless. I already know that, but he said a more complex cataract surgery on the right eye is a possibility. And the odds are pretty good."

"Merrick. That's incredible!" I said, a beaming smile on my face, ignoring the niggling feeling of nervousness at the thought of him actually seeing me.

"Yeah, it is," he replied, a little dejected and maybe even a little frightened. "What do I have to lose, right?"

My smile faded as I got a good look at his expression. There was something wrong. "What is it?"

"I don't know. I can't figure out why the decision is so difficult. I mean, I should have said yes right away."

"You didn't?"

He shook his head slowly. "I needed to think."

Completely reasonable when I thought about it. How does one suddenly make a decision like that when the chances had been so impossible before? Then again, this was Merrick. Since the very beginning, he felt so much anger about not having his sight. I never would have guessed he wouldn't immediately say yes to the surgery.

"I don't understand."

"The odds are good, Grace, but they aren't certain. What happens if it doesn't work?"

I sat there, just blinking. Confused. "Is that what you're really afraid of?"

He lifted his shoulder in a half shrug.

"Is that why you didn't tell me?"

His hand dropped away from mine and rubbed down his face. "I didn't want you to have hope when it isn't a for sure thing, but I couldn't keep it from you forever. I just didn't know how to say it or if you would even understand why I can't decide."

"Is it worth the chance for you? The *possibility* that you might see again."

He shrugged. "I just don't want anything to change."

My heart started to race, all those insecurities I locked away breaking out. "What would change?"

He didn't answer for a long moment, his expression blank. His eyes normally made an attempt to point toward me, always trying to find me in that darkness he said was always there.

But for the first time in a long time, he actually moved them away from me.

"Merrick, what would change?" I demanded, my chest tightening with emotion. That empty pit in my stomach was growing every second that passed without an answer.

"Me. You. I don't know. Everything."

I sat up all the way, hugging my legs to my chest as I scanned his expression, searching for the actual answer. Then it hit me.

"Do you honestly think it matters to me whether you are blind or not?"

He frowned, lines forming between his brow and his eyes coming back to where I was sitting. "Doesn't it?"

"No, it doesn't."

After that whole episode in the kitchen – reminding me that he loved me, that he wanted me – he actually had the nerve to forget how *I* felt.

"Merrick. I'm with you because I love you."

"What if things change? What if I have to fight through all the shit I've overcome these past few months?"

"Then I'll be here. Yeah, it'll be hard, but that's what this is all about. I wouldn't leave just because things got tough."

"But *what if*, Grace?"

Why was he arguing with me about it? Didn't he know I loved him? That I would stand by him no matter what? Unless ... unless it wasn't *me* he was talking about.

Suddenly, the whole idea of what happened in that kitchen made me nauseous.

"Are you saying ... Merrick, are you suggesting that things might change for *you*?"

"No," he emphasized, then paused, his brow furrowed with uncertainty. "I don't know."

It was a direct blow to the chest. I thought he was different. I thought he wouldn't let anything come between us, not after everything we'd fought through together. All the shit I went through with Jason came swiftly crashing back into my mind. Clanging around every memory until the only option was to believe that it was happening again.

All the effort to tell myself otherwise no longer mattered.

How quickly it happens. The hurt from the past rising up to take control. It wasn't because I was weak, just human.

"I see," I said, deadpan.

"Grace, that came out wrong. I'm not saying anything will change for me, I just don't want you to get your hopes up. I don't want you to get hurt because I–"

"Stop. Please. I don't want to hear anymore," I interjected.

"Grace–"

"No, I get it."

"No, you don't." He started to sit up, reaching for me, but I was already off the bed. "Where the hell are you going?"

I shoved my legs into my pants and yanked my shirt over my head. "I need to go."

"What? Why? Come back here and let's talk about this. You misunderstood."

"Maybe, but I still need a minute to think."

He was scooting to the edge of the bed, his muscles flexing like they always did, distracting me from my eminent escape.

I turned and hurried to the door.

"Grace, stop! Please."

I didn't. I made it out into the hall and almost fell over from the dizziness swarming my head. I leaned against the wall and took a few deep breaths. His steps followed me and I glanced back to see him reach for the door frame. He wasn't paying attention to his steps so he couldn't find it and he ended up catching his foot on the edge.

I wanted to cry. This was just cruel. Leaving like this. But if I didn't leave now, I'd end up right back in a place I didn't want to be.

I continued down the hall only to stop when he shouted. "Damn it, Grace, will you just listen to me? I can't chase you, but I'll fucking try."

I turned to face him. He stood in his doorway, clad only in his underwear, that glorious chest heaving and the worry on his face clouding his features. When he didn't hear me move, he stepped forward.

I took a step back and that super hearing of his caught it and made him freeze.

"Baby, don't do this."

I sucked in a breath, holding back the damn tears that were begging to fall. "I'm sorry, Merrick. You needed a few days to think and you got them. It's my turn."

"Why won't you listen to me?"

"Because I already know what's going to happen!" I screamed.

"Really? You think I'm *anything* like that fucker?"

I refused to answer that because I knew he wasn't, but it didn't change the fear I had that he would be. Eventually.

"Maybe that's what the problem actually is, then. Maybe it's *you* with all the issues. Not me," he snapped.

Another blow to the chest.

"You're right, Merrick. It *is* me. So, maybe you should just let me go before you get stuck with a head case."

He flinched, as if I had physically slapped him across the face. Then his expression twisted, pained and full of regret. "This isn't over, Grace. Not by a long shot."

I wanted to believe him, but after the hurtful things we had just said to each other, I couldn't. People changed all the time. They changed their minds, their beliefs, and they were unpredictable. Life was unpredictable. That's what made it so difficult to survive without a scratch on the surface. Or even deeper.

I spun away, steadying myself when the lightheadedness took over. The enormity of what just happened didn't actually hit me until I'd made it to Keara's, twenty minutes later.

That's when the tears rushed out and my chest cracked open.

My best friend opened the door to find me on my knees, gasping for air that just wouldn't come.

"Grace!"

Her arms came around me as I buried my face in her shoulder, immediately soaking her shirt with unending tears.

"Oh, God. Please tell me you're okay, sweetie."

I shook my head and let out another sob.

"Merrick called me," she whispered.

That just made it worse, because that's when I knew ...

I was the one that had changed in a matter of seconds.

Chapter Twenty

Merrick

I had somehow fucked up and there was no way for me to fix things. Not when Grace refused to answer any of my calls. I spent three days trying to reach her, but no one could help me. Or they just *wouldn't*.

I couldn't control anything anymore. I was miserable and desperate one minute, then moody and abrasive the next. By day three, the numbness had taken over. Then, without warning, regret and shame.

I replayed our conversation, over and over again. To anyone listening in, it was clear that Grace had misunderstood me and she was too upset to give me a chance to explain. But I didn't blame her.

When she asked if I was worried that things would change for *me*, I immediately said no. Then, something came over me and I really couldn't be sure. *I don't know.* It came out of my mouth so damn fast, I had no chance of stopping it.

I *didn't* know if things would change for me, but those things had nothing to do with Grace. It was me I was worried about. Whether or not I would regress back to the pitiful excuse I was before. I was scared that everything I had worked for, would just disappear in a heartbeat.

And suddenly, being in the dark this whole time, didn't seem so bad.

What I should have said ... it doesn't matter anymore because she wouldn't let me say it.

I got angry again, careless. I drank anything I could get my hands on, then when I couldn't even hold myself up, I promised myself I'd fix it.

Grace stayed away. The only person that had seen her was Mom and she didn't think she would be able to help without making it worse.

No, I needed to do this myself. I needed to show her how sorry I was for even *thinking* that she was the problem. It was a moment of insecurity and impulsiveness, and I didn't mean it.

But it was too late.

Her father called me on day four and asked if I had made my decision. He didn't bring Grace up and when I tried to, he knocked it down.

"These things have a way of working themselves out, son. Plus, we're men. We're allowed a free pass now and then, you'll see."

He waited for my answer. It only took me a minute to lock it in.

Yes. I was doing the surgery, risks and all.

But not because I deserved to see again.

I was doing it because I wanted to fix things with Grace, and since it had come to chasing her down, I kind of needed to be able to see out of at least one eye to do it.

He scheduled it for that Monday. I had two days to prepare for a surgery that might change everything for me.

Mom and Dad stopped by that weekend to celebrate with me, but I begged them to just go away.

"We don't know, yet," I insisted. "So, I'm not going to hold my breath."

I spent Saturday night planning out how I was going to convince Grace to hear me out. It was perfect. No way she would reject what I had in mind. I even called Micah to make sure he could be available to help me if I needed him.

He was hesitant, but my brother knew how much Grace meant to me. He'd seen what her light had given me.

Sunday morning came and the doubts crept in. I was an idiot. A woman like Grace didn't deserve to be hurt the way I hurt her. Why the hell would she ever take me back?

So round and round it went.

Hope. Doubt. Hope. Doubt. Anger. Depression.

I was starting to think I was never a real man with the drama playing out in my mind. Ryan posed the same question when I told him what was going on.

"You're a dumbass, Merrick, but you're too strong to give up," he encouraged. "Plus, you've got two working hands and ten working fingers. And if you really know how to use them, no way she'll stay away."

It was the first time I had smiled since Grace walked away from me. But by Sunday night, I was a mess and decided to just leave it up to fate.

I sat at my window, like I'd done every night since she left. I waited for her each night, but there was nothing. No music, no talking. She was never there. When I wouldn't hear anything for a while, I called Keara who confirmed she was at home every time.

Every night for six nights, it was the same thing.

She was making it a point to avoid me.

I would be doing the same thing.

My head started to fall from the lack of sleep. After accepting that I would just have to wait until after the surgery, I started to stand so I could get in bed. The procedure was in just a few hours. I couldn't do anything until then. Until I knew I could find her myself.

A soft click resonated in my ears and I froze. Footsteps, the closet door opening, a loud zip. Wait. That sounded familiar.

"Grace?"

Silence. Not even a breath.

I started to wonder if she had already walked out of her room. My hearing was good, but even I could have missed that with the staggering effort she was making to stay away from me.

"Answer me, baby."

A sigh. Then, "Hi, Merrick."

Relief, unlike any I ever felt before, surged through me. "I'm sorry."

"Merrick—"

"Please, just listen."

She hesitated, then there was the sound of her door clicking shut. I knew she hadn't left because I could practically hear her heartbeats. It could have been in my imagination, but it was enough to convince me to keep talking.

"I didn't mean the things I said to you. And what I was trying to say was that I'm absolutely terrified to have this surgery. I'm terrified to see again and worried that, if it works, I'll go right back to being the fucked-up mess I was before you came into my life." I drew in a long breath, my racing pulse urging me forward. My plan was to tell her how I felt, then leave the decision up to her. It was her life I actually cared about and I just wanted her to be happy.

"I've been overwhelmed ever since I found out there was even a possibility. The first thing that ran through my mind was that I'd finally get to see you. I'd get to see your smile and what your eyes looked like when you do. I'd get to see those eyes I've dreamt about so much.

"Then the possibility that it wouldn't even work made me feel like I'd already gotten it back and lost it again. It was depressing and infuriating," I admitted.

It was hope torn to shreds.

"I didn't want you to have to see me at my worst. Believe it or not, I was a lot worse before you showed up. I don't even know why my family still even talks to me. And I'm ashamed to even consider the chance that I might go back there. To that man that truly *doesn't* feel like he deserves you."

I heard a sniffle and my stomach dropped. I didn't want her to cry. Not when I couldn't wipe away those tears myself.

"I love you, Grace. I'm not leaving you. I'll be here. Blind or not, I'm yours and nothing will change that."

Another sniffle, then a quiet sob.

"No, baby. Don't cry."

"I can't, Merrick."

"Can't what?" I asked, swallowing thickly.

"You were right. There are things I need to fix in my life, to get past. You have enough to worry about without me. So, I can't do this right now."

My mouth went dry. I couldn't even think of a response that didn't involve getting on my knees and begging her.

"You deserve better, Merrick."

I shook my head, resolving to give her the distance she thought she needed. At least until I could do something about it.

"Funny, that's how *I* always felt about *you*."

Two weeks, and still, I just couldn't get used to it.

I could see.

My depth perception was shit, but I could finally see.

Once the cover came off, I was completely lost. Months of nothing, then suddenly, everything. Light hurt, color hurt, and without Grace ... everything was meaningless.

It was the first time since that day Grace showed up at my door, that I didn't really want to try. But I had to. For her.

I spent two weeks making sure I wasn't going to have a mental breakdown. I still felt all the heaviness I knew would only go away with time. The squeal of tires, the slam of a door, even the sound of a diesel passing by the house; it all sent my pulse racing, but it wasn't any more than before.

I still felt the day to day frustrations. Maybe even more now that I could see, but I had them under control. Or at least, I knew they were *out* of my control. Knowing that made accepting them a whole lot easier.

Watching a person run by the house in the morning, just for exercise, was like seeing that look on Eric's face all over again. When would it all come crashing down? It was difficult, but it was something I knew I could face head on with the intention of fighting through it.

Grace gave me that. My family gave me that. Hell, *I* gave me that.

It also helped that I kept myself preoccupied with trying to catch a glimpse of Grace in the morning or at night. I had given her the space she needed and I was about to reach the end of my rope. When I didn't even get a peek at her in the two weeks since my surgery, I knew I needed to act fast.

Keara and Josh kept in touch. Unfortunately, it was without Grace's knowledge. Something I would have to make up to them at the first opportunity. Keara informed me that Grace had actually moved out of the house the day of my surgery.

I knew something was suspicious about her sudden appearance that night. She was packing to move to some apartments not too far away.

Keara, bless her, 'accidentally' told me the apartment number and I was going to see her. Today.

I just had to get this follow-up appointment over with. The last one for my arm.

It was only the second time I'd driven and I did so without having permission. Dr. Samuelson was still waiting the regulated amount of time before he gave me the go ahead for restricted driving. With one eye still out for the count, it was a little riskier.

I was done inconveniencing my mother, though. Driving sucked, don't get me wrong. I twitched more than I actually drove, but I could *see*. That was better than nothing.

One step at a time, with a gracious outlook on the future.

I didn't miss reading. Magazines were full of lies and crap that didn't matter and finding a book to read that didn't give me a headache was ... well, a headache. I tossed the dreadful magazine down on the table and sat back in my chair, rolling my shoulders to release the tension of being inside the hospital again.

Grace was here every day, but I didn't give hope to the possibility that I might run into her. Not unless God had a hand in that.

I missed her.

Life just wasn't the same without her voice, her laughter. I didn't want to think about what the next months would be like if I didn't see her. I closed my eyes and took a few deep breaths. I had a plan. It wasn't a very good plan, but it was a plan.

Alaina might get annoyed, but it didn't matter. If Grace refused to see me, I was going to see her parents every day, maybe even several times a day, and even at night. If I could get them to convince Grace to give me another chance, then just maybe I would get one.

Today.

I would go for it as soon as I left this cold, unforgiving building.

"You ready to go home?" I heard a nurse ask.

I looked up, quickly realizing that no one was actually speaking to me. I dropped my head back and closed my eyes, smiling when I could still see the presence of light in the right one. Then I prayed that the doctor would call me back soon.

"I think so. Just have to fill out a few charts and I'm out of here."

Every muscle in my body tensed.

That voice. I knew it better than I knew my own voice.

Grace.

My eyes flew open and I frantically searched the room. She was here. So close to me. I was going to see her for the first time. Dizziness swept over me, but I pushed it back. My first impression as a blind man wasn't the greatest for her. This one *would* be.

I caught a glimpse of two women at a desk. One behind it and the other leaning against the front of it. The nurse who was seated, was blonde, a bright blonde that hurt my eyes, and her lips were a deep red.

The nurse who was standing, had dark brown hair with strands of gold shining throughout. The exact color I pictured on Grace. Shiny and vibrant. Thick enough to bury my fingers in. She was short, no taller than five feet three inches. Her hips flared out in the most sensual way and her neck ... it looked delicious.

I couldn't see her face. Not yet.

"You've had a long couple of weeks. You sure you're alright?" the blonde asked, frowning worriedly at the other nurse.

She sighed and combed her fingers through her hair. I swear I almost felt those fingers against my own scalp. "I'm fine, Cindy. Just got a lot on my mind."

"You need to take a vacation," Cindy said with a sweet smile.

Wait a second.

Cindy.

I recognized the name from so many conversations with Grace. I quickly glanced up at the sign over the desk.

Homecare Department.

Fuck me.

I was going to start praying more often.

The nurse dropped her head and rubbed the back of that beautiful neck with her hand. A hand I knew had touched me.

I didn't know I was moving, didn't even know I was standing until I was a few feet behind her. She turned her head to look at a clock on the wall beside her and I caught the first glimpse of her profile.

A small nose that pointed up slightly. Full lips, the lightest shade of pink. Long eyelashes that almost brushed her cheeks when she blinked. Rosy cheeks that would definitely brighten with pleasure and a chin I knew only too well. It was a profile I had memorized eagerly, over and over again, and it made my fingers twitch.

I took another step forward, hearing a gasp come from Cindy. I didn't look away from Grace. My Grace.

She was so fucking gorgeous. I knew she would be.

I stood directly behind her, inches from her back. Her spine instantly straightened, her shoulders tensing. I watched goose bumps rise on the back of her neck, savoring the moment, and held my breath as she turned to face me. So slowly.

I was wrong.

Grace wasn't just beautiful. She was the very definition of beauty.

Freckles dotted her nose, mascara was lightly smudged under her widened eyes. Those eyes. So many colors. Bright and complex. The colors swirled together and then I saw them. The small spots of golden brown. I wanted to count them like I'd imagined doing so many times before, but I didn't have time. Not now.

I reached forward, gripping her trembling shoulders. "It's you."

She didn't look frightened or angry. Just stunned into silence.

Didn't matter. She wouldn't need to speak for what I had in store for her.

"Grace," I whispered before pulling her against me and roughly – so effortlessly – colliding with her lips. I moved my hands to the sides of her slender neck, a neck that felt all too familiar. Tilting her face up with the pads of my thumbs under her jaw, I held her in place and kissed her like a starving man.

I had starved myself over the last couple of weeks. Frantic for her taste and now that I finally had it …

A small moan vibrated in her chest and it spurred me on. I traced her lips with my tongue, begging her to open for me. She didn't disappoint. She *never* disappointed.

These lips were made for me. This body, for me.

This woman.

Made. For. Me.

Her arms came around my neck and she fell into the kiss. I buried a hand in her hair, the familiar smell of her shampoo wafting over me, and I kept her head where I wanted it, to deepen the kiss. Our tongues tangled, my chest burned with the need for air, and my head was floating.

I kept my eyes open, taking in every flutter of her eyelashes as she lost herself to me.

"Holy shit, that's hot."

Grace pulled away at the sound of Cindy's voice, swollen lips and wide eyes staring back at me.

"I–"

"I love you," I declared.

Another gasp from behind the desk.

"Merrick–"

"I love you, Grace. I don't care how many times I need to tell you. I'll say it even after you finally believe it."

Her eyes glistened and that adorable chin trembled.

"I *see* you, baby. And I want to see you forever. So, do what you have to. If you feel like there are things you need to get past. Get past them. But don't leave me out of it."

Her face was still in my hands when the first tear fell. I swiped it away with my thumb, relishing the privilege. Even when she cried, it was beauty she radiated.

"We both have our issues, Grace. But we're stronger together than we ever were apart. And I want you, because I know, right here," I stated, lightly pounding the spot over my heart, "that you're the one for me."

I bent down to kiss her tears, gliding over her jaw and finding that safe spot in her neck I discovered just a few weeks ago. She tilted her head to give me more room to work and I took advantage. Her hands came up to my shoulders, holding on tightly. Giving me the sign that she was in this with me now.

"Really?" she whispered, trembling in my arms.

"Mmhmm, and I've got news for you, love." I kissed her soft, flawless neck, inhaling deeply before pulling away to look at her. Those hazel eyes shimmered back at me and that curious grin was even better than I'd imagined. "I'm the one for you, too."

Chapter Twenty-One

Grace

Three weeks of no Merrick was like a lifetime of no laughter. No happiness. Nothing.

It took everything I had to stay away from him, but I needed it. I needed to figure out what I wanted and how I was going to get it. Being afraid of something so completely out of my control, isn't worth the grief it causes, so I set out to change ... me.

I regretted every word that came out of my mouth the night I left Merrick in that hallway. But it set me on a path to fix the things I had only safely tucked away before. The wounds that kept opening at the first spike of fear; I worked on stitching them back up just right.

I wasn't there yet, but I was closer.

I already knew what I wanted and I had currently been working on how to get it.

Then Merrick showed up, his presence as powerful as it always was. Only now, he could see it for himself.

I knew it was him before Cindy even looked over my shoulder. I could feel it. Every pore and every vein flared to life. I only ever felt that with *him*.

Turning around to see him looking down at me, those striking blue eyes meeting mine for the first time; I don't remember a time when I felt more proud of *anyone*.

If there was one person on this earth that deserved true happiness, it was Merrick Thatcher. He worked so hard to get where he is and even though the road in front of him was filled with obstacles, he knew he could get through it.

That's the only thing that really mattered. That he would do it to honor the men that died for him. That he would do it for me.

"Tell me what it's like," I requested, as he drove us to my apartment in my car. He was actually driving. I couldn't get over how amazing that was.

He hadn't really given me an option to leave without him, all but dragging me into his appointment, admitting that he didn't trust me to wait for him.

He was right.

I was still anxious, but after processing everything he said to me in the middle of the hospital, where several people overheard, I couldn't say no.

Because I still loved him fiercely.

"It's ... painful," he chuckled. "Sometimes I go to bed and my eye aches more than it did in the beginning. It wasn't even a year spent being blind and already my brain has to reprocess everything I look at. It's exhausting."

I couldn't comprehend that, but I took his word for it.

"Is it clear?"

"Yes. I see everything clearly. The only issue is depth perception, but with practice, I can get around that."

I smiled at him when he glanced over. He only took his eyes off the road for a moment, but seeing them focus on me instead of somewhere around me ...

"I'm so happy for you, Merrick. Really."

He reached over and grasped my hand, lifting it to his lips. All the while, his eyes stayed on the road. Not taking any chances.

"I've got a job at the base. The same one they were considering for me before. I start next week."

"And?"

"And I can't wait," he said, grinning with excitement.

We pulled into the apartments and he followed me to my door. Another possibility I hadn't considered. He no longer needed anyone to lead the way for him.

I couldn't stop the beaming smile that covered my face.

"What's that for?" he asked, curiously, maybe even a little breathlessly.

I lifted my shoulder in a half shrug.

We stepped into my apartment and I shut the door while he got a brief glimpse of the living room. I dropped my purse on the table by the door. When I turned around, I smacked right into his chest. My hands came up to stop the collision, but it was no use.

When I stepped back, he pulled me right into him again.

"What's that beautiful smile for, Grace? And if you don't mind, show it to me again," he requested, his voice gruff.

Smiling was difficult when the only thing I could focus on were his hands around my waist. I wanted him to kiss me again. To push me against the wall like he enjoyed so much and take me back to where we were before.

"Don't look at me like that unless you want me to do something about it," he muttered, his gaze gliding back and forth over my face.

He zeroed in on my lips, making me lose my breath for a moment.

A low rumble rose up his chest and that's when I saw it. His right eye dilated, completely covering the blue of his iris. I remembered the time that happened before and my mouth fell open in surprise.

"What?" His eyes darted back and forth between mine, the left one not as active as the right, but still strong.

"It was meant to be all along," I whispered.

He lifted an eyebrow, the scar slashed through his left eye standing out. "If you're talking about us, then I already knew that."

I smiled, bigger than before. He drew in a sharp breath while those arms tightened around me, drawing me closer.

"Make love to me," I demanded, not even caring how desperate I sounded.

He squared those massive shoulders and took a good, long look at me. Making sure I really wanted it.

Oh, I wanted it. I had always wanted it.

I just couldn't see past everything else, but I was getting there.

I was lucky that Merrick actually loved me enough to join me on that journey. That he was strong enough and devoted enough to fight those insecurities right along with me.

What was in front of me no longer mattered because of who wanted to stand behind me. Merrick was worth any risk.

Loving him was worth everything.

Something in my eyes must have satisfied him because in the next breath, he had me lifted in his arms and was wandering through the apartment in search of my bedroom.

I pointed the way then took his face in my hands and pulled his head down for a kiss. He paused, tangling his tongue with mine before picking up the pace and finally finding the bedroom.

He tossed me onto the bed, a squeal leaving my throat as I flew through the air.

"I've always wanted to do that. Now I finally can," he growled, crawling over me.

He pinned me to the bed and kissed me madly. My legs and arms automatically came around him as he shifted us both up the bed into the pillows. Those hands tore at my clothes until they slid under to find the skin beneath. His lips tore away from mine and he sat back on his knees, staring down at me with an intensity I'd never seen before.

"What's wrong, Mer?"

He shook his head and looked down at his hands resting on my hips. They constricted and started to slowly, gently, push my shirt up. The skin beneath was revealed and his fingers slid over my stomach, leaving goose bumps behind.

He stopped suddenly, closing his eyes.

I reached up, smoothing my fingers over the lines on his forehead. "Babe, what is it?"

He blew out a long, slow breath. His eyes stayed closed.

"Are you afraid to see me, Merrick?" I asked, knowing the answer before I even asked, but needing to say something to get him to open those eyes.

He didn't disappoint.

They popped open, a deep frown transforming his entire face. "No. I'm not afraid," he insisted, emphasizing it with a firm shake of his head.

I let my fingers drop to his chest, resting my hand over his heart. "Then what is it?"

His eyes blazed with desire, the blue more vivid than ever, and his hands started to move again. "It just doesn't seem real to me. Being here, seeing you for the first time. I've dreamed of this moment, prayed for it. Now that it's finally here, I don't want it to end."

"It doesn't have to."

He bent forward, planted his hands on either side of my head, then kissed me.

"I still have a lot to work on, Grace. I'm not worthy of you. Not yet. But I'm going to be. I'll do my best to fight the monsters we face and I'll stop being afraid of the dark. Because with you, there's always light. I know that now." He kissed me again, then shifted so we were both on our sides, looking at each other. "I'll be the kind of man you can be proud of."

"Oh, Merrick." I ran my fingers over his face, tracing the scar from his eyebrow, down to his jaw. "I'm already proud of you and I love you."

He smiled. "I know, baby. But a man should never stop making his wife proud."

I froze.

What did he just say?

Merrick chuckled, his eyes darting down as his cheeks filled with color. "Not the smoothest proposal, but we haven't really had the smoothest road, have we?"

"Merrick. Are you ..."

"Yes, Grace. I'm asking you to marry me."

I was in shock.

It wasn't what I was expecting at all. I thought we would have wild and crazy sex for a good week, then make a plan for ourselves and take it one day at a time. But marriage?

Warmth spread through my chest at the idea of marrying Merrick.

We're stronger together than we ever were apart.

"It doesn't have to be today. Hell, it doesn't even have to be this year. I'll take any day you choose. I just want you to know that I'm in this, all the way."

I took a deep breath and exhaled with a smile. "Okay."

"Okay?"

I nodded. "Whenever I give you my answer, it'll be yes. So, okay."

He slowly rolled back over me, settling in the cradle of my thighs. The whole time, his eyes were on me, a brighter light in them, now.

"Okay," he sighed. "Now, lie back and relax, baby. Because I have a lot to see, all day to see it, and you know I like to take my time."

An anxious moan left me as he lifted my arms above my head and slid my shirt off.

"Christ, that's a sight," he whispered.

My bra was nothing special, but to him, it was fascinating. He fingered the straps, gliding down to the cups. Those fingers slid over the material, around it, beneath it. Until I couldn't take anymore.

He took his time, just like he promised. Rediscovering every inch of me.

At one point, he turned me onto my stomach, a low groan on his lips when his hands landed on my ass. There was a sharp slap and before I had time to flinch, he covered me with his body and started kissing my shoulder, my spine, my hips.

Then, he flipped me back over, starting it all over again.

It was sweet, blissful torture. I didn't want it to end either.

"Open up for me, love. I've got some fantasies to play out."

I giggled as his hands spread my thighs open, only to gasp when his fingers found my core.

I closed my eyes.

"Let me watch you, Grace. Open those beautiful eyes for me."

They fluttered open and he pressed a finger inside of me, watching my face closely as he brought me higher and higher.

"Exactly the color I imagined," he said.

I didn't have a chance to ask what he meant, because I was already there and he wasn't about to stop and chat.

"Show me that light, baby. Blind me with it," he commanded.

I watched his head drop and his shoulders pushed my thighs opened wider. It only took that first touch of his mouth to send me over. All the while, Merrick watched.

He spent the rest of the day and well into the night, making love to me, worshipping me the way I worshipped him.

It was when neither one of us could keep our eyes open that I realized, being broken doesn't mean it's the end. Cracks can be filled with new paths, new friends, new love, and a lot of sweat and blood.

If anything, being broken is kind of a beginning.

And ours would last a lifetime.

Epilogue

Merrick

Two years later

We are all broken, that's how the light gets in. – Ernest Hemingway.

I kept staring at the quote on the wall of my mother's living room. It had hit me like a brick wall the second I walked in the house.

While everyone else sat around the dinner table talking about their plans for the summer or what movie they wanted to see next, I kept thinking about that quote.

I had come back from war a broken man. Living in a darkness I thought would never end. But there was a reason for everything that happened back in that desert.

The things that broke me, actually saved me. Because I could feel the light seeping in through those cracks.

Every time I looked at my wife, our beautiful baby girl nestled against her chest, I could feel that light shining through me.

The day Grace said yes to marrying me, I felt one of those cracks seal up tight. The night she told me she was pregnant, happy tears filling her eyes, another one sealed. More cracks opened up here and there. Struggles and obstacles we faced together would always leave us a little scratched, but they wouldn't break us.

The night Grace shook me awake, telling me it was time, I felt one seal up while another opened.

We were both scared, neither one of us knowing what to expect. Grace confided in me that she didn't think she could handle anything like the loss of her child ever again. She wouldn't have to. At least, not alone. Not ever again.

That trip to the hospital was tense. The ride up to labor and delivery even more so. But the moment we both heard that tiny heartbeat, strong and steady, we knew everything was going to be just fine.

Another crack sealed.

Then, every trial either of us had ever faced in life finally made sense. Every single one of them led us to that moment. I thanked God for giving me a second chance.

Seeing our beautiful daughter – this tiny miracle – come into this world, I broke down. And Grace was right there with me.

Who was I to raise a child, so perfect and pure, in a world with so many rough roads? But she was my future and so was Grace. They were both given to me to protect, to love. I'd fight for both of them, as long as I was breathing.

"It's time for a nap, I think," Grace said quietly. The conversation around us continued as she stood to take little Erica to a quiet room.

I followed after her, always eager to hear her sing our daughter to sleep. It had the same affect on Erica as it did on me. She always immediately calmed, her precious face relaxing from the sound.

I spent most of my nights following these two around, making sure I didn't miss a single thing.

I stood in the doorway, watching my beautiful wife rock our child to sleep. That soothing voice sending warmth through me for the millionth time in my life.

I'm trying. The images from being overseas still haunt me, but that's because I don't want to forget what happened. I want to live through it and know that those men died for me. I want to honor them for their bravery and remember them for everything else.

I'm going to live for *them*. For Grace and Erica.

For me.

The End

L   O   V   E

Special Operations Warrior Foundation

http://www.specialops.org/

Like many other foundations, the Special Operations Warrior Foundation provides assistance to injured soldiers as well as their families. SOWF also focuses on one of the most important challenges those families face; 'getting to their hospitalized loved ones as quickly as possible'.

With grants immediately provided to the family, they can travel to be bedside with their loved one, especially for those crucial first days.

SOWF also provides a scholarship program, family services (including clinical social workers, scholarship counselors, and family services counselors). With on-going support and helpful counseling to all families of fallen members in every branch of the military, they are able to help in all the ways that count.

The SOWF was highly recommended to me by a recent veteran who served in Iraq. Therefore, I am thrilled to be able to help them in any way possible.

Every little bit counts.

SOWF Mission Statement

The Special Operations Warrior Foundation ensures full financial assistance for a post-secondary degree from an accredited two or four-year college, university, technical, or trade school; and offers family and educational counseling, including in-home tutoring, to the surviving children of Army, Navy, Air Force and Marine Corps special operations personnel who lose their lives in the line of duty.

The Special Operations Warrior Foundation also provides immediate financial assistance to severely wounded and hospitalized special operations personnel.

Vivid Playlist

Damien Rice - I Don't Want To Change You

Weezer - Say It Ain't So

Weezer - Hold Me

Bright Eyes - First Day Of My Life

Bright Eyes - An Attempt To Tip The Scales

Acknowledgements

There are quite a few people to thank, but first and foremost, I want to thank my brother, Jeff. For your service in the Army National Guard, the sacrifices you made to protect this country, and the never-ending devotion to your family. I love you and I am so proud and honored to be your little sister. Thank you for being so willing to share your experiences in Iraq with me and allowing me to make an attempt at putting those experiences into words.

To my husband. I honestly don't know how you put up with me and my constant habit of burying myself in a story. Your patience and support means the world to me. Thank you for always being a sounding board and a reminder that true love is *completely* possible. To my baby girl, I love you more than anything. You are the light of my life and I am so grateful for the privilege of being your mommy.

To Erica. I honestly don't remember life before you! I don't want to! You've been my rock through this entire journey. Not only with writing, but life in general. Thank you for the late night conversations that end with my face hurting so much from smiling and laughing. For the encouragement and support you have always given me. For your devotion to getting the word out there about my books. Like I always say, YOU ARE SUPERWOMAN! Without you, I wouldn't know what the hell I was doing. You are my best friend and you mean the world to me. I love you! This just isn't enough, I feel like I didn't even hit the nail on the head. So I'll show you! I'll cherish your friendship and hopefully one day you will understand how much you mean to me. A shout out to your beautiful blog, Always Behind a Book. Thank you for all the cover reveals, blitzes, spotlights, tours, trailers ... everything! You are amazing!

To Keara. Seriously, where do I begin? What would I do without you? Your friendship means *everything* to me. You have changed my world so much just by being you. Thank you for always being there for me, for your enthusiasm, and your never-ending support. For being the Keara that *this* Grace will never stop loving. Without you, my world would be dark and lonely, sad and Dean-less (*wink wink*). Thank you! I love you! I cherish your friendship, and since words are never enough, I'll show you, too!

To Tracie, Jess, Amy S., Blythe, Amie, Jamie, Loraine, Amy A., Kass, Ginelle, Lisa R.D., Leah, Christy, Sarah, Joy, Tricia, Samantha, my Wilde Ones Street Team (you know who you are), and so many more! Thank you for your friendship, your shares, your encouragement, and your support. You help me more than you realize and I'll never forget it.

To all the beautiful bloggers out there that have stuck with me through it all - I just can't thank you enough. Each and every one of you has helped me and so many other authors tremendously! Without you, the book world would be bleak. So, thank you. Please keep doing what you're doing. Whether you are big or small (To me there are no 'small' blogs! You all rock!), just starting out, or have been around for years, you make a difference! You make THE difference!

To my gorgeous readers. Thank you for sticking with me. For taking a chance on me. For your messages and love, your reviews, your bribes to get me to finish the next one (Yes, I said that), your shares and comments. For being the reason I do this! I love each and every one of you from the bottom of my heart. Thank you for reading my heart and soul, and for handling them with care.

And finally, to the men and women in all branches of the military – past, present, and future – and to your families, wherever you are. Thank you for your sacrifice. Thank you for your courage and commitment. Thank you for being the strength that holds us together through the good and the bad. Our prayers are with you.

About the Author

I live in Morgan, Utah with my husband, beautiful daughter, and a couple of spoiled pups. If I'm not deeply involved in writing my next book, then I'm probably reading in the safety and quiet of my closet. I love yoga – which I now practice regularly – playing hide and seek with my daughter (only to have my hiding spots revealed by one of the pups), and I love Fruit by the Foot, Twizzlers and Peace Tea. These are great ways to bribe me into revealing secrets about what's to come.

I have an unhealthy obsession with Supernatural, The Walking Dead, and The Big Bang Theory. I also enjoy talking about them, so if you like them, too, come find me.

Writing has become an enormous part of my life and every book I write holds a special place in my heart. If you read one of my books, I hope you have the same experience.

Connect with Jessica Wilde

Facebook
 www.facebook.com/AuthorJessicaWilde

Twitter
@JessicaWilde9

Coming Soon

Book #2 in the Rise & Fall Series by Jessica Wilde

Reckless

Read the prologue to Ricochet, Book #1.

Prologue

Fear.

It's the last thing I remembered.

I was afraid.

Afraid to fight, afraid to run… afraid to breathe.

Then, everything had gone dark. As if life was finally hearing my pleas, my cries to end the torment. To end the fear.

But even in the dark, I still felt it.

I always felt it.

The rush of useless adrenaline, the sound of my heart frantically beating against my chest like a drum. The churning in my gut that made me want to fold into myself for some kind of reprieve, to close my eyes and imagine that none of it was really happening, that it was all just some fucked up nightmare that would go away with time. But it never went away and I was still afraid.

But this time… *this time* there was something new that came after the fear. There was light, there were soft voices instead of the harsh, cold one spitting in my ear to wake up, only to be afraid all over again. There was still pain, but this time, someone was waiting for me to wake up that didn't want me to be afraid.

"Don't let him win," the voice said. "Don't let him have your strength. Take it back… take it back and *never* let it go."

Then, the darkness came over me once more and instead of fear, I felt hope.

Instead of pain, I felt peace.

And instead of doubt, determination.

My life had been a ricochet of one event leading to the next. Bouncing back and forth from good to bad. Happiness to despair. Hope to fear.

I was done.

Enough was enough.

Made in the USA
San Bernardino, CA
08 May 2016